PLAY WITH DUKES, GET BURNED

Dukes in Danger

Book 9

Emily E K Murdoch

Text by Emily E K Murdoch
Cover by Dar Albert

Dragonblade Publishing, Inc. is an imprint of Kathryn Le Veque Novels, Inc.
P.O. Box 23
Moreno Valley, CA 92556
ceo@dragonbladepublishing.com

Produced in the United States of America

First Edition January 2024
Print Edition

ARE YOU SIGNED UP FOR DRAGONBLADE'S BLOG?

You'll get the latest news and information on exclusive giveaways, exclusive excerpts, coming releases, sales, free books, cover reveals and more.

Check out our complete list of authors, too!

No spam, no junk. That's a promise!

Sign Up Here

www.dragonbladepublishing.com

Dearest Reader;

Thank you for your support of a small press. At Dragonblade Publishing, we strive to bring you the highest quality Historical Romance from some of the best authors in the business. Without your support, there is no 'us', so we sincerely hope you adore these stories and find some new favorite authors along the way.

Happy Reading!

CEO, Dragonblade Publishing

Additional Dragonblade books by Author Emily E K Murdoch

Dukes in Danger Series

Don't Judge a Duke by His Cover (Book 1)
Strike While the Duke is Hot (Book 2)
The Duke is Mightier than the Sword (Book 3)
A Duke in Time Saves Nine (Book 4)
Every Duke Has His Price (Book 5)
Put Your Best Duke Forward (Book 6)
Where There's a Duke, There's a Way (Book 7)
Curiosity Killed the Duke (Book 8)
Play With Dukes, Get Burned (Book 9)

Twelve Days of Christmas

Twelve Drummers Drumming
Eleven Pipers Piping
Ten Lords a Leaping
Nine Ladies Dancing
Eight Maids a Milking
Seven Swans a Swimming
Six Geese a Laying
Five Gold Rings
Four Calling Birds
Three French Hens
Two Turtle Doves
A Partridge in a Pear Tree

The De Petras Saga

The Misplaced Husband (Book 1)
The Impoverished Dowry (Book 2)
The Contrary Debutante (Book 3)

The Determined Mistress (Book 4)
The Convenient Engagement (Book 5)

The Governess Bureau Series
A Governess of Great Talents (Book 1)
A Governess of Discretion (Book 2)
A Governess of Many Languages (Book 3)
A Governess of Prodigious Skill (Book 4)
A Governess of Unusual Experience (Book 5)
A Governess of Wise Years (Book 6)
A Governess of No Fear (Novella)

Never The Bride Series
Always the Bridesmaid (Book 1)
Always the Chaperone (Book 2)
Always the Courtesan (Book 3)
Always the Best Friend (Book 4)
Always the Wallflower (Book 5)
Always the Bluestocking (Book 6)
Always the Rival (Book 7)
Always the Matchmaker (Book 8)
Always the Widow (Book 9)
Always the Rebel (Book 10)
Always the Mistress (Book 11)
Always the Second Choice (Book 12)
Always the Mistletoe (Novella)
Always the Reverend (Novella)

The Lyon's Den Series
Always the Lyon Tamer

Pirates of Britannia Series
Always the High Seas

De Wolfe Pack: The Series
Whirlwind with a Wolfe

Chapter One

1 June 1811

It was never particularly pleasant to be awoken in the middle of the night, and this time Daniel Vaughn was not going to put up with it.

"Go away," he mumbled as firmly as he could manage while keeping his eyes closed. *Just another hour—surely the sun had not even risen yet.* "Go—"

"Sir," said the hurried, muffled voice just within earshot. "Sir, you must wake up!"

Daniel groaned.

Must? Must was a far too serious word for the middle of the night. As far as he could recall, his head had only just touched the pillow. Wasn't he permitted at least one night of complete slumber? Was his service to the Crown really so vital that—

A hand shook his shoulder. "Sir!"

Daniel groaned loudly. "What in God's—"

"I am sorry, but you must wake up!"

It was the panic in the man's voice that finally alerted Daniel to the fact that waking up may be the only option. At the very least, it seemed to be the only way to make whoever was disturbing his repose go away.

Very slowly, hating that he was forced to waken, he opened one eye. He almost closed it again immediately. Horrendous brightness dazzled his pupil. Someone was holding a lit candlestick far too close to his face.

"Jesus wept, you couldn't move that thing a little farther back?" muttered Daniel, forcing his other eye open.

The blinding light moved, dimming slightly, removing the overpowering brightness from his eyes. The circle of glimmering light around the candle's flame illuminated a man in his nightclothes, a look of fear on his face. His hand trembled. The candle flickered.

Daniel blinked. "Campbell?"

His valet nodded feverishly. "You must wake up."

"Yes, yes, I am awake," said Daniel heavily, pulling himself up and leaning against his pillow.

What was it this time? There was always some emergency in the Vaughn family, and being the only child of the three of them with any sort of wits about them . . .

Well, that wasn't exactly fair. Amelia tried her best, and if she had ever been given her own income by their brother, perhaps she could have maintained her own household and forged her own path in Society. As it was, however . . .

"You have to get up," his valet said urgently.

Daniel sighed heavily. "Dear God, I hope not. What time is it?"

"Near two o'clock in the morning, sir, and—"

Daniel's groan drowned out the rest of the man's speech.

Two o'clock in the morning! He had managed to go through his whole life without ever seeing that particular time, from either direction. If he went out carousing with his friends—something he did far less lately—he was always happily in bed by one o'clock. On the rare occasions he needed to rise early to travel, Daniel refused to even countenance breaking his fast before six o'clock.

But two o'clock in the morning? "Why on earth would you wake me up at—" Daniel began, weariness tinging every syllable.

His words were short when Campbell interrupted. "Something has . . . happened." This time, the man's terrified tone was enough.

Daniel sat straighter, his eyes focusing on the trembling man. "Happened?"

Happened. It was such a small word, really. Yet it could contain multitudes. Could it be a message about a case with the Crown? A desperate plea from one of the men he served? Or something closer to home? With the Vaughn family, it truly could mean anything—any disaster, any scandal. Anything.

"You have to come now," said Campbell, placing the candlestick on the dressing table on the other side of the room and picking up his master's dressing gown. "I promised—"

"Promised?" Daniel pushed back the bedlinens and rose out of bed. His feet moved sluggishly, as though they had as little interest in awakening as he did. "Promised who?"

There were only two people his valet would even consider taking directions from—other than his housekeeper, of course. Daniel tried not to smile at the idea of Mrs. Stafford issuing orders. She was a quiet woman, shy and nervous. But she ran his little home like clockwork. She would never send Campbell to get him up at this ungodly time of the night.

Other than her, there were the Vaughns. His sister Amelia and . . . his brother.

Daniel sighed as he allowed his valet to attire him with his dressing gown. "Don't tell me. David—"

"I truly think it is best you come downstairs, sir," said Campbell wretchedly, inexplicably refusing to meet his eye. "Please."

Daniel felt a flicker of discontent at the man's evasion, but he was no monster. There were plenty of masters in Bath, he was sure, who would deride his softness with his servants, but Daniel saw no point in berating them for any part of their service which did not immediately suit his needs. They were only people, after all.

"Fine, fine," he muttered, pulling a hand through his hair and trying to make a mental note to make an appointment with his barber. As though he would remember it once he returned to bed. "Come on then."

Campbell followed Daniel closely as they left the bedchamber and strode along the corridor toward the staircase.

At least, Daniel attempted to stride. His mind was still groggy, and his legs definitely wanted to return to the comfort of the mattress. When he took the first step down, he almost stumbled.

"Careful—"

"Yes, yes, I don't need your arm," muttered Daniel irritably. *Dear God, what did the man expect, woken at such a ridiculous hour!* "I can make my way perfectly . . . perfectly . . ."

His voice trailed away as someone standing in his small hall, dressed in a pelisse and heavy woolen bonnet, emerged into view.

Daniel reached the bottom of the stairs and found his mouth no longer worked. How could it? Now he had seen who his valet had been desperate for him to speak to, he could quite understand the man's eagerness. The woman standing in his hall was beautiful. She had almost white-blonde hair, an imperious expression, and silent tears rolling down her cheeks.

"Amelia."

His sister looked around. She had been staring blankly at a wall, unseeing, unmoving. As her gaze lighted on him, something odd flashed in her eyes, something Daniel had never seen before. Something he was certain he never wanted to see again.

"Daniel," she murmured, then without any warning, she curtsied. *To him!* "Damn. I mean, Your Grace."

She remained in a low curtsy position as Daniel stared. What on earth was going on? Why was his sister acting so strangely?

It wasn't the cursing. That was a natural part of Amelia, a part of her character which had been there for so long, he barely noticed it anymore. And there was no possibility that—no, Amelia had never touched a drop of alcohol in her life. She wouldn't start now, at the age of one and twenty, would she?

So what could explain this most bizarre action?

"Oh, get up, Amelia," Daniel said quietly. "Thank you, Campbell, that will be all."

His valet was gawping at the curtsying woman and Daniel had to get him out of here. He had only a few servants—two maids, a footman, a housekeeper, and Campbell—but the last thing he wanted was for the five of them to be gossiping about the most outrageous behavior his sister was exhibiting.

Turning up at his Bath townhouse in the middle of the night! Using that ridiculous and entirely unwarranted title with him and curtsying? When was the last time Amelia had curtsied to him?

"Your Grace," she said softly, "I came as soon as I—"

"Don't call me that," said Daniel roughly. "It's not amusing."

Another tear rolled down Amelia's face. "And I am not laughing."

"Look, this is a very strange jest, and I am sure I will laugh about it in the morning," snorted Daniel, thinking privately that he certainly would not. "But this is simply not on, Amelia." He rubbed his eyes tiredly. "It's too late for you to go back home now, but I have a spare bedchamber. You can—"

"I will not be returning to that cursed house, Your Grace—"

"Amelia," said Daniel, more sternly. *What on earth had got into her?* "I said, that is not amusing. David may be unwell, but—"

Amelia met his gaze steadily, and Daniel's stomach lurched. His words died in his throat. *No. It wasn't possible.* She had said not another word, but it could not be clearer now what news his sister had come to his home to bring. The worst news. The very worst. In his sleep-deprived state he'd simply been too slow to see it.

All warmth disappeared from his face. Daniel was certain he must look pale, as though he were sickening for something. Perhaps he was.

Perhaps this was all just a misunderstanding, something that could be cleared up instantly if his sister just stopped weeping for five minutes together.

"No," said Daniel, his voice hoarse. "No, Amelia. It can't be."

His sister nodded slowly. "He . . . he died about an hour ago. Christ, I wasn't going to cry—I wanted to be the one to tell—"

"No," Daniel said, more firmly now as his mind whirled. *It couldn't be.* He wouldn't let it. After all these months, David had been improving. "The doctors said he was getting better, that he would live—"

"Doctor Walsingham did not," Amelia said softly.

Daniel waved a hand, showing her without words precisely what he had thought of Doctor Walsingham's prognosis. "The man barely knew our brother's situation, he—"

"He was right," said his sister, tears continuing to fall. "I am sorry, Daniel. I know you would never have wanted it to be this way, but it's . . . it's true. David is dead. And you are now the fourteenth Duke of Thornfalcone."

His sister's words echoed around the hall.

Daniel staggered backward, half sitting, half falling onto the staircase.

It couldn't be. David was going to live forever. That was what he had always said when they were children—that he would be the thirteenth Duke of Thornfalcone, and there would be no others, for he was going to live forever.

And now the bold, brash, and occasionally blackguardly ways of his brother were over.

Either Daniel's head was spinning or the whole world was—he could not tell which. A hand touched his shoulder and he jumped.

Amelia tried to smile. "It's a blasted shock."

Daniel nodded. "Of . . . of course."

"Your Grace," she added.

He winced. "Don't call me that."

Daniel had never given much thought to what would happen when the head of the Vaughn family died. When their father had gone, suddenly and in the middle of a game of cards, they had grieved, but there had been an heir. His twin brother, David, had been three and twenty, more than old enough to take on the family name and the burden of representing the family to the world and to Society, and that had been that.

David had dealt with it all. Oh, Daniel had offered to help. And perhaps if his offer had been more hearty, his brother might have accepted it.

Or not. His brother always liked being the one in control, after all. That was perhaps why, days after his sister's late-night revelation, he was standing in his brother's study, faced with the consequences of setting to rights the affairs of a controlling man who never seemed to open a damn letter.

"And this is the last of it?" Daniel said with a sigh before he opened another drawer and groaned.

The room was absolutely covered in paper. Every inch of the place. The desk, the chairs, the floor. Even the tops of bookcases, as far as he could see, were dusted with white parchment and paper.

"Goodness," Amelia said faintly from just behind him. "He wasn't very tidy, was he?"

Not very tidy, Daniel thought darkly, *was an understatement.*

When the solicitors had sat him down and told him that, as his brother's heir, he had inherited everything—title, fortune, property, and estate—it had taken them almost half an hour to list it all.

Daniel had forced himself not to snort with laughter throughout the whole experience. As though he did not know the family's possessions! He had grown up in half of them.

But he had let the man speak—in truth, he'd been too tired not to. He'd only managed a couple hours sleep after Amelia's appearance in his hall, but he had known that there would be much estate business that simply couldn't wait. And he had subsequently spent the last two days going through the Bath townhouse that had been the Vaughn family home whenever they were here for the Season. David and Amelia had been living in it together the last few months—his sister desperate to return to Egermour Manor in the country, his brother equally determined to stay until the very last member of the *ton* had disappeared off to their own country estates.

Daniel had resided in his own townhouse. It was small, far smaller than the Vaughn home, but that hadn't mattered. He hadn't been one for the pomp and ceremony his brother had preferred.

What he had not realized was that David had become . . . well, there was only one word to describe it. *A hoarder.*

"Four pianofortes!" Daniel grumbled as he waded into the study, the paper dragging at his heels. "What does a man need four pianofortes for? *Forte* on one piano wasn't enough?"

"It was the six violins that surprised me," said Amelia, poking at a mound of papers and jumping as it cascaded into the mess. "I didn't even know he played."

"He didn't," sighed Daniel, glancing about the study and wondering where on earth to start. "And the numerous paintings just propped up against walls—"

"To be fair, every inch was covered in other paintings," his sister pointed out.

Daniel shot her a look. "How on earth did you live in all this?"

It was a sore reminder that he had been sadly absent from his brother's life these last few months. Something that thankfully, no one had mentioned in his hearing. But after the fiasco in Edinburgh, when he had attempted to find a doctor for David and the man had attempted to—

Well. The less said about that, the better.

Suffice it to say, David had ordered Daniel out of his presence, and Daniel had been so irritated with the man that he had complied.

Something he would regret, now, for the rest of his life.

"There must be hundreds of letters in here," said Amelia, attempting to reach the desk but finding it impossible to move through the swathe of paper.

"If not thousands," said Daniel with a sigh.

How was he ever supposed to organize all of this? Would he ever reach the end of it?

"And more letters are arriving all the time, Keynes said," said his sister brightly. "You may find yourself with more before you've even started."

"Thank you," Daniel said, trying not to smile. "That's very encouraging."

There was a knock at the door. Two faces peered in, one in fascination, one boiling with rage.

Daniel attempted to take a step back. Arms flailing, he sank into the sea of letters.

"Sir!" he heard through the rustling sheaves.

"I think you will find he is Your Grace," snipped a second voice.

Daniel looked blearily up at the two women. *Ah. The second of his problems today.*

"I-I am terribly sorry to bother you, sir," began Mrs. Stafford.

"I told you, he is Your Grace!" cut in Mrs. Markl, the housekeeper for his brother. "And you would know that if you had ever been a housekeeper for a duke!"

Daniel's heart sank. *What did a man do with two housekeepers?*

"Amelia," he said, inspired by a moment of madness. "Would you please ask Mrs. Stafford and Mrs. Markl for some help with my brother's—"

"But Your Grace," Mrs. Markl said primly. "I don't—"

"I was under the impression you are here to serve me, Mrs. Markl," said Daniel, more harshly than he wished, but he had to end this nightmare.

The two women had been accosting him on an almost hourly basis, desperate to find out what was to become of them. He quite understood. He was still wondering what was to become of him.

"Amelia," Daniel said, looking beseechingly at his sister.

She sighed but plastered on a smile. "Ladies, I would greatly appreciate your advice in the ballroom. You see . . ."

The three women departed from the study as Daniel blinked, still lying on the letters. *Ballroom?* Since when was there a ballroom in this place?

Oh, it was all such a mess. David could not have left his affairs in a worse state, and it was now his responsibility, apparently, to untangle it all. But it was all so complicated! Debts to names Daniel did not recognize, debts owed to David—now to him—from people he did not know. Bills and invoices, horses David was halfway through selling, an antiques dealer who had arrived with three crates of items his brother had apparently just purchased . . .

If only there were something simple, Daniel could not help but think. Something he could immediately resolve, give himself the sense he had an iota of control over the whole thing.

He picked up a folder. It was a large one, the sort he rather assumed a solicitor or an accountant would use. Inside the file were several letters. They were all written in the same hand, a delicate and old-fashioned one, all addressed to the Duke of Thornfalcone.

Me, Daniel thought wryly. *At least, now it was.*

Hardly considering what he was doing, he unfolded one of the letters.

My Lord Duke,

You promised me assistance and yet I have not seen you now for almost five days. Have you left Bath for London? Are you so swift to abandon me that you would make false promises to a desperate woman?

Please, return to Sunview Cottage at your earliest convenience.

Your humble servant,
Nora

Now that was most interesting. Daniel had never known his brother to be particularly charitable, but evidently this old woman had depended on him for something. Most peculiar.

With a rising sense of interest, he unfolded another letter.

My Lord Duke,

I have never begged for anything in my life, but after the hint you gave yesterday about assistance, it would be remiss of me not to.

Please, I would be forever in your debt. And you know how I could pay off that particular bill.

Your most humble servant,

Nora

Daniel half smiled. Whatever the woman thought she could do, he doubted a duke would need knitted gloves, or a scarf, or whatever charitable act she thought she had to offer.

A third letter revealed the following.

My Lord Duke,

I have heard that you are unwell, which I hope is the reason for your abandonment. The moment you are better, please come to Sunview Cottage. I am in dire need, and you did vow to help me.

Nora

Daniel slowly began picking his way toward the door. Well, he had hoped for something small and tangible. The woman probably needed a few shillings, perhaps a small bill paid off to ensure she could keep a roof over her head. Something simple for him but truly meaningful for her. It was perfect.

"Campbell," said Daniel, striding across the echoing hall—nothing like his own. "Have you ever heard of Sunview Cottage?"

The man frowned. "Sunview Cottage? No, I don't think—oh, perhaps . . . it's not . . . well, I hesitate to name her before you, sir—

Your Grace, sorry. But . . . Nora's place?"

"That's the one," said Daniel, pleased that they were making quick progress. "Directions, my good man."

The valet's eyes widened. "You, er . . . you want to see Nora?"

Clearly the old woman was fearsome, Daniel thought. If she could strike fear in a servant, perhaps they teased her as a witch!

Ah, well. It would be a small diversion, something to keep him out of the house and away from that pit of loose paper and unopened letters.

"Directions," Daniel repeated. "And tell Cook—oh, goodness, it's a different cook here, isn't it?"

Campbell hesitated. "Yes. And, if you forgive me for saying so, sir—Your Grace, sir . . . there's a ducal valet here."

Daniel almost swore under his breath. Of course there was. How did other dukes do it? When they newly inherited a title, how did they merge and mingle two entirely different households? Or did they not? Did they simply let one set go and keep the others?

"I will sort all that out later," he said firmly, far more certainly than he felt. "Directions to Sunview Cottage, if you would be so good."

It was not hard to find. Daniel sighed happily as the sun poured down on him and his horse. It was good to get out of Bath for a while—though he wasn't that far from it. The road to Bath was just a few hundred yards away, and he could see the glittering town on the hill from here.

Still, it was fresh country air he breathed as he carefully dismounted outside the cottage he had to assume was Sunview Cottage. Soon he would be speaking to the elderly Nora and would put something right in the world.

Daniel knocked smartly on the door. The poor dear. She had been waiting for the Duke of Thornfalcone, and now she would receive . . .

Well. The Duke of Thornfalcone.

Daniel half smiled. It would be rather a shock to the old thing.

Perhaps he should break it gently—

The door opened. The most beautiful woman he had ever seen, with flaming red hair and a scowl across her face, glared up at him.

"What?" she snapped. "What in God's name do you want?"

CHAPTER TWO

Eleanor Harvey glared up at the man who was staring as though she was someone who had come back from the dead.

Honestly. She did not look that bad, did she?

True, she had sold the looking glass a few days ago and so technically had no idea what she looked like—but she had grown so accustomed to pinning back her hair without it, surely it could not be that different?

The man's jaw had dropped. Was he just going to stand there like an idiot?

Nora sighed. She would have to say something. Why was she always doing the hard work of conversation with men? Couldn't they just act like human beings for five minutes?

"What?" she snapped. "What in God's name do you want?"

Immediately, Nora wished she had waited just a half second more before jumping down the man's throat.

He had obviously been recently bereaved. The mourning coat was long, longer than she had thought fashionable—though she had been out of Society so long, it was hard to know what the styles were these days.

There was a heavy look in his eyes and bags underneath them that suggested he had not slept well in days.

Regret tugged at her. *Perhaps she had been too harsh.*

"I mean, good afternoon, sir," Nora said, trying to sound cordial. "Is there a purpose for your visit?"

And try as she might, she could not stave off the hope that rose as she considered this man's presence here. Was it possible that . . . that *he* had sent this man to her? That even though he could not come to her himself, he had sent a servant to do his bidding?

The trouble was, this man did not look like a servant. He appeared to be a gentleman, now Nora took a closer look. There was something strangely familiar about that face . . .

"I . . . I . . ." The man swallowed. "I am looking for Sunview Cottage."

Nora nodded. "You have found it."

"No," said the man instinctively.

What was wrong with the man? Had she not been perfectly clear?

Nora took a deep breath and tried to push all the day's frustrations—none of which had anything to do with this stranger—from her mind. She did not care that the roof was leaking. She did not care that she was out of firewood. She did not care that the larder was empty. She did not care—

"Sunview Cottage," repeated the man. "I . . . I was told—the directions I was given—"

"This is Sunview Cottage, for its sins," said Nora, unable to keep the dryness from her voice. "You have found it, sir. The directions you were given must have been good."

And hopefully you were sent by a duke, she wanted to say but managed to swallow. At this point, she'd take any help she could get. It didn't need to have a title attached.

Where was he? After all those promises, after vowing on his own life he would return within a week, what had it been now—four? Five? Nora had started losing count, which was a sure sign it was far too long.

The blackguard. She should never have trusted him.

"But . . ." the man swallowed. "Are you certain?"

It was everything she could do not to laugh in the man's face. Certain? Of her own address?

"Yes, I am certain," she said aloud. "It's been Sunview Cottage for near a hundred years."

That's what her grandmother had said. The cottage would last forever, she said.

Nora almost snorted aloud at the memory. To be sure, any building could last forever if it was cared for properly—but that took coin, and she had precious little of it right now. And precious few ways to earn it.

At least, she had thought so.

"I . . ." The man cleared his throat. "May I come in?"

Nora narrowed her eyes. "Why?"

It was a reasonable question. It was an unreasonable request, in her mind. What man—what gentleman—would consider it appropriate to enter the home of a woman like her, alone and unmarried, without a chaperone?

Not that it had stopped the Duke of Thornfalcone, of course. But then, he had not been a gentleman.

He didn't answer right away, and Nora opened her mouth to simply give a negative response—but she hesitated.

Her eyes met those of the man, whoever he was. They were tired eyes, it was true, but there was also something else in there. Something dark and yet soft. Something in those gray irises that told her he would not hurt her. Something powerfully trustworthy.

Something she did not see very often.

Nora hesitated. *Well, what difference would it make to her reputation now?* It was already ruined. It could hardly be made worse.

"I . . ." Lord, now she sounded like him—uncertain. "You wish to come in?"

The man nodded slowly. "I . . . yes. I think the conversation we must have would be better conducted inside, rather than on a doorstep."

The hope that a moment ago had flickered in Nora's heart grew. He had to have been sent by the Duke of Thornfalcone—there was no one else who would need to have a conversation of any import. Finally, he had come to his senses. Finally, he had realized that making a vow such as the one he had made required following through.

Finally, she was about to receive what she deserved.

"Well, I suppose you had better come in," Nora said, as graciously as she could.

Before she'd had a chance to step to the side in the doorway, the man strode through. His sleeve brushed up against her chest, and his smell intoxicated her. For just a moment, she was suddenly conscious of his breadth, his masculine power—

And then it was over. He continued on inside without giving her a second glance.

Nora breathed out slowly, hardly aware of the breath she had been holding in. *Good God.* The man was power itself. How had she not seen it? How did he suddenly come into his own as he moved?

He was not moving now. The man was standing in her kitchen, the room the front door of her cottage opened into, with a rather uncertain look.

"I . . . erm, where shall I sit?" he asked awkwardly.

Nora raised an eyebrow. "Did I invite you to sit down?"

It was perhaps a jest at his expense for her own amusement, and not a very clever one at that. But as she watched a flush tinge the man's cheeks, she rather wished she hadn't made it.

It was, after all, a fair question. The table in the center of the room was dark oak, heavy and weighty, but its matching chairs were absent. One had gone the way of the fire—that had been a particularly hard winter—and four had gone the way of the rag and bone man. The last was in her parlor.

Not that this man, whoever he was, would be seeing her parlor.

"I am afraid this is a working kitchen, not a place I typically receive guests," Nora said, as airily as she could manage.

She was not going to permit herself to feel ashamed of her living situation. It was hardly her fault. It was all—

"I see," said the man slowly. "Do you—well. Do you have a drawing room, or—"

His voice was interrupted by Nora's laughter. "I am sorry, did you not see the size of this cottage when you approached it? You think there is space here for a drawing room?"

Honestly, who was this man? Had he never seen a house before?

The man's flush deepened. "I . . . I do apologize, I—"

"Oh, I would not worry about it," Nora said with a bracing smile she hoped communicated her regret for making the jest in the first place. "It was foolish of me to . . . you have come from the Duke of Thornfalcone, haven't you?"

The name had slipped from her lips before she could stop it. Desperation did that to a woman.

Unable to look at his embarrassed face any longer, her turned her eyes to anything else in the room. The bread cooling on the table. The kettle on the fire—or at least, where a fire would be if she had any coal. The pitcher of milk on the side, as far from the warmth of the window as possible.

And that was it. Bread, milk, and perhaps a few eggs she could boil later. If the man asked for tea, what on earth was she going to do?

"I . . . you know the Duke of Thornfalcone?"

Nora turned her gaze back to the man. She would have to be careful, here. She had no wish to antagonize the brute, and any servant or friend the duke had sent would surely take back a report. She did not wish to lose what little favor she already had.

Though she wasn't entirely sure if you could call it favor. What was it, being offered the world, then not hearing from the blackguard in over a month?

"I thought he would have come himself," Nora said slowly. "After his promise."

The man stepped closer. "His promise?"

"Many promises, actually—but then you'll know all about that," she said, forcing herself to smile. "And I will admit, I am glad to see you."

The man's eyebrows rose. "You are?"

The man was either very dense or attempting to be gallant. Nora was unsure which. Surely he knew the . . . the arrangement she and the duke had come to?

"Yes, of course," she said, as lightly as she could manage. "It is about time."

"It is?"

Nora tried to take a deep, calming breath. It was rather difficult to conduct this sort of conversation at the best of times. So much one needed to say, so much one could not say directly.

But this man seemed to have no compunction in merely repeating half of what she said. Did he not have anything to contribute?

"You are Nora, aren't you?"

Nora reached out for the kitchen table, as though to steady herself.

She did not know why. The instinct had flashed through her so swiftly, she hardly knew where it had come from.

There had been something . . . well, not threatening, precisely, but darkly meaningful in the man's voice. Something that suggested there was more going on here than met the eye. Certainly more than she knew about.

Well, she was not going to permit this sort of nonsense any longer.

"I am Nora, yes," she said aloud. "And you are?"

It did not seem to be a difficult question. Nora was sure everyone in England knew how to respond to that question. All she wanted was a name, not a life story.

But the man, inexplicably, hesitated. "Ah."

"Ah?" repeated Nora, irritation bubbling in her stomach. "Look, sir, if the Duke of Thornfalcone did send you—"

"He did. In a manner of speaking," the man said with a strange sort of smile.

And Nora's heart sank.

Oh, God.

She had always worried someone might discover the agreement made and believe they could take advantage of her. *She was not that kind of woman,* Nora thought desperately. She did not offer herself for nothing—she had never offered herself at all! And if this man thought he could overhear the Duke of Thornfalcone boasting about her, and just turn up here—

"Look, you clod, I am not available for—for that," she said fiercely, gripping the kitchen table hard. "I don't know what you have heard of my agreement with the Duke of Thornfalcone, but I can assure you—"

"No—no, it's not like that!" The man looked truly outraged she would presume such a thing. "It's just . . . I am the Duke of Thornfalcone."

Nora stared. She took in the words, one at a time, and carefully examined the man's face to ensure he was not jesting.

And then she laughed. "Very good, very good. And your real name is?"

But the man did not laugh. "I am the Duke of Thornfalcone."

"You must think me a complete fool," said Nora sharply, laughter fading in her throat. "I have met the Duke of Thornfalcone. Not once, but several times." It had taken several times to negotiate the agreement. "And I can tell you quite definitely, you are not—"

"I know this may be hard to accept," said the man, slowly taking a step around her kitchen table. "But I am the Duke of Thornfalcone."

Nora opened her mouth to protest, but her words faded.

There was such certainty, such determination in the man's face, it was almost impossible to think about arguing with him.

How was it possible? There could not be two Dukes of Thornfalcone, could there?

Panic rushed through Nora's veins. There was a chance, even if it was remote, that the man before her was telling the truth. He did not look like a rake, now she came to look at him. His mourning clothes were not overly elegant. He wore no rings save for a signet ring, and his pocket watch chain was simple and discreet.

In short, true examples of gentility. No brashness, no apparent desire to impress, but everything about his person was precise and well made.

But if this was the duke, then that would mean . . .

Nora had never questioned him. The man who had arrived outside her cottage almost two months ago. He had called himself the Duke of Thornfalcone, and she had seen no reason to disbelieve him.

Who would argue with a man who was promising you the world?

But what proof did she have, Nora asked herself with a sinking feeling, *that the first man had truly been the Duke of Thornfalcone?* What if he had lied? What if he had been no duke at all?

The panic flaring in her stomach reached her lungs, making it difficult to breathe. What bargain had she struck if it was with a man she did not even know? How could she find him again? All her letters had been addressed to the Duke of Thornfalcone . . .

The panic turned to nausea. Was that why this man was here? Had he started receiving her letters and, at a complete loss to understand why she was doing something so uncouth as to write to him, decided to come to meet her himself?

Nora swallowed. Anyone could lie about being a duke, couldn't they? She had no way of ascertaining the truth. She was at the mercy of any man who arrived at her door.

Any man . . .

"I have met a man," she said quietly, her voice hoarse. "He called himself the Duke of Thornfalcone. You cannot both—"

"I think," interrupted the man with quiet eyes, "you met my brother."

"Brother?" Nora stared. "Your brother?"

And suddenly her mind was able to put together the clues it had spotted but not quite understood. The same hair. The same build, probably within an inch of the same height. Oh, they dressed differently, and this man was certainly more understated, more gentle. But they were similar. The same color eyes, even if this man looked at her with pity and confusion, and the first had looked with desire. A need to possess. A demand to have her.

Nora swallowed. *If they were brothers . . .*

Well, that could only mean one thing. Nora did not have a great acquaintance with the nobility. Even when she had been a part of Society, when her attendance at card parties in particular had been demanded by women as well respected as Lady Romeril, she had rarely encountered actual nobility. But she did not need to be intimately acquainted with them to know the rules about how titles changed hands.

"He's . . . is he dead?" Nora's voice was a whisper.

The new Duke of Thornfalcone nodded.

How could this have happened? The chances were astronomical—it was surely a complete coincidence that just as she had made an agreement with this man, he would die and render the assistance void.

Nora sighed quietly. Was that all she cared about, she wondered with shame. A man had died, and she was worried about herself?

A quiet drip fell from the ceiling into the bucket she had placed only last night. Nora winced. Well, it was easy to worry about yourself when there was so much to worry about.

"Nora?"

Nora focused on the man in her kitchen—a man who was significantly closer to her now. Somehow he had stepped around her kitchen table without her noticing. He was only a foot away.

She stumbled back. "What is your name? I know your title, but—"

"Daniel Vaughn," he said quietly.

Nora swallowed. Vaughn. Yes, the other Duke of Thornfalcone had said his name was Vaughn. There was no reason to disbelieve the man before her.

A new Duke of Thornfalcone. And what was to become of her?

"I found some of your letters to . . . to my brother," said Daniel awkwardly.

"Found them?" repeated Nora. "Why would you—oh."

Heat flushed her cheeks. Of course. David Vaughn was dead, and so his brother—his younger brother—would be sorting through his possessions. How strange, to think that one's life could be picked up by another. In this case, every part of it. Houses, riches, title . . .

And women.

Nora swallowed. "I-I don't know what you read—"

"Not much, but enough to know my brother was in some sort of agreement with you," said Daniel softly, his gaze fixed on hers. "And I would like to know about it. All about it."

Of course he did. What was wrong with gentlemen—did they only think of one thing? Were they interested in nothing more than gratifying the flesh? Was it impossible for them to look at her and see not someone they could possess or demand pleasure from, but simply a woman who faced the world alone?

Nora finally managed to find her voice. "Get out."

Daniel—the Duke of Thornfalcone's—brow furrowed. "I beg your pardon?"

"I said, get out," said Nora stiffly, walking around the other side of the kitchen table as though that could protect her from his presence.

How did he do it? Fill the place with a sense that all here was created for him and him alone?

"Nora, I don't—"

"It's Miss Harvey to you, Your Grace, and I will thank you to leave my property immediately," said Nora as sternly as she could manage, reaching the front door with relief and pulling it open. "Good day."

For a moment, she was certain he was going to argue with her. And what then? She could not eject him bodily from the place. She doubted whether she could pull him forward one inch.

But as Daniel looked at her, gray eyes flooding with an emotion she did not understand, he nodded. "As you wish."

He was gone in the space of a moment, his mourning coat tails flapping in the wind. Nora did not wait to see if he had anything else to say. She did not even look out at him through the door.

Slamming it, she leaned against it and tried to catch her breath. What on earth was she going to do now?

CHAPTER THREE

5 June 1811

DANIEL CLEARED HIS throat and shuffled his feet.

He was not nervous.

Probably. Most irritatingly, the nerves did not disappear the moment he informed himself that he was not nervous. It had never worked, not even as a child when he had been willing to believe almost anything.

But he was here. That was the main thing. Wasn't it?

Brilliant summer sunshine poured down on him, making the mourning coat even more uncomfortable. Who was it who had decided black was the only suitable color for those who had been bereaved, anyway? Why not a lighter color, one which would not make him feel so discomforted?

But he wasn't here to criticize Society's stylistic choices. He was here to make good on a bargain, whatever it was, that had been made by someone who had borne the title he now held. He had to make it good.

For his family's honor.

Daniel lifted a hand and knocked on the door. "Miss Harvey?"

There was absolute silence.

Well, almost. The leaves continued to rustle and birds continued to sing in the trees, but it all rather emphasized the fact that no one had rushed to open the door and welcome him in.

Which, after the way he had been ejected from Sunview Cottage just days ago, should not have surprised Daniel. The little sleep he'd managed to gain before seeing his solicitor and then immediately diving into David's sea of clutter and unanswered correspondence had not been enough—nor had any rest he'd had since. Not enough to prepare him to both see to his new ducal duties and see Miss Harvey. And he'd made his choice.

He knocked again. "Miss Harvey!"

His pulse was throbbing rather painfully in his ears, something Daniel told himself was natural. He was meeting someone new—something he loathed—and he had clearly got off on the wrong footing with her.

How, he did not precisely know. He had said very little, and the little he'd said had been harmless. At least it had been harmless as far as Daniel could make out. He had spent an afternoon running through every line he could recall, but it did not seem to make any difference. Nothing he had uttered appeared to justify the rude dismissal he had received.

"It's Miss Harvey to you, Your Grace, and I will thank you to leave my property immediately. Good day."

Daniel shifted on his feet. She was in there. Nora. Eleanor Harvey, as he had discovered from Campbell when he had returned to the family house, dejected.

He really should be considering it *his* house. One day, perhaps he would.

Eleanor Harvey, it turned out, had a reputation. And not a very savory one.

"I assumed you knew, sir—Your Grace!" his valet had protested when Daniel had inquired delicately about the woman he had met that day. "I mean, everyone in Bath—"

"Not everyone," Daniel had said wearily. "Not me."

It had been impossible to return here as swiftly as he had wanted. Daniel had been determined to revisit Sunview Cottage with flowers, some sort of gift, an apology—though he knew not what for—the very next day.

As it had turned out, that had been an unrealistic plan.

"The funeral of course is tomorrow," intoned his new butler, Keynes, in a low voice. "You will need to visit the solicitors again, meet with your steward, choose the next eighteen bottles of wine from the cellar, and confirm all servant appointments now you are combining both households."

Daniel had nodded, head spinning, bewildered as he sat alone at the massive dining table.

Honestly, who had a dining table this large? When their parents had been alive, one of the smaller drawing rooms had been made into a family dining room. It had a table for six—perfect for the family of five. What on earth had David done with it?

There appeared to be a great deal to do as Duke of Thornfalcone—which was strange, because his brother had never seemed to do anything.

"Right," he said. "And—"

"Your valet informs me—both of your valets inform me, actually, Your Grace," said Keynes pointedly, "that you require an entirely new wardrobe, as befitting the new duke. Your tailor will visit all day the next day, and the day after—"

"Am I not to have a day to myself for weeks?" Daniel could not help but mutter under his breath. All he wanted to do was return to Sunview Cottage and see Nora. Miss Harvey.

As it turned out, he had not spoken under his breath enough.

The butler cleared his throat with a raised eyebrow. "This is the ducal burden, Your Grace, and I am sure you would not wish to disappoint. Now, the silverware needs to be reviewed by you—"

"Reviewed?" Daniel had asked.

"Yes, reviewed," the butler said carefully. "It is tradition, Your Grace, that after the death of one duke and the emergence of another, the new duke reviews the silverware."

Leaving aside the fact that he was being described more like a chrysalis than a man, Daniel said, "Reviewed, though? What for? Marks? Out of ten, hahaha . . ."

His attempt at a jest was met with a dour look from Keynes. "Very amusing, Your Grace."

Daniel swallowed. *And this was why*, he told himself firmly, *you do not make jokes*.

"It is merely a formality, to ensure none of the silverware has been stolen in the interim period, Your Grace," the butler continued.

That made Daniel's eyes widen. *Stolen?* Was this a typical sort of concern in ducal households?

It was a foolish question. He had been raised in one, knew the odd sorts of formalities that crept up over the years. Traditions no one understood, servants with odd titles who performed only one role. Parts of this house had been closed up in the summer of '72 and had never been seen since.

"Ah," Daniel had said helplessly. "Right. Well, if you want to bring the cutlery through now—"

"There are four hundred, eighty-seven pieces of silverware in the possession of the Duke of Thornfalcone," said Keynes smoothly. "I will have them laid out on the ballroom floor."

The man had disappeared before Daniel had been able to ask where on earth this ballroom was that everyone kept talking about. There had been no opportunity to inquire about Miss Harvey, or any bargains or agreements the previous duke may have made.

And so here he was, days later, finally escaping all the requirements of a duke, half of which he had never heard of.

And Nora—and Miss Harvey was not answering the door.

"Miss Harvey?" Daniel said, a little deflated.

He had decided against the flowers, in the end. Flowers could have made his appearance look . . . *expectant*.

A flush tinged his cheeks as he recalled the way Nora had looked at him, in horror, when she thought he was demanding her affections.

It was bad enough that he admired his brother's mistress—he could at least admit that much to himself. But it was worse that she had been so repulsed by even the suggestion that he—

Not that he would, Daniel told himself firmly. There were some things in life one simply did not do, and bedding your brother's mistress was one of them. There were some lines you just did not cross.

He cleared his throat. "Miss Harvey, I know you are in there."

It hadn't been too hard to deduce. There had been a sudden ruffling of the curtains, drawing them tight as he had cantered up to the place on his horse. And then the sound of what could have been a chair being tipped over had also echoed around the cottage. Daniel wasn't sure what the noise had been, in truth. He had not seen a chair in the pitiful kitchen he had been welcomed into, but he presumed there was another room in the place with at least one chair.

Dear God, he hoped so.

How had his brother allowed this place to get into such a state? Though to be fair, Daniel himself had hardly looked at the cottage when he had first arrived. He had been convinced he would see the old dear within, give her some money, then be off.

He had not expected to be so touched.

Daniel shook his head ruefully. Not that it had. He was no green gilled boy—he was a man of nearly eight and twenty!

But he hadn't been so distracted by the sensuous beauty of the woman who lived at Sunview Cottage that he had ignored the dilapidated roof, the peeling paint around the windows, or the way that every stick of furniture which could be sold obviously had been.

"Miss Harvey? I . . . I have brought food," Daniel said lamely.

He hated the plaintive tone in his voice the moment it emerged from his lips, but he could not help it.

Had any woman ever captured his attention as she had? Had he ever been so lost in a woman's eyes, so completely adrift in a woman's presence?

He was being a fool. Daniel had never been a ladies' man. His brother had more than fulfilled that role in the family. So why was he standing out here, a basket of food in one hand and the other knocking once again at the door, when he should be in the townhouse, trying to find the floor in his brother's old study?

Daniel sighed. He couldn't wait any longer. He had to use the last resort, the phrase he had promised he would not use unless it was absolutely necessary. But if she was not going to answer the door . . .

"Miss Harvey," Daniel said, raising his voice. "I have some good news for you."

There was an irritated snort through the door. "I doubt it!"

A slow grin crept across Daniel's face.

She was in there. More than that, she was standing right on the other side of the door. Nora was far more curious about why he was here than her silence had let on.

Besides, it was refreshing to be spoken to in such a manner. For all his life, Daniel had been a younger son. Younger by about twenty minutes, but younger, nonetheless. David had never permitted him to forget it, and neither had their father. Or their tutor. Or most of the other nobles they were permitted to associate with.

In truth, it was only men like Samuel Dellamore, the Duke of Chantmarle, Daniel thought darkly, *who treated him as someone even worth knowing.*

The last few days, of course, all that had changed.

Now Daniel couldn't go five minutes without someone bowing or scraping. Everyone kept insisting on calling him "Your Grace" even after he asked them to stop. His sister, Amelia, had even taken to calling him Thornfalcone instead of Daniel, which was most disconcerting, though thankfully that had ceased when she had gratefully agreed to go to their country manor, where she had wanted to be all summer.

But Nora? Oh, no, she was more than happy to be rude toward him, and it fired a small furnace in Daniel's chest.

Forced politeness? You could keep it. But the subtle rage of a woman who had no wish to open a door? That was more like it.

"I promise you, Miss Harvey, I speak the truth," said Daniel, calling through the door and wishing to goodness she would open it.

So that she could hear him plainly, of course. Not so he could once again take in the beauty of her eyes, the curves of her—

"I said that I doubted it, and I stand by my statement!" came her sharp words.

Daniel smiled. "I have paid off all your debts, Miss Harvey."

As he had expected, there was no quipped reply to that remark.

There was, however, the sound of a heavy bolt being flung back into its casing. The door opened slowly, and a face peeked out from behind it.

Just as he had predicted, Daniel thought. If there was one thing that would almost guarantee that Nora would open the door, it was that news.

But it was not a look of blind adoration, or even just gratitude that met his. No, though the fiery red hair was the same, and the simple blue gown she had been wearing days ago was again today's attire of choice, there was a far more suspicious glare on Nora's face than Daniel had ever seen. On her, or on anyone else.

There was also a strange white patch in her hair.

Daniel blinked. He did not recall Nora having graying or white hair. Surely he would have recalled such a thing. The door opened wider, and Nora brought her hand through her curls as though unwilling to face him. More white appeared in her hair.

His gaze dropped to her hands. They too were white. She was . . .

baking?

"Why?" Nora snapped.

"Why what?" Daniel asked, bewildered.

Any man would be. Had anyone ever stood in the face of such beauty—

"Why have you paid off all my debts?" Nora said, eyes narrowing. "If you have. Which I doubt."

Whatever had caused Nora Harvey to be so suspicious of men, Daniel thought with a sinking feeling, *it could not be good.* Why were men so cruel, he wondered. He had seen much of the worst of men. One could not attend university and be a grudging member of the Dulverton Club without seeing it.

But how had a woman like Nora encountered the worst of men?

"I have done so," said Daniel aloud. "At least, all those I could find."

"Find?" she said quickly. "You've been asking about town after me?"

"No, of course not, that would be most dishonorable," Daniel said quietly, still holding the heavy basket. "I would never—you sent a note listing all your debts to my brother. It was sent the day before he died, as a matter of fact." Another thought occurred to him. "I suppose you did not incur any additional debts in the meantime."

He should have considered that before. Perhaps he should have asked his butler to make discreet enquiries. But then Daniel would have to explain it all to Keynes, and he wasn't sure he understood the full story himself.

"Oh," said Nora faintly. "Oh. That was . . . but why?"

Daniel drew himself up proudly. He may not have been a duke for very long, but he knew the etiquette that respectability demanded.

The moment he had worked it out, he had known what he had to do. His brother had never been particularly open about his mistresses, but Daniel had always known he'd had them. As long as their sister did not know, Daniel had said to David once, that was quite all right. And after Nora Harvey had turned out not to be the little old dear Daniel had first assumed, he'd read again the letters he'd found with a wiser eye. The only conclusion to draw was that she had been one of those mistresses.

Well, David would have cared for her if he had lived. Now it was his, Daniel's, responsibility to do so.

"It was a matter," Daniel said as grandly as he could manage, "of honor."

Nora snorted. "You're pulling my leg."

Daniel blinked. He had expected gratitude, thanks, wringing of his hands, and perhaps even—his stomach lurched—an embrace.

Nothing sordid, naturally. Just enough to demonstrate her relief and to warm his heart.

But instead, Nora was looking with a raised eyebrow and an expression which told him he was not going to receive a single one of those things. In fact, he would be fortunate if he were not subjected to another sharp remark.

"No, really," Daniel said, bewildered. "My brother—well, he would have continued to support you throughout the duration of your . . . ah, agreement."

Why, oh why, did his cheeks have to burn at this very moment? She would think him an absolute fool! Daniel was no innocent—no gentleman was once he passed the age of about twenty. So why did he find it so mortifying talking about this sort of thing?

Perhaps it was because it was with his own brother's mistress. Nothing to do with her beauty or the way his gaze was constantly drawn to her breasts. Nothing like that.

"I made a commitment to take care of all my brother's affairs," Daniel began.

Nora laughed bitterly. "There were that many, were there?"

"I mean, all his affairs of business," said Daniel, cheeks fully aflame now. "And I would hate to think a single person had suffered because of his death."

There was a strange look in her eyes as something passed across Nora's face. Something Daniel did not quite catch, but looked remarkably like—

But no, it couldn't be. Why would one of his brother's mistresses be angry?

"I see," she said dryly. "Is that for me?"

"What—oh," said Daniel lamely, wishing to goodness he had thought to give it to her before Nora eagerly snatched the basket from his arm. "Yes, yes, it's for you."

His voice trailed away as he watched the hunger in her eyes. Not for him. *He wasn't that lucky.* Besides, as he had told himself firmly the day they had met, he would never cross that line. His brother's mistresses were off limits.

No, Nora's hunger for food was the desire here. She pulled the napkin off the roasted ham, the dish of spiced chicken, the loaf of bread, slab of butter, jar of pickled beans—

"This is for me?" she repeated, suspicion dripping from every syllable.

Daniel tried not to look at the almost bare kitchen behind her. "I-I thought . . . well . . ."

"You thought I was hungry," said Nora plainly, meeting his eye.

He swallowed. *Yes*, he wanted to say. And it's been killing me these last few days, thinking of you here, in this damp, moldering cottage with nothing to eat and no furniture to speak of. I've been sitting in my new home, trying to confirm to my new butler that all sixteen candelabras are polished to perfection, while you've been here, starving.

"I . . . I want to look after you," said Daniel helplessly.

The words had been pulled from his tongue before he could stop them.

Nora flushed. "That means nothing."

It meant everything. Daniel hardly understood what he was doing, but he knew that he could not live while Nora suffered like this. It was burning a hole in his conscience as nothing else ever had. Could she not see that?

"If I could just come in," he said, finally allowing his gaze to flicker into the cottage behind her. "Then I could explain—"

"Absolutely not," Nora said firmly, moving to shut the door.

Daniel just managed to wedge his boot into the doorway. It caused a great shooting pain up his leg, but it was worth it. He could still just make out Nora's face.

"I want to talk to you," he said quietly. "I want to—"

"Well, I do not want to talk to you," said Nora, cheeks flushing. "You think you can just come in here, thrust a basket at me—"

"You took—"

"—tell me all my debts are paid, which I highly doubt," Nora continued, her color rising, "and expect gratitude and a welcome inside! You may be a duke, Your Grace, but this is my castle, and I am afraid to say you are not welcome!"

A sudden kick against his ankle made Daniel withdraw it with a hasty intake of breath.

And then it was too late. The door slammed before him.

Daniel sighed heavily and leaned his forehead against the door. If he had any sense—which ordinarily he had a great deal of—he would turn around, mount his horse, and never come back here again. Never subject himself to such humiliation. Never torture himself with the prospect of seeing Nora while unable to have a proper conversation with her.

If he had any sense.

Blast it all to hell.

CHAPTER FOUR

6 June 1811

NORA GLARED AT the green painted door as though it had done her a grievous injury.

In a way, perhaps it had.

"Oh, fiddlesticks," she said with a sigh.

She hadn't even wanted to come into Bath. It had been months since she had last done so. That had been the last time, after all, that she'd had any coin. She had purchased everything she could think of, as many dried foods and jars of pickled meats, as much firewood and coal as the man who had ungraciously brought it all back to her cottage could carry. And she had known she would not return to Bath unless absolutely necessary.

Unless she was desperate.

Nora frowned at the door before her. She was desperate now.

She would just have to hope that Hamish wasn't also in town. The blackguard had already got in trouble with the law two times that she knew of. It was a small relief that the justices in Bath knew she had nothing to do with her brother anymore.

The door was larger than her own. Almost twice as wide, painted in a crisp, grassy shade. There was a brass knocker on it and a bell pull to the side, making it a tad confusing which she should use to attract the attention of those inside.

And though she was tempted to walk back down the three steps that led up to it and return to the pavement, Nora knew she had to do this. She couldn't live with herself if she did not say what she had to say. Even if she hated to do it.

Nora sighed, stomach twisting. She had promised herself she would never have to worry about feeling dependent on a gentleman again. What a shame it had been the new Duke of Thornfalcone who had come a-knocking that day.

Steeling herself for what Nora knew would be a most unpleasant encounter, she lifted a hesitant hand.

Door knocker? Or doorbell?

Oh, what did it matter? The gossip would soon be all around town that Eleanor Harvey had returned, whatever choice she made here or anywhere else, she thought darkly. She lifted both hands together and knocked with one and rang the doorbell with the other.

The clattering noise that followed was enough to raise the dead—*though*, Nora thought awkwardly, *she probably shouldn't think that*. She hadn't been able to ignore the black ribboned bow that adorned the top of the doorframe.

This was a house in mourning.

And then—

Nothing happened.

"Oh," Nora said aloud.

Now this, she had not expected. She had presumed there would be a footman—or someone—to open the door. But perhaps if the house was truly in deep mourning, as would befit a duke, they were not receiving any visitors?

Hope sprang in Nora's heart. *Well, that was perfect!* She could return to her cottage, conscience clear. If she ever felt a quaver of regret, she could . . . could write a letter. Yes, that would surely be sufficient!

Nora had almost reached the pavement when the door behind her opened.

"Yes?" said a cold, low voice.

Her shoulders slumped. Why was it always so hard interacting with the world? Why did men seem to go out of their way to make it more difficult for everyone around them? Could they not just be kind for two minutes?

"Good afternoon," she said softly as she turned.

There was a butler, or what appeared to be a butler, standing in the doorway. "Is it?"

Nora sighed as the man scrunched his nose. *Did every butler have to be so . . . so snooty?* Did they have to make a point of looking at her pelisse—which admittedly, had seen better times—and her gown with disdain? And it was a perfectly serviceable gown. It was one of her only gowns, now.

Nora raised herself up and attempted to project a sense of superiority. It was rather a challenge.

"I am here," she said imperiously, "to see the duke."

The butler looked at her, clearly unmoved, then said in a expressionless voice, "I regret to inform you that the Duke of Thornfalcone is dead."

Nora almost laughed. It was rather amusing. "I had gathered that," she said dryly, clasping her hands in a posture, she hoped, of quiet respect. "I actually meant the new one."

The butler glared. "Why?"

All careful manners were gone, replaced with wariness, Nora noticed. It seemed she was not the only one who had turned up in the hope—or the expectation—of meeting the new duke. And he had clearly informed his butler to keep as many people from darkening his doorway as possible.

Now that was interesting. What duke did not wish to be fawned over, told he was the best and most shining example of manhood that Society had? What man in the whole of Bath did not wish for visitors, now the rush of the Season was over?

Despite herself, despite the chance to curtsy and leave just as she had planned moments before, Nora hesitated. "I think the duke will wish to see me," she said demurely.

"I doubt it."

"Well as neither of us knows his mind," Nora said, more sharply, "I suggest you inquire."

She tried to put as much dominance into her tone as possible. She may not be part of the highest echelons of Society, but she was not a servant, and she was not going to permit one to talk to her like that!

The butler hesitated, indecision flashing across his face for just a moment. He must be as unsure of her social standing as she was. Then he nodded stiffly. "If you would not mind waiting, Miss—Miss?"

"Miss Harvey," Nora said, hating that she had to give her name. "His Grace knows me."

"I am sure he does," the butler said sardonically before closing the door in her face.

Nora's mouth fell open. "Of all the rude—"

She should not have expected any better. *Servants typically responded that way when they heard her name,* Nora thought dully. Even some shop owners now heard the name and suddenly discovered they were no longer able to serve her. It had been a miracle she had been able to order that piece of mackerel before the news spread around the fishmongers.

She waited. Then she waited a little more. Then Nora started drumming her fingers on her arms as she crossed them.

This was getting ridiculous. Either this Daniel Vaughn, Duke of Thornfalcone wanted to see her or he did not. What on earth could be taking this long?

Nora glanced at the basket on her arm. It was remarkably light, but then, so was her reticule. But if the mackerel within it wasn't going to go off, she needed to put it in the coal store as soon as possible. It was the coldest part of the cottage, and—

The door opened.

"His Grace will see you in the Japanese drawing room," said the butler in a disapproving tone, as though he had argued against the decision but had been unsuccessful.

Nora blinked. "Japanese?"

Why would a man name his drawing room? It was most odd.

The butler nodded, opening the door wide for her to enter. "As opposed to the French drawing room, and the Scots drawing room. The previous duke had a particular sense of style."

So Nora saw. As she was ushered into the cavernous hall—and noticeably not invited to hand over her pelisse, gloves, and basket—her eyes widened as she attempted to take in the magnificence of the place.

A high ceiling, covered in paintings of what appeared to be cherubs. A wide fireplace to her left, with porcelain lions either side in what Nora guessed was a Chinese style. A large rug in the center of the hall that covered the marble patterned floor, and such a chandelier—

"His Grace is waiting," said the butler pointedly.

Nora started. She had completely forgotten both butler and duke. Who could focus on mere men, when such splendor was around her?

"Oh, yes, of course," she said vaguely, following the man toward a door which she presumed was the Japanese drawing room.

She was wrong. Nora's eyes darted about the long corridor which the door opened into, amazed at the beautiful paintings on the walls and the gold gilt frames that surrounded them. Door after door led off from the corridor, all of them closed.

How large was this place, exactly? The man couldn't own the whole street, could he?

"Miss Eleanor Harvey, Your Grace," the butler intoned, opening a door and waiting for her to step through it.

And for the first time since she had left her little cottage, Nora swallowed with not anticipation but with fear. Had this been a mistake? Would it have been better to simply accept the kindness offered by a relative stranger? Did she have to come here in person to thank the man for it?

But it was too late now. She was here, just outside the Japanese drawing room, and the butler was frowning.

"Go on," he hissed under his breath.

Nora almost stumbled over her skirts as she stepped forward into—

She would hardly call it a room. The place went on and on, for yards and yards. Sofas and armchairs, a pianoforte—no, two pianofortes. Statues, and a chandelier, and more console tables than she had ever seen before. A chess set, laid out on a table. Two footstools, several rugs, a marble pillar, a cabinet of curiosities, a pair of fans which at least explained how the room had acquired its name. Two bookcases, a globe, a telescope near a window—

"My brother was something of a collector, Miss Harvey," came a gentle voice. "I must say I am not sure what he was collecting. Dust, I think."

Nora swallowed. Seeing Daniel Vaughn, Duke of Thornfalcone, here in his own surroundings, the man seemed entirely different.

Not just more impressive—more real, somehow. As though he had not truly existed when he had come to visit her at Sunview Cottage, but here he was fully realized.

Perhaps it was the fact he was not wearing mourning. *Not that he had to, in his own home,* Nora reminded herself. Maybe that was why the butler was disinclined to permit her entrance. It would be scandalous, after all, if she whispered to anyone in Society that the new Duke of Thornfalcone was not sufficiently mourning his brother.

If there was anyone in Society who would even credit her, it certainly would be a cruel rumor to start.

Nora tried to curtsy, but her legs simply would not obey. "I . . . goodness."

"I think he was attempting to be something of a true collector and collected anything he thought had particular beauty," said Daniel, weaving his way through the plethora of items in the drawing room as he approached her. "You would know all about that."

Nora flushed, hating the heat blossoming in her cheeks but unable to stop it.

Well, how dare he speak to her like that! As though she were an object, something his brother collected simply because he wanted to possess her!

Her anger must have been visible, for the duke suddenly flushed just as dark as she was sure she had. "I m-mean—I did not mean . . . obviously you are not something he collected, I only meant—my brother's recognition of beauty, he . . . oh, hang it."

He looked most awkward, which Nora had not expected. Were dukes always this uncouth with their tongues, or was Daniel unique in that? But of course, he had only been the Duke of Thornfalcone about a week, Nora reminded herself, curiosity piqued. This was a man who had never expected to hold such a title.

Now that was interesting.

"I did not expect to see you here," Daniel said quietly. "Not after . . ."

Nora tried to smile at the remembrance of her last words, shouted at him through a small gap in a rapidly closing door.

"You may be a duke, Your Grace, but this is my castle, and I am afraid to say you are not welcome!"

"Yes, well," she said lightly. "I did not expect . . . may I sit, Your Grace?"

"Oh, Lord, of course," said Daniel, hastily stepping to the nearest sofa. "Here, let me."

The sofa, though large and plush with a red and gold stripe in its silk, was sadly unsuitable for a person to sit on. That was because it was covered with what could only be described as . . . well, everything. Cushions and papers. Books, sheets of music, a quill, two daggers which looked Arabic in nature, a pipe, a collection of tinderboxes.

"I am struggling to find places to put things that don't then get in the way elsewhere," said the duke helplessly. "Let's just do this."

With a sudden sweep of his hand, he pushed the things on the sofa onto the floor—well, some of them—making space enough for her to sit.

"There," he said cheerfully, as though that were a permanent solution. "Please, make yourself comfortable."

Comfortable was not the word Nora would have used as she slowly lowered herself into the gap on the sofa. She hardly knew what to do with herself.

She had intended to speak to the Duke of Thornfalcone in his hall, thank him curtly for paying off her debts as he had said—and she had disbelieved—then be on her way. Nothing else.

Finding herself seated amongst such a surfeit of objects, with the duke seated in an armchair opposite her from which he had already removed two shepherd ornaments and a small Wedgewood vase, was rather disconcerting.

"So," said Daniel inelegantly.

Nora drew herself up. *This was ridiculous.* She had come to thank a man for a favor—*one she could not and would not repay,* she told herself. And that was it. She could be off home, and the mackerel in her basket would—

The duke sniffed. "Oh dear, I am sorry to say I think my brother must have deposited some food here or something."

Shame rippled through Nora. "I'm afraid that's me."

Daniel's eyes widened. "You—"

"Not me, precisely," Nora added, hating that she had not explained that better. *What, she was declaring to dukes that she smelled like fish today?* "I purchased some mackerel from the fishmonger's. It's in my basket. This basket," she added rather necessarily and pointed at the basket on her lap.

She immediately wished she had not done so. The duke's eyes snapped to the basket, then lingered on what appeared to be just above it. Her breasts.

Nora cleared her throat. The duke's eyes snapped back to hers.

"I wanted to thank you," she said stiffly. "I accused you of lying about paying off my debts. I know now I was wrong and that you have paid them—all of them. Thank you."

There. It was said.

Nora rose in a rustle of skirts. "And now—"

"Oh, you can't leave now," said Daniel, rising also. "I—well, I am glad you are here."

She looked at him helplessly. *Why*, she wanted to ask. What on earth could you think you and I might have in common? You're a duke, and I am a woman with no reputation who was half encouraged, half forced to leave Bath.

He paid debts. She could only accumulate them.

"Please, sit," said Daniel softly, sitting himself. "It truly was not a problem. As I said, I wished to ensure all debts my brother accrued, whether directly or indirectly, were paid. It was only right."

Despite her better judgment, Nora allowed herself to slowly sit back onto the sofa.

Only right. This was a man very different from his brother.

"You look surprised," he said with a smile.

Nora tried to return the smile, but she was certain hers was far less relaxed. "I . . . it's just that the interactions I have had with gentlemen before—"

"I presume my brother would have made good on his agreement with you, had he lived," Daniel said firmly.

In such a firm voice, Nora thought with a flicker of recognition, *she was certain the man was trying to convince himself.*

"After all, you were his . . . ahem, his mistress," continued the duke, his voice hoarse for a moment. "Though I have never been involved so . . . ah, intimately in his affairs before, I know what is due a mistress. Due to you."

Nora opened her mouth, hesitated, then closed it. *So that was it. The man believed that she was his brother's mistress.* She had suspected he thought so, but it felt different, hearing him say it out loud.

For a moment, Nora considered telling him the whole story. One she was half-certain the new Duke of Thornfalcone—this one, with manners, and a conscience, so unlike his brother—would not accept.

But what would it gain her?

Guilt swirled in her heart, but a desire—a need—to protect herself won out. *There was nothing to be gained by explaining the true story to this Daniel Vaughn,* Nora told herself sternly. Nothing but further heartache and the possibility of greater problems. No, it was done. David was dead. Her debts were paid. That was an end to it.

"Well, I am grateful," Nora said quietly, trying to convince herself even as she spoke that the man did not deserve greater clarification. "More than I can say, in fact. There is only . . . there is just one more thing."

She almost winced as she said the words. Being in another's debt was something she loathed. That was why, though this conversation was most excruciating, she had to ask.

"One more thing?" Daniel said, eagerly leaning forward. "Of course—that is, if I can be of any assistance, I would be glad. To help you."

Nora's conscience prickled once more. It was not too difficult to see what was happening here. The man admired her. Well, a few had, once. When she had her good name and her presence at a party did not instigate a rush to leave.

But it would be wrong, wouldn't it, to play on that admiration? To use his like of her to manipulate him to get what she wanted, merely because she was a woman of some beauty and he was a man obviously starved for affection?

"I would like my letters back," said Nora quietly.

Daniel barked a laugh as he leaned back in his chair, and her heart sank. *Was he to deny her this?*

"Fine," he said quietly. "But only if I can bring them to you myself."

Nora frowned. "Bring them to me? No, I want them now."

She would not give him any further excuse to come to Sunview Cottage. That was her place, her sanctuary. She would have no more men in there.

"You cannot have them now, simply because I still have my brother's study to clear and I must be sure I've found them all," Daniel was saying. He gestured around the Japanese drawing room. "As I am sure you can imagine, clearing the study is a far greater task than I had first thought. I still have a quarter of the floor to clear."

Of the floor? "How many letters did your brother—"

"Most of them are about the estate, not other women, if that is what you are asking," Daniel said.

There was such sarcasm in his voice, Nora almost started with surprise. It was a dark seam in the otherwise bright personality she had seen.

"Besides," the duke added. "This way, I will have another excuse to see you again."

His gaze flickered over her face, lingering for just a moment on her lips, before it returned to her eyes.

Nora swallowed. Those gray eyes were not cruel. They would not insist, not force, not cajole. He was not his brother.

But that did not mean she had to agree.

"Burn them," Nora said succinctly, rising to her feet. "Good day, Your Grace."

She had almost made it to the corridor, though goodness knew how she would find her way to the front door again, when the Duke of Thornfalcone's words made her hesitate.

"I will see you, Nora," said Daniel softly, "in a few days. Letters in hand."

Nora looked back. He was still seated, but there was a strange sort of power in his look. One that told her in no uncertain terms that, although Daniel was unlike his brother in many ways, they shared the same determination to possess her.

Nora swallowed. "The letters I will be glad to see. But do not expect a long visit."

Chapter Five

10 June 1811

Daniel knew it was her the moment he saw the lone figure on the path.

Not because he had been doing nothing but thinking of her from the moment he had last seen her, he told himself firmly. Not because that fiery mane, that elegant figure, and the way she held herself had been indelibly marked into his mind.

Not entirely, anyway.

His butler, Keynes, had been astonished at his determination to complete the review of the study at the earliest opportunity.

"But Your Grace," he had said plaintively. "There are many other calls on your time, far more important than reading through letters—"

"I have a duty to discharge the previous duke's business," Daniel had said, sitting cross-legged on the floor of the study and prizing out the letters which had slipped under the large mahogany desk. "I am sure you appreciate—"

"There are three tradesmen wishing to confirm the ducal seal!" Keynes made everything seem so dreadfully important when he said it like that.

Daniel had looked up. "Ducal seal? Sounds catching."

The butler had nodded, ignoring the jest. "Certain tradesmen are permitted to display the ducal seal at their places of work, to denote that the Dukedom of Thornfalcone purchases goods exclusively from them. It's a badge of honor!"

It sounded, Daniel had thought with a sinking feeling, *like more paper would be involved.*

Why had no one told him being a duke was mostly nodding at what other people said and signing things? He had never signed his name more frequently in his life. No, not his name. His title.

Duke of Thornfalcone.

Daniel shuddered every time he did it. His father's name, his brother's. He had never thought the blasted title would one day come to him.

It was most inconvenient. One struggled to move through the seedier parts of London, Bath, Brighton, Edinburgh, if one was pointed out by all and sundry to be the newest duke to discover blue blood.

He had yet to speak with Chantmarle. The duke would expect a report soon, but Daniel had been so distracted by this ducal business that he hadn't finished his duty to the Crown. Blast.

"Your Grace," his butler had continued. "I really think—"

"Yes, well, it turns out it's far more important what I think," Daniel had said, hating the imperious note in his voice but resigned to the fact that it was the only way the blessed butler would listen. "And I made a promise to someone, Keynes, that I would . . . would locate some papers for them. The last is somewhere in this study, so I must—"

"Why did you not say so before, Your Grace?" For some reason, the servant had looked suddenly horrified. "A promise from a duke is a most sacred thing!"

Though not as horrified as Daniel as the butler had dropped to his knees and started rifling through the letters still scattered on the floor. One of them, written by a Miss Yates who was most insistent she receive a reply, had happily slipped through a floorboard.

"Your Grace, I am more than happy to be of assis—"

"No," Daniel had said firmly. "No, I—I rely on you to keep this house in order, Keynes. I would not dream of demeaning your . . . your impressive intellect."

He had chosen the correct wording. Keynes had risen with a satisfied look on his face and a remarkably happy note in his voice.

"Of course, you can rely on me, Your Grace," he had said pompously, finally veering toward the door, though he missed it on the first attempt. "Anything you wish, however, the bell—"

"Yes, yes," Daniel had said in a vague tone. The letter he had just picked up ended with the name he had been attempting not to think for days, but it had only grown more and more enticing with every time he pushed the thought away.

Nora.

Now, riding from Bath once again toward Sunview Cottage, Daniel patted his pocket, just to make sure. There was no possibility the stack of letters he had carefully tied with not only two lengths of string, but a ribbon as well, could have slipped from his pocket. No possibility at all.

That knowledge, however, was not preventing him from checking with a gentle pat every hundred yards or so. And it was why, as Daniel spotted Miss Nora Harvey just ahead of him on the path, his heart swelled.

This was perfect. No door to keep them apart. No specter of his over-enthusiastic, collecting brother to make conversation awkward. Just the two of them in the English countryside in the sunshine. What could be more perfect than that?

It was therefore with a sinking feeling that Daniel saw, the moment he drew his horse alongside Nora, that she rolled her eyes.

"Are you following me, Your Grace?" she said archly as she glanced up.

Yes, he wanted to say. "No, I—"

"Because it certainly feels that way," Nora said, returning her gaze to the path.

He tried not to be offended by the dismissive attitude. *She was in mourning*, Daniel thought to himself, guilt searing through him. So was he. They were both mourning the loss of a man who was supposed to be important to them.

What a pity it was that David had lost his brother's respect, trust, and even Daniel's ability to like him long ago.

The decision Daniel made next was not a conscious one. He was not even sure, if he had been asked about it later, that he could pinpoint the moment he decided to do it. But he dismounted, much to Nora—to Miss Harvey's surprise, and started to walk alongside her.

"What do you want?" she asked immediately.

The muscles in Daniel's neck tightened, just for a moment. "Who said that I want anything?"

It was a foolish thing to say, he thought as he watched a flush creep across Nora's cheeks. Looking as she did, being what she had been to his brother, was it any wonder Nora expected a man to make certain demands?

"You are following me, aren't you?"

"I'm afraid I don't follow you," he quipped.

She stared at him blankly.

"I have no idea what could possibly give you that idea," Daniel said bracingly, looking ahead of him and ensuring, despite the great temptation, that he did not look at the woman beside him. "After all, it has been an entire four days since I last saw you."

"Counting, are you?"

Even without looking at her, he could sense the artfulness in her reply. Cursing himself under his breath, Daniel tried to remind himself he was from the house of Vaughn. He was part of a great family, one who—

No, wait a minute. He was the Duke of Thornfalcone. He could draw on that, could he not?

"I brought you your letters."

Now that gained her attention. "You did? All of them?" Her voice was eager.

"All that I could find," said Daniel, risking a glance at her. The rolling Avon hills stretched out before them as they walked, but he had ceased to notice. How could he concentrate on the beauty of nature, when the most beautiful thing he had ever seen was looking at him like this?

"You did not go to too much trouble, I hope," said Nora slowly.

Daniel pushed aside all memories of that study: the hours he had spent reading through every single piece of paper, the difficulty in eventually dismantling the desk to get at those letters which had fallen between two drawers, the late nights into early mornings he had spent there.

"No," said Daniel vaguely, conscious he was flushing but hoping Nora would ascribe it to the heat of the day. "No, not too much trouble."

"Where are they?" Nora said, her gaze flickering over his person.

Well. He would have gone to a great deal more trouble if he had known Nora would look at him like that. As though he were the only thing she wanted in the world. As though she could not wait to get her hands on—

On the letters, Daniel reminded himself sternly as he pulled the sheaf of papers from his pocket. Them and nothing else.

She was your brother's mistress!

"You . . . you did not read them all, I suppose?" said Nora hesitantly.

They had just arrived outside Sunview Cottage. She halted, twisted her fingers together as though uncertain whether to invite him in or just snatch the letters from his hands and run inside.

Which was the last thing Daniel wanted. No, he should have dragged out the revelation that he actually had the letters on him. Why had he been so foolish as to show them to her immediately?

"Will you take a walk with me, Miss Harvey?"

The words had spilled out of him before he could stop them—before he could remind himself Miss Harvey had a reputation—of a sort—to maintain and that being seen in his presence, in the middle of the countryside, with no chaperone could be damaging. Well, it wouldn't do *his* reputation any harm, but that was how Society was. Men could do what they liked.

"Why?" Nora said sharply.

Daniel shrugged, letting out a huge sigh. This was getting ridiculous. He wasn't a flirt, and being circumspect wasn't getting him anywhere. He might as well try being straightforward.

"Because I would like to spend a little more time with you," he said. "Before you slam that door in my face."

Nora's gaze darted to her cottage, to what was obviously home and safety and security, then returned, hungrily, to the letters in his hands.

Daniel swallowed. "I'm not holding you ransom, you know. I would never—I'm not one to force. Here." Heart hammering, he reached out, took one of Nora's hands in his own, and placed her letters in it.

Too late, he realized the impropriety of the motion. It wasn't just that he had reached out to touch her. Oh, no. It was far worse than that—Nora had not been wearing gloves. And thanks to the heat that morning, neither was he.

Daniel stood there, stock still, with Nora's hand in his. Her skin was warm, almost scalding to the touch, burning through all his resolve to be the resolute and impartial duke he knew he had to be. The warmth was flickering down his arm, tightening his lungs, making it impossible to—

"Th-Thank you."

Nora's murmur was enough to break the spell. *Or whatever it was that had happened,* Daniel thought vaguely, mind drifting in and out of focus.

His hand dropped to his side. He balled it into a fist, just for a moment, as though that would dissipate some of the heat which had so unexpectedly roared through him. But it was no good. He was branded.

"You . . . you really were just going to give them to me, weren't you?" Nora said slowly.

"I'd very much like to give it to you," he said without thinking.

"I beg your pard—"

"Nothing," he said hastily, cursing himself for allowing his tongue to speak.

Daniel forced himself to meet her eye, and immediately wished he had not. Not because she was not mightily pleasant to look at. That was unquestionable. But because there was mingled distrust and wariness in her expression which no one had ever looked at him like before.

He was Daniel Vaughn. Dependable, slightly dull compared to his brother—he'd heard the gossip. Plain old Daniel Vaughn.

Not a duke. Not an impressive gentleman about town. In fact, the only vaguely interesting thing about him was—

"Yes, Your Grace."

Daniel blinked. "I'm sorry?"

How was it possible to be so lost in thought while standing opposite a woman like Nora Harvey?

Perhaps it was the simple fact that she dazzled him. Her very presence was intoxicating. It was—

"I said yes, I will take a walk with you," said Nora, a teasing look in her eye. "Have you already forgotten the very kind invitation you offered?"

Daniel was half certain she was laughing at him, half certain he did not care if she was, and half aware that what he was about to agree to was probably not a good idea.

The mathematics tutor he'd had as a child would be horrified.

"Excellent. Excellent, good, yes," he said, hearing how foolish he sounded but seemingly unable to stop himself. "Good. Do you wish to—right. Yes. A walk."

"A walk," repeated Nora, a smile dancing across her lips. "I won't be so bold as to ask to take your arm. That would be ridiculous."

Daniel swallowed. "Ridiculous."

Oh, hell.

"You . . . your cottage," he said aloud as they started to walk past Sunview Cottage. "It is very . . . pleasant."

And very small, Daniel realized, seeing it again with fresh eyes. Dear Lord, the whole thing could probably fit inside the entrance hall in the ducal residence in Bath, let alone Egermour Manor.

"It is," said Nora firmly.

Daniel waited for what felt like an eternity but was probably no longer than half a minute. "So, when did you first begin residing in the cottage?"

"The day I took possession," Nora said succinctly, not looking at him.

"Which was?"

"When I inherited it."

Daniel wasn't sure if the strange stirring he felt was irritation or enjoyment. How did she manage it? Pushing aside every question, every polite query, with such elegance—and yet such firmness. Delicacy alongside the determination.

It was bewitching.

"Ah," he said helplessly. "From your father, I suppose."

Nora did look at him then, but only for a moment. "You suppose incorrectly."

The path took a gentle slope at that point, for which Daniel was grateful. He was already marching uphill in the conversation. The last thing he needed was an incline for his feet as well as his mind.

"Your mother, then," he attempted. "How charming."

"Wrong again," said Nora brightly. "My, what fine weather we are having."

Daniel swallowed his retort—suitable for a gentleman, not a lady—that the weather was nothing to the bracing conversation he was enduring.

Why did she not have any interest in telling him about herself? Surely, if he had been rude enough to read all the letters she was now clinging to so ardently, he would know about her anyway. He would not have to ask these questions. He would just know.

And yet he had attempted to be the gentleman! He had tried, desperately, to demonstrate that he had nothing for her but goodwill!

Well. Perhaps something else.

"Who was it you inherited Sunview Cottage from, Miss Harvey?" Daniel asked heavily.

There was nothing to lose in being direct if all other attempts had failed.

Nora shot him a quick glance but allowed her gaze to drift away from his face almost immediately. "My . . . grandmother."

It appeared that revealing that small morsel of information was a great compromise. She looked out at the hills while Daniel attempted not to look at her.

He was playing with fire here, he could tell. One did not need to know a great deal about Nora to know that Miss Harvey was not one to be crossed. In fact, it was even clearer by her dislike of sharing any personal information. If Daniel wasn't careful, he would be burned by more than just a passing touch.

So why was he still walking alongside her, highly conscious of the way her right hand hung by her side just inches from his left?

"Have you always lived in Bath?"

"Not at all," said Nora, a teasing lilt in her voice. "Since I inherited Sunview Cottage, I have lived there."

"You know what I meant," said Daniel, breathing a laugh. "Goodness, you are difficult to talk to, aren't you?"

He thought at first he had gone too far, but she chuckled in response. "Yes, very."

Well, Daniel could not fault her. And if she had been one of the informants he had worked with in London and Edinburgh, he could not have respected her more. Daniel Vaughn had copious experience getting someone to talk.

Though his brother had loved being a duke, had valued the ability to be impressive and have the whole room turning on his every phrase, the thought of the limelight had always caused Daniel's chest to constrict, not swell.

It was far more interesting to spend his time with the common people in whatever city or town he happened to be living in—London, Edinburgh, Bath—then ensure that the information he learned from them was shared with someone who could do something about it. Samuel Dellamore, the Duke of Chantmarle, for example.

Wheedling the truth out of people, knowing precisely when to wait and allow a person some space, and when to press in, was a skill he'd crafted over years.

But Nora Harvey?

She was a master. *A mistress*, Daniel thought. Every question he asked, she managed to push aside, or answer in a totally bland way. And she knew it.

Blast. He was impressed.

"Do you not have better things to do?"

Daniel blinked. Nora had halted, pushing a curl of hair back behind her ear as the wind tugged at it.

Something else tugged at his loins. "Better things?"

"You are a duke," she pointed out, as though he might have forgotten. "Don't you have to . . . I don't know, name ships or order butlers about?"

Daniel thought privately that the only orders he was able to get his butler to obey at the moment were those which aligned precisely with what Keynes wanted to do in the first place.

Not that he was about to admit to that, of course.

"I used to have a great deal to do," he admitted, choosing his words carefully. He could not be that open. "I used to . . . help justices and judges, I suppose."

Daniel realized he'd made a mistake—though he wasn't immediately sure what it was—when Nora flushed. She immediately looked away, her shoulders tensed, and it could not be clearer that she had absolutely no desire to talk to him any longer. Or be seen with him.

Oh, damn it. Of course, the last thing she wanted was to be reminded of justices and judges. A woman who lived in a cottage like that . . . *well, it would be no surprise if she had accidentally found herself on the wrong side of the law*, Daniel thought wretchedly.

"I see," Nora said coldly.

"Mainly to help catch criminals," Daniel added hastily. "People who had broken the law, you know. Robbed and killed and all that. Real crimes."

Nora raised an eyebrow. "As opposed to . . .?"

He swallowed. *Oh, hell.* How did he seem to be managing to dig an even deeper hole with every breath?

"As opposed to what I do now, which is nothing," Daniel said slowly, managing to deflect a question himself. Though it was strange, in truth, to be admitting this to a woman he barely knew, but he had to tell someone. Amelia kept telling him in her letters what an honor it was. She didn't understand at all. "I just sit around all day, nodding at servants and inspecting silverware."

Nora crinkled her nose. "Inspecting silverware?"

Daniel laughed, shaking his head. "I don't really understand it either."

How was it possible to speak to her as he had never spoken to anyone before? How could his words simply open up as it was impossible to do with another?

"That sounds most odd," said Nora softly. "And . . . and lonely, I suppose."

Daniel swallowed. "I've never much been one for company."

That was certainly true. Society had a rather dim view of gentlemen who could not properly quip without needing five minutes to think of a witty response.

Nora's gaze raked over his features, as though hunting for sincerity, and her eyes widened as she found it.

Daniel wasn't sure whether to be gratified that she believed him or offended that it was so obvious he was no duke.

"I have some more time," Nora said quietly. "If you wish to continue walking."

For a moment Daniel thought he would not be able to reply, but then he found his voice. "Y-Yes. Yes. Thank you. I . . . I would like that."

CHAPTER SIX

13 June 1811

NORA PUMMELED IT as hard as she could, really making sure her knuckles connected. She breathed out heavily with the effort but continued on just as harshly as when she had started. She had to make sure this was done properly or she would just find herself doing it again.

Her elbows ached, her shoulders throbbed, but her hands did not cease their pummeling.

Eventually, brushing away hair from her eyes and sighing as she saw a floury streak immediately appear in her curls, Nora leaned back and examined the dough.

Yes, she had probably kneaded it sufficiently. It was hard to tell with some of the larger loaves, but she was almost certain.

But more pummeling would not hurt. Nora hated a dough that did not rise sufficiently throughout, and she only had one coin to give the baker of the nearest village. She did not wish to eat stodgy bread for the next week.

The work was hard, but it was a relief to escape into the physical demands of the dough for a few minutes. After all, her mind had not permitted her a single moment's rest ever since that ill-fated walk with the new Duke of Thornfalcone.

"That sounds most odd. And . . . and lonely, I suppose."

"I've never much been one for company."

Nora snorted as she pushed back her curls once again. Ill-fated was perhaps the wrong way to describe it. She had not completely embarrassed herself, though it had been mortifying, attempting to keep the handsome—no, the *inquisitive* man away from any truth about her. But she had not come this far just to give away information, after all.

And she had been perfectly polite when he had, at length, escorted her back to her cottage.

"Well," Nora had said, as briskly as she could manage. "Thank you for the walk, Your—"

"When can I see you again?" the duke had said eagerly.

It had been all she could do not to meet his eye. *Oh, he was so eager.* So charming, albeit in an accidental way. Perhaps that was where the charm itself came from.

So unlike his brother.

"I don't suppose you will," Nora had said, far more airily than she had felt. "I have my letters now, after all, and—"

"Would you like to go on a ride together?" the duke had persisted, clearly ignoring her hand which had crept onto her front door handle. "There are some simply splendid routes around the Bath hills, we could—"

"How sad for me that I have no horse," was the only thing Nora could think to say in the moment. "Good afternoon, Your Grace."

"That is indeed a shame," said the duke, his voice now soft. "A great shame."

And though Nora had known it was best to simply step into her cottage and never see the man again, she had hesitated. Why, she did not know. But there was something about him—something about the way he looked at her.

He desired her, yes. But it was not a possessive desire, the kind she had seen on so many men's faces before. She was not even sure if it was a desire the man would act on, which was stranger still.

It was . . . more innocent. No, not innocent—more reverential.

Nora punched the dough and watched with satisfaction as it squelched with a most delightful sound. It was fortunate indeed that all those days ago she had not entirely lost her head. No, she had said not a word to the duke after that but simply marched into her own home and shut the door in his face.

Shut the door on a life that was tempting, at least for a moment.

"Do not be foolish, Nora Harvey," Nora muttered to herself as she started to shape the dough into a loaf. "Do you want to invite danger back into your life?"

And was there anything more dangerous than a duke?

She shivered, despite the warmth of the day, at the recollection of a conversation she'd had with another Duke of Thornfalcone—though he was as different from his brother as night was from day.

"You will be mine, Nora Harvey."

"I won't—"

"You'll do what you're told. Eventually, you'll come back to me begging," David Vaughn, Duke of Thornfalcone had said with an ugly smile. "You'll be desperate. Then you'll want our agreement. Then you'll give yourself to me without question."

Nora swallowed the panic that the memory always brought with it. But she hadn't given in.

Well. She had, actually. The letters she had burned the moment she had watched Daniel Vaughn, the new Duke of Thornfalcone, ride out of sight had been proof of that, though her weakness had never been acted upon.

She *had* become desperate. And she'd had nowhere else to turn. So she had written the letters she had promised herself she would never write, offering herself to a man she had vowed she would never touch, and the agreement had been made.

"And now that chapter of your life is over," Nora said firmly, looking with pleasure at the impressive loaf of dough she had managed to make. "That chapter was only going to bring danger. But now—"

A strange noise made her turn, heart pounding.

When would she start to believe she was safe? When would she stop looking over her shoulder, nervously only entering Bath when she was absolutely out of any other possibilities? Would this nightmare never end?

Nora's eyes raked across the small window. There was nothing unusual to be seen through the cracked panes of glass, just the countryside as it always was. The harvest was starting to golden, and it would not be long before all the villagers on this side of Bath would be called together to help bring in the harvest.

The pair of oak trees she had lovingly called "Adam and Eve", all twisted in each other, branches knotted together, were still there. There was no one she could see on the path that meandered a few yards from Sunview Cottage. Nothing to be seen at all.

Except a shadow.

Nora stepped away from the kitchen table where she had been preparing her dough, and toward the window. It could have been a trick of the light, but there were no clouds in the sky. It was perfect June weather, brilliant sunshine with not a shadow on the ground.

Her heartbeat sped to a painful patter as she reached the window and looked out as best she could. It had to be Hamish—there was no one else it could be. But after that argument with her brother, why would he return?

No shadow.

She must have dreamt it, she told herself wearily. Just as she had imagined there was someone moving about downstairs a few nights ago. Nora had crept downstairs, candlestick in hand as it was the only weapon she could get her hands on, and what had there been?

Nothing. Not a thing. The entire place had been empty.

Nora exhaled slowly.

It was not Hamish. And even if he were about, he would not have been creeping about the cottage in the daylight. No, her brother was the sort to turn up in the dead of night, light a fire in her grate—if there was any coal—then demand his dinner.

She was just about to turn away from the window, satisfied there was nothing outside her cottage to alarm her, when something teased her out of the corner of her eye.

A shadow. A large one.

Nora whirled around and saw . . . something most odd.

Pulling off her apron and covering the dough with it, she stepped to the back door and opened it, half expecting to find she was imagining things. *After all, what on earth would a . . .*

A horse. A horse was in her garden outside the back of her cottage.

It was just a small one. The garden, that was. Potatoes, beans, carrots, parsnips, and whatever flowers she could grow without worrying too much about the slugs. And standing in the middle of it, happily munching on the tops of her carrots, was a horse.

Nora blinked. "I'm dreaming," she breathed.

The horse snorted.

"Perhaps not," she conceded, although why she should be talking to a horse, she had no idea. "But . . . but where's your owner?"

Nora took a few hesitant steps toward the beast, but it did not bolt nor rear, as she had half expected it to. No, the horse merely continued eating her carrots, the rascal.

Her shaking hand gently patted the horse's neck. It completely ignored her.

Looking around her, Nora could see no one. Not a rider running toward her cottage, not a hunt which had lost a spare steed, nothing. There was not a single person as far as the eye could see.

And usually, that was how she wanted it. Sunview Cottage provided her with the chance to be alone, finally, and she valued that.

But it made no sense. Nora looked more carefully at the horse. It appeared, as far as she could see, to be well cared for. It was shod, its mane was in good repair, and there was nothing about the creature suggesting it was neglected.

Nora bit her lip. "Well, you are a mystery," she said quietly to the horse, patting it once again. "A completely mystery, even if you are a beauty."

"I knew you'd like her," said a delighted voice.

Nora did not need to turn to know who that voice belonged to. In fact, she purposefully did not turn, for she knew in that moment her face would display her emotions precisely, without a filter, and that was only going to end in tears.

His tears, of course.

"David Vaughn, Duke of Thornfalcone," Nora said to the horse instead, carefully stroking its mane. "You appear to have lost your horse."

She had lost her sensibilities, too, not to have noticed him before now. Where had the man come from? Had he been hiding around the side of her cottage—and why? Why would he do this? Just to gain her attention?

"Oh, I haven't lost my horse," the duke said cheerfully. "You've found yours."

That was what made Nora look around. Inch by inch, she slowly turned until she was looking directly at the man who had just spoken those completely idiotic words.

The duke took a step backward. "That is—"

"What in God's name are you talking about?" Nora asked, entirely perplexed and momentarily forgetting she was standing beside a creature that was taller, wider, and stronger than she was. The horse stepped away, nickering as though to chastise her.

She stepped toward the duke, who took another step backward. "Look, Your Grace—"

"Daniel."

She halted, a frown deepening across her forehead. "What did you say?"

The man before her was just as handsome as he always had been, not unlike the previous duke, worse luck. Now she knew the two men were brothers, Nora could see the similarities. It was actually rather like looking at one man who had lived two very different lives. Both versions of the man had some weariness around the edges, but for this one it came from hard work, not spendthriftiness and rakery.

"Daniel," repeated the duke, a lopsided smile creeping across his lips. "It's my name."

It's his name. Nora would have thrown her hands up to the heavens if she weren't so restrained.

He was impossible!

"You think I can just call you by your first name, as though we were siblings?" Nora said with a snort.

Daniel's expression darkened. "I most certainly do not think of you as a sibling."

She swallowed. There was such passion in that voice, determination she had never heard before. An absolute certainty they would be something to each other . . . and brother and sister was hardly an appropriate way to describe it.

"And . . . and I would like to call you Nora."

That forced Nora back to the present, to the gentleman with whom she was having the most ridiculous conversation. What on earth did he think he was doing?

If she did not know any better, she would presume Daniel—that the Duke of Thornfalcone was attempting to seduce her. But she had already seen enough of the man to know that was not his way. He was far too reticent for that.

So what was all this? The sudden appearance? The name? The horse?

"Look, Your Grace," Nora said firmly, ignoring the strange stirring in her stomach as she avoided his name. "I don't understand. This horse—"

"Your horse," said Daniel cheerfully. "I wanted to call her Beauty, but then I thought, you should probably choose her name."

Nora's mind was whirling. She must not have eaten enough that day, because her intellect was insufficient to understand what the man was talking about. Why would she be naming one of his horses?

Then understanding dawned. It was a strange sort of compliment, she supposed, but then she did not get the impression this Duke of Thornfalcone knew how to admire a woman.

"Oh, you wish to enter her into races," Nora said with relief, her shoulders sagging. "I have heard of men asking ladies to name their horses. It brings good luck, they say—"

"Why would you enter your horse into races?" Daniel cut across her, brow furrowed.

Oh, it was so infuriating, Nora could scream! "Stop saying that!"

"Saying what?" the duke asked, taking a step toward her.

Nora did not step away—she was not going to be the one to back down. She was not the one trespassing on someone else's property. She was not the one permitting their animal to eat another person's carrots!

So from where she stood, she shooed away the horse as best she could from what remained of her vegetables, then turned back to face the duke.

The duke who was suddenly much, much closer.

"Look, the horse is a gift. For you," said Daniel quietly. "I thought—well, you said it, did you not? You could not come riding with me because you did not have a horse. And now you do."

Nora's mouth fell open as memory of the offhand comment she had made a few days ago echoed in her mind.

"Would you like to go on a ride together? There are some simply splendid routes around the Bath hills, we could—"

"How sad for me that I have no horse. Good afternoon, Your Grace."

"That is indeed a shame. A great shame."

Surely he did not think—surely no rational gentleman would believe her words had been a subtle request?

"I did not mean—I did not ask for this horse," Nora said firmly, pointing to the beast now helping itself to what remained of her beans.

Her breathing felt tight as the strain of the moment was taking its toll. The last thing she needed was an excuse to feel indebted to another man. Had she not suffered enough? Had she not paid her dues again and again to the men who insisted on attempting to help her even when she did not ask for their assistance?

And the one time she had finally given in and written to David . . . she was left with this. His brother. And a horse. A hungry horse.

"I know you didn't ask," Daniel was saying brightly. "It's a gift! Here, I'll—"

"You have to take it back."

Nora had not intended to speak so plainly, but it was impossible not to be blunt. This duke—this *Daniel*—seemed entirely unable to register either the delicate hints or the not-so-delicate hints she had given that she no longer wished to see him. Even if part of her rebelled, the rest of her knew it was a mistake.

"I don't need your charity," Nora lied, trying not to think of the empty coin purse in her reticule, or the single loaf of bread she would be subsisting on that week. The rest she made would have to be sold to pay off her other debts, though she'd still need to find a coin for the baker to bake the bread in the first place. *Oh, hell.* "I don't need anyone's charity, Your Grace. I am my own woman—"

"It's not charity!" Daniel looked horrified. "Do you think I frequently give horses to people?"

Nora swallowed. *She would not see more in his words than was already there*, she tried to tell herself. She was nothing special. This was a passing fancy—he had met her, desired her, and would soon tire of her. She had to bring this to an end.

"We hardly know each other—we were never even formally introduced," Nora said, attempting to appeal to his sense of honor. "It is most inappropriate—"

"Oh, I don't care about that," said Daniel with a wave of his hand. "I want you to have her. Don't you like her?"

Nora hesitated, glancing at the horse. How long had it been since she had ridden? Years. Too long. If anyone had told her when she had first entered Society that within five years she would be without friends, without family to all intents and purposes, and without funds—without a horse!—she would never have believed them.

Shame flowed freely through her. He must know—this Duke of Thornfalcone, he must know about her fall from grace. He must be aware of the great scandal it would be if anyone knew he had been speaking with her. And that told her, in no uncertain terms, that he had absolutely no intention of anyone finding out.

Anger flickered alongside the shame. Nora would not be someone's dirty little secret that a man tried to keep hidden. *Not again.*

"You don't understand, do you?" she said harshly, allowing her frustration to leak into her words. "What do you think I am supposed to do with such a beast?"

Daniel plainly did not understand. He was still smiling. "Why, enjoy her! I would wish for you to ride every day. Gentle exercise is, I have heard, very good for—"

"How?" interrupted Nora. "With what saddle? With what reins? In what riding habit, using what riding boots?"

The duke opened his mouth, hesitated, then said, "I can arrange—"

"I don't want more gifts from a man I cannot possibly repay!" Nora cried, pain in every syllable. "How can I take the time to exercise the beast when I have to work?"

"Work?" blinked Daniel.

"How can I afford to feed it?" persisted Nora, hating how this revealed her poverty but unable to think of any other way to make her point. "What stable will I put her in? What blanket will I cover her with, what—"

"Ah," said the duke weakly. "I . . . I see."

"Do you?" Nora's shoulders were tight and there was a throbbing at her temple which she knew would lead to a headache, but she could not stop. She was only just starting to make the clodpate realize what a fool he was making of her. "Your Grace, I am sure in your world, in your life, the arrival of an additional horse is an afterthought—if you even think of it at all! How many horses are in your stables this very minute?"

She felt satisfaction, sharp and burning, as she saw the duke swallow. "I—I don't precisely—"

"I am tired," said Nora, her voice breaking. *Oh, how she hated it when her voice did that.* "I am tired of wealthy men like you acting like you can just turn up at my cottage and push into my life, somehow believing you can—or have even been given leave to—solve all my problems. With a horse?"

"It wasn't like that," Daniel said stiffly. "I—damn it, woman, I—"

"Goodbye, Your Grace, and I hope this is the last time," Nora said firmly, blinking tears from her eyes and wishing to goodness she did not have to spell out her poverty to this man who had never-ending opportunities to make a life for himself. The sort of life she had already forfeited and had no further desire to dwell on. "Please, just—just go."

Slamming her back door would have felt a great deal better if three things had not happened.

Firstly, if Nora had not immediately burst into tears the moment the door had closed.

Secondly, if a small patch of ceiling, cracked after months of disrepair, had not fallen onto the floor beside her.

And thirdly, if she had not heard, only just within earshot, a voice through the fractured window.

"Oh, Christ. You're a fool, Vaughn."

CHAPTER SEVEN

19 June 1811

"GOODBYE, YOUR GRACE, and I hope this is the last time. Please, just—just go."

"You have me all wrong," said Daniel, striding forth with a powerful look that immediately quelled Nora's words. "I am no ignorant man who merely thinks spreading largesse will solve your problems!"

He gloried in the way her lips parted, her astonished eyes wide.

"I . . . I . . ."

"I too have known the challenge of poverty," Daniel said grandly. *Well, relative poverty.* Not being able to afford to attend a third house party last summer. "And I can well understand your frustration, my love."

"Ahem."

"Oh, Daniel! I never thought anyone would understand!" breathed Nora, her cheeks pink as she hurried forward to step into his embrace. "If you would just hold me, kiss me, love me—"

"*Ahem,* Your Grace."

Daniel flailed so wildly he almost fell out of his armchair. The newspaper which had been resting across his eyes slipped to the study floor and the brightness of the room made his head spin.

Keynes was standing before him.

He was not still outside Nora's cottage. He had not stepped forward with those bold words and made her see, somehow, that they were perfect for each other. And Nora had certainly not leapt into his arms. He'd only arrived back from London twenty minutes ago, now he looked at his pocket watch, after a hard journey of riding on a mail coach horse he'd hired for its endurance. But he'd needed to finish that business with the Duke of Chantmarle, and the man's London wedding reception had been the most efficient way of doing it. Though he had to admit he was exhausted and his behind was punishing him for it now.

"Keynes," said Daniel hastily, clearing his throat as though his servant could somehow see into his daydreams. "Did you want anything in particular?"

Yes, that was it, be as haughty as you can. That's what they expected, wasn't it?

Daniel's heart sank to see how positively the butler responded to his aloof manner.

"Yes, there was something in particular," the butler intoned. "We have received some additional post intended for the late duke, and I wondered if you would like it brought here?"

For a moment, Daniel simply blinked. It was such an innocuous question. If it had been asked by anyone else, he would have thought they were being foolish. Of course all correspondence should be brought in here. This was the study, after all. Where else would it go?

"In . . . in here?" he repeated, just to make sure.

"Indeed, Your Grace," said his butler with a slight bow.

Daniel hesitated. There was something else going on here, and he wasn't sure what. He wasn't even sure what time it was. Or what day. All those things had started to feel immaterial, the moment he had mortally offended Nora.

"I am tired of wealthy men like you acting like you can just turn up at my cottage and push into my life, somehow believing you can—or have even been given leave to—solve all my problems. With a horse?"

He almost groaned aloud at the memory. How could he have been so foolish? It was obvious, the moment Nora had laid out how completely impossible it would be to care for a horse. What had he been thinking? He may as well have taken her a dolphin, for all the good it would do her.

He had been the very worst of a gentleman: thoughtless.

Ironic, really, as all he seemed able to do was think of her.

"Do you have any other suggestions about where these letters should go, Keynes?" Daniel asked slowly.

Perhaps that would untangle whatever secret it was his butler appeared to be hiding.

The man cleared his throat. "If I were to make a suggestion, Your Grace, something I rarely do and would not wish to be seen as . . ."

Daniel permitted him to meander for a minute, watching for the movement of the longcase clock behind him, then cut in. "I asked for your opinion, Keynes, and I do wish you would give it."

The butler gave him a reproachful look. "I was only elucidating, Your Grace, how rare it is for a servant like—"

"Keynes—"

"The ballroom, Your Grace."

Daniel blinked. He must have misheard. It was this business with Nora; nothing had been right since. Everything he had attempted to do had backfired most irritatingly, his fingers getting scalded with the heat of her fury every time he came close.

A lurch in his loins told him he wasn't entirely unhappy about all of that. Well, a woman with that much fire—who knew what she would be like outside the drawing room and in the bedroom . . .

"Yes, the ballroom, Your Grace," the butler said, replying to his unspoken but obvious confusion. "May I be so bold—"

"I wish you would," snapped Daniel, pushed beyond all endurance.

Keynes smiled, as though congratulating himself for proving that this new duke was no duke at all.

Or perhaps that was just Daniel's imagination. It was difficult to tell, the last few weeks had been such a whirlwind. There were rumors, of course. Gossip that his brother had been a fine Duke of Thornfalcone whereas *he* had done nothing to claim the name. No ball hosted in his brother's honor, no parties held, no official entrance at Almack's.

Well, perhaps they'd like to clear out the second kitchen he'd discovered last week, Daniel thought grimly. Packed to the rafters with pots, pans, dishes, spoons, stools. It was no wonder the kitchen staff had been forced to move into another one. But what sort of master decides to build a second kitchen rather than clear out the first?

"I would recommend, Your Grace, that I show you," his butler was saying.

Daniel sighed heavily but rose from the armchair and made certain not to tip over one of the piles of paper he had carefully stacked about the room. In just a few more days, this tidying lark would be over—mostly over—and he could return to the most challenging problem he had ever faced.

How to apologize—truly apologize—to Nora Harvey.

"Come on then," he said irritably, following the butler down the corridor and around the corner. "I honestly can't see why the ballroom would be a suitable . . . suitable . . . oh hell."

There were no other words for it.

The ballroom, such as it was, could not match some of the grander ballrooms in the London houses of the nobility. Lady Romeril's ballroom was twice this size, and the Duke of Penshaw's three times. But still—it was a ballroom. It had enough space for a line of twenty dancers, musicians at the side, and food and drink on tables on the other. It was a ballroom.

It now appeared to be a postal sorting office.

"I had one of the footmen bring through the dining table," said

Keynes placidly, raising his voice over the noise. "We just kept running out of room."

Daniel's eyes widened as he took in the scene. Four footmen were trailing bag after bag of letters into the room, emptying them out on the dining table and what appeared to be a billiard table, both set at the side of the ballroom. In the center were two maids, carefully examining each letter and attempting to put them into two piles.

One pile was significantly bigger than the other.

"Dear God."

"Yes, that's what I thought," murmured the butler beside him.

It was almost impossible to take in. "Why, there must be hundreds—"

"We actually believe we are into the thousands, Your Grace," said Keynes with a sigh. "Molly and Abigail are dividing them up as we speak."

Daniel's eyes rested once again on the two piles in the center of the ballroom. It was disconcerting how much larger one was than the other.

"And the two piles are—"

"Debts owed *to* the house of Thornfalcone," said Keynes delicately. "And debts owed *by* the house of Thornfalcone. I couldn't quite read—I mean, the maids are sorting them out."

He did not need the butler to point out which was which. He knew enough of David to know, without a shadow of a doubt, that the "house of Thornfalcone", as the old servant put it, was in a great deal of trouble.

How could this have happened? Oh, David was a reprobate, he had always known that. Daniel rather thought their parents had known, too, even if they had always extolled his older brother's virtues to the hilt. He and Amelia had known his character better, but what was the point of arguing?

It had only got worse when their father had died. David then had access to the Thornfalcone coffers, and he put them to . . . well, Daniel would not call it good use. But he certainly put them to use.

And now David was dead, and he was faced with . . .

"Right," said Daniel with a sigh. "Right."

He'd thought he had a grasp of David's excesses. After all, how many times had Daniel been forced to ride in and find a surgeon after a duel? Find a doctor after a bout of drinking? Find any loose change to pay a woman off?

"We are starting to run out of room, I am afraid, Your Grace."

Daniel blinked. There was something rather unusual in the butler's tone there, and if it had come from anyone else, he would have said it was . . . shame. Perhaps not in Daniel, but certainly in the situation they were faced with.

Daniel took a deep breath. "Send for my steward. Sit with him—yourself, Keynes, I don't trust anyone else to do this. Prioritize debts owed to us and selling the furniture in the Japanese Drawing Room."

"All of—"

"All of it," said Daniel heavily. *Dear God, give him some breathing room in this place.* "Then look at the debts we owe to the most important of debtors. Pay them first. You'll know the difference."

The butler's eyes were widening. "But Your Grace, how will I—"

"Whichever letters contain the most threats, pay first," said Daniel heavily. He may have only managed informants for the Crown, for those spying dukes with far greater power than he, but he knew enough to be able keep scandal from his door. God willing. "Not a word to—"

Keynes drew himself up. "I would never bring scandal to the house of—"

"Good, good," Daniel said hastily, patting the man on the arm and realizing immediately that dukes don't pat butlers on arms. "I—I have to go out, Keynes. I'll leave this all in your capable hands."

Casting the piles of letters one more despairing look and wishing to goodness he had never discovered the ballroom at all, Daniel strode out of the room and to the one place he knew would provide escape.

He did intend to come back eventually. Probably. Though why, at this point, he did not know. Debts coming up to his eyeballs, rooms crammed with furniture, it was a wonder David had been able to do anything!

Other than endanger himself, of course.

When he arrived at the stables, the groom did not need instruction. Daniel's face must have been thunderous, for the man quietly tacked up his mare as swiftly as possible and stepped back as the duke threw his leg over his mount and settled himself in the saddle.

He had to get out of here. Out of Bath, away from the stares, certainly away from all those letters.

What else did Daniel not know about his brother?

"Yah!" He kicked at the horse's sides, and she launched forward.

Within minutes, the heavy ache in Daniel's heart was starting to dissipate. *What was already past couldn't be changed*, he tried to tell himself as the busy streets of Bath faded away, and the calming brilliance of nature started to fill his vision.

The past was gone. David had played with fire too many times, and whatever sickness he had caught had quickly worked through a body run ragged by debauchery.

And now he was the Duke of Thornfalcone, Daniel thought ruefully as he slowed his horse to a trot and looked out across the stunning hills. Now he had to be the one to maintain the family honor, what was left of it.

If anyone saw the state of his ballroom right now, he would never retrieve it.

Daniel sighed. "But here, I am alone."

There wasn't another person to be seen. Emptiness, rolling fields and woodland, was all his eye could see. You could almost be forgiven thinking he was the only—

A figure.

Daniel's attention snapped over to it, the only moving thing in the entirety of what his eye could distinguish. If he had been one to believe in myths, he would have said it was a centaur. It was certainly a rider, but the way the horse and its rider moved, they appeared to be almost one. Cantering gracefully, every movement was fluid as though they thought with one mind.

It was truly lovely, almost poetic. Daniel pulled his horse to a standstill and watched, appreciating the way the woman—for it had to be a woman, with that figure—rode. Her riding habit flowed out behind her, creating a picture of—

Daniel's stomach lurched. It couldn't be.

It was Nora.

He saw her cheeks flush as she approached, riding the mare he had taken her all those days ago. But how could this be?

Daniel's thoughts whirled in his mind as he attempted to put the story together. He had been upset, irritated with himself, hating how swiftly Nora had managed to outline his offense—

He had just ridden away. He had left the horse there.

But no, that didn't make sense, he thought rapidly. He would have sent his groom back to get the horse, he would never have just left. But had he? After the sharp words from Nora, had he told the groom? Or had he merely marched up to the house and hidden himself away in the study?

Daniel had a sinking feeling in his gut. That sounded about right. *How could he have been so—*

"Your Grace," said Nora stiffly, drawing her steed to a stop just before him.

Daniel attempted to look up, but it was like staring into the sun. One could easily become dazzled, almost blinded to reality, if one looked at Nora too long.

When he finally met her eyes, his whole chest tightened as the breath was drawn inexplicably from his lungs.

Dear God, she was beautiful.

Her hair, fiery red, was unpinned and flowed down her shoulders. She wore no hat, and what he had believed to be a riding habit was naught but a gentleman's greatcoat—much too large for her—which she wore unbuttoned.

Instead of a side saddle, Nora had eschewed any such thing and was riding—Daniel had to swallow here—bareback and astride. Her cheeks were flushed, her eyes bright, and she was . . .

Warmth pooled to his loins as Daniel tried to clear his throat. *He was not going to think about how beautiful she was. How radiant, how—*

"Miss Harvey," he said aloud, thankful his distraction had not leaked into his voice. "I . . . goodness. I thought . . . I believed you would be unable to keep her."

Daniel hated himself the moment the words had slipped his lips. What, the first thing he would say to her was an implicit accusation that she had lied?

Nora must have sensed the unspoken censure, for she flushed and looked at her hands clutching the reins. "I . . . I spoke the truth when I said—"

"Oh, I am sure you did," Daniel said hastily, cursing his idiocy. "I only meant—"

"But she was left in my garden and I—"

"—should have sent back my groom, totally unconscionable that I did not—"

"—so I made a deal with someone," Nora said in a rush. "To stable her."

Daniel opened his mouth to reply, realized he had absolutely no idea what to say, then closed it.

Was the sun always so damned hot? When had it grown so? He had not thought the weather so changeable today.

"Ah," he said helplessly. "Good."

"Yes, it is rather convenient," said Nora softly, her eyes briefly meeting his own, then dropping once more to her hands.

Daniel's throat was dry, and he could barely see anything but the beautiful woman atop the horse he had thought absolutely perfect for her. He needed to leave. He needed to incline his head, express his relief that she had found a solution to her problem—*the problem he had created*, he thought awkwardly—then be on his way.

He should not remain here. Daniel knew it, as certainly as he knew the letters building up in his ballroom would not be contained there for long.

Nora Harvey was dangerous.

Oh, not in the way of most people. He knew how to take care of himself, and he had a few slight scars across his hands from when blades slipped that could prove it.

No, she was dangerous in entirely different ways. She could tempt him to do almost anything. He could be so easily captivated by her that he would not even know what he was doing. She could tantalize in a way no other woman had, and if she asked him to do something, how could he refuse?

He needed to leave.

So why wasn't he?

"Yes, the deal was most simple, and . . . well, I did want to keep her," Nora said in a mildly defensive tone.

The deal. Daniel tried not to think about the sort of deal Nora, who had almost nothing, would have made with someone to take on the serious expense of keeping a horse. There was only one sort of deal that a woman like that would make.

"Ah," he said helplessly.

The trouble was he hadn't been raised to be a duke. He hadn't even had a title, which was rare amongst ducal heirs and something Daniel had grown accustomed to over time. His brother, on the other hand, had been taught refined etiquette, the arts of conversation, ways of making people feel so at ease around him . . .

Granted, it was so he could swindle them, Daniel could not help but think. But that was beside the point.

"I . . . it's very sunny," he said aloud.

The full body cringe he experienced at hearing his voice say the words almost unseated him from his horse. His mare stepped to the side, unhappy at the sudden movement.

"Yes. Yes, it is," said Nora lightly. "I wonder, Your Grace, if you would like to ask me to ride you—ride *with* you!"

Daniel blinked. *Did she say . . .*

"Do you want to ride alongside me or not?" Nora snapped, eyes flashing.

His gaze met hers. *She most certainly did say it,* Daniel thought with a flash of joy. And what's more, she knows it.

Well, that was interesting.

"I would be honored to *ride alongside* you," said Daniel, holding her gaze as he spoke with specific intonation. He was rewarded with another hearty flush. "Which way are you—"

"Any way, it doesn't matter," said Nora, clearly flustered. "Come on."

She nudged her mare forward and Daniel drew up beside her, conscious that because she wasn't riding side saddle, her leg was remarkably close to his own. He permitted himself a single glance and was rewarded. Dear God, he could almost see her knee!

"And how are you faring today, Your Grace?" Nora said stiffly, not looking round.

Daniel opened his mouth to give the polite yet dull response that was expected but discovered himself, much to his own surprise, saying something completely different and far more honest than he'd intended. "I've been looking at a pile of my brother's debts on a ballroom floor."

Nora turned sharply. "His what?"

He tried to smile. "It's rather amusing, actually . . ."

It was impossible to tell precisely why Daniel felt he could share this with her. He had just left Keynes with strict instructions not to permit anyone to know of the shameful goings-on occurring in the Thornfalcone residence, and here he was, spilling the truth to a woman he barely knew.

And yet knew so well. He knew her. In truth it felt as though they had been separated once but fate had been drawing them back to each other ever since.

"I can't believe I'm telling you all this," Daniel said with a heavy sigh. "I didn't want anyone to know, but . . . I feel like I can talk to you. Is that strange?"

She was certainly looking at him as though he were strange. "Yes. No. I don't know."

"I don't know much either. At least, that's how it feels," Daniel said, the words pouring out. "I feel all at sea, honestly. I always used to speak to my brother—"

Nora interrupted his words with a snort. "I never bothered with my brother."

He glanced at her, saw the redness of her cheeks, saw her discomfort, and decided not to pursue that particular line of questioning. Not right now.

"It all sounds like a monumental undertaking," said Nora softly.

Daniel warmed at the kindness in her voice. "It is certainly not something I would wish on anyone."

"But it seems as though you are managing."

He managed a laugh as the path curved to the left. "I'm not so sure, Miss Harvey—"

"Nora."

"I—I beg your pardon?" Daniel stammered, turning in his saddle, once again upsetting his horse.

He could not have heard correctly. Surely she had not—after he had asked her days ago, and they had argued—

"I think, once a man gives me a horse, he has probably earned the right to call me by my first name," said Nora. Her cheeks were flushed, but her look was defiant. "I will have to call you Daniel, naturally. That would only be fair."

Daniel swallowed and forced his mind out of the gutter as it immediately imagined Nora calling him by his name but in a much less appropriate setting. Say, underneath him while naked and being pleasured by him, for example.

"Right," he said, his voice a croak. "Well, Nora. I cannot help but feel out of my depth."

Their horses had slowed to a walk now, and Nora was able to flash him a smile. "I tend to have that effect on gentlemen."

Dear God, how was he supposed to keep up with this woman? Daniel hardly knew whether she would boil hot or burn ice cold—every moment in a conversation could tend a completely different direction. He had never felt more lost.

He had never felt more alive.

"I meant with the debts," Daniel clarified, allowing himself a small smile.

Nora's eyes twinkled. "Of course you did. Well, you'll come to the end of them eventually. And debts are something everyone has. You did not presume your . . . your brother had them, too?"

Daniel was not so completely dazzled by her that he missed the slight hesitation, but he could not think of it now. He was too preoccupied with her eyes. So blue that the sky itself seemed put to shame.

"Daniel?"

"Blue," he blurted out.

Blasted tongue, why did it just keep—

"You are not much of a conversationalist, are you?" Nora said, eyebrow raised.

Daniel swallowed, but there was no point in attempting to hide it. He was quickly becoming an open book to her—besides, he was not one to attempt to keep secrets in his private life, even if he could manage it. That was part of his line of work, actually one of the more difficult parts of his life serving the Crown—a life he would have to leave behind, while he sorted out this dukedom thing.

"Not with you, no," he admitted. "You, Nora Harvey, have a marvelous habit of undoing all my planned speeches."

He had expected her to blanche, to be offended, perhaps, or to roll her eyes at his stupidity.

What he did not expect, as their horses brought them under the canopy of the trees and dappled green light scattered over them, was for Daniel to see a rather shy smile on Nora's face.

"Yes, I can see that," she said softly. "I rather like it."

Daniel almost fell off his horse. "You do?"

"There is nothing more tiresome than a gentleman who believes he knows how to please," Nora said, her voice gentle as a rod of steel ran through it. She looked away, toward the path. "I have no time for a gentleman who is certain he knows how to seduce."

Daniel swallowed. "Well, no problem there."

Chapter Eight

21 June 1811

"This is not a habit, you know," Nora said sternly as she closed her cottage door and carefully locked it with the large key.

"Doesn't look like a habit to me," agreed Daniel with that cheerful air he always had whenever he was making a terrible pun. "Looks like a gentleman's greatcoat."

Nora groaned. The man was truly a terrible joke teller. Every jest he made was somehow worse than the one before, and each time she thought that impossible—until he impressed her.

Well, impressed was not quite the right word.

"You know what I meant," she said as she placed the key in the flowerpot by her front door. "I meant this is not a habit. Riding together each day."

Even if it was the third day in a row they had done so, a traitorous voice in the back of her head muttered. Even if you find yourself invigorated by his company in a way you could never have predicted. Even if you spent all last night thinking about your conversation, wondering if you had said too much—

"Isn't it dangerous, leaving your key in a flowerpot?" came Daniel's voice, thankfully interrupting the annoying one in her own head.

"No one is going to break into my cottage," Nora said aloud, turning around to look at the duke atop his horse. "There's nothing worth stealing in there, for a start."

Something that the whole village nearby knew, she thought darkly. They had to, the number of times she had attempted to pay for wares with bread she had baked, or tried to push back her repayment date to the following week, or had to—most humiliatingly—send in a "gentleman friend" to pay off her debts.

Never again.

Though of course, there was Hamish . . .

But surely her brother would not be so foolish as to come here again, Nora thought with a flicker of concern. She had been most stern, most clear.

He had abandoned her when she had most needed him. Now she never wanted to see him again.

"Then why lock the door in the first place?" Daniel asked in a reasonable voice. "In any case, you owe me a ride for all my trouble, as I very kindly took the liberty of collecting your horse for you. You can consider it a gift. And you can't look a gift horse in the mouth, can you?"

Nora snorted, grateful for the excuse to tease the man for his terrible jest, rather than answer the question. "Your sense of humor is abysmal, Daniel."

A rush of satisfaction crackled up her spine as she spoke. *Calling a duke by his first name.* Well, it wasn't the first time—not that she would ever admit it to the amiable man fast becoming the only company she enjoyed.

No, Nora told herself firmly as she walked over to her horse and carefully mounted, using the fence as a mounting block. No, she had been down that road before. No more getting entangled with gentlemen—either her heart, or her legs. She wasn't going to make that mistake again.

"Not a habit," Nora repeated as she settled herself in the saddle and glared for good measure at the smiling duke. "At any moment I will surely tire of you, and that will be that."

She attempted to put a great deal of dry wit, and more than a little harshness, into her voice.

The last thing she needed was for Daniel Vaughn, newest Duke of Thornfalcone, to realize she was starting to get soft on him.

Daniel grinned. "Whatever you say, Nora."

Nora frowned, as though that would remove all the happiness bubbling in her stomach from hearing her name spoken by a man who had three things most men in her past never had.

Integrity.

Honor.

All his teeth.

It wasn't a particularly long list, Nora thought, *and yet so many men hadn't quite come up to snuff.*

"So, where do you want to go?" Daniel's words cut through her thoughts. "We've not ridden out toward Bath yet."

"No," said Nora firmly.

"No?"

"No," she repeated, casting him a firm look. "Let's go this way, the views at the top of the hill are quite spectacular."

It was rather pleasant to be giving orders to a man, Nora thought, *particularly a duke.* What was so disconcerting was seeing them obeyed.

Every other gentleman she had known had been very particular about always getting his own way. Hearing what she thought, even admitting Nora may have her own opinions? Oh no, that would never do.

But Daniel was more than that. Daniel not only cared about asking for her opinion, he actually listened to what it was. It was most peculiar.

Nora felt the tension in her shoulders from kneading dough that morning melting from her shoulders.

Whatever this man was doing to her, she needed to bottle it. She'd make a fortune.

Nora glanced at the duke—the Duke of Thornfalcone!—riding alongside her. There was a peaceful, half grin on his lips, and his eyes were taking in the spectacular countryside her cottage was surrounded by. He did not speak. He was not even looking at her.

He was just . . . companionable.

It was most alarming. Every man had an angle, Nora knew. Every man wanted something. But it appeared, from all the evidence, that all Daniel Vaughn wanted was her company.

Most suspicious.

"So," Nora said, finally breaking the silence in an attempt to decipher precisely what on earth this duke could possibly want from her. "Tell me about . . . about your family."

Her stomach immediately clenched. *That was a poor decision.*

"I mean—"

"Well, you've already met my brother," said Daniel, turning to meet her gaze.

Nora tried to smile, she really did. But how was a person supposed to do that with their insides tied in knots and their heart sinking?

She should have told him the truth. Right when the man had first turned up at her door and she had believed him an inconsiderate fool who was only seeking one thing, she should have told him.

But it had been easier, hadn't it? Just to let him believe she and his brother had been lovers. Nora had thought it would give her a modicum of protection. What man would attempt to bed his own brother's mistress? What man would harm her then? As it turned out, though she could not have known it at the time, she had no need to fear Daniel.

And now . . . now it was too late.

"And do you have any other siblings?" Nora managed. *Please God, let there be others.*

"I have a sister, Amelia," said Daniel with a grin. "Lady Amelia, I suppose, though I have never seen her like that. She's a rather sweet woman with a heart of gold and a mouth that swears like a sailor."

Nora blinked. It must be the heat of the day. She could not have possibly heard—

"Yes, most people don't believe it," laughed Daniel, reading her expression easily. Their horses took a right at a crossroads, hedgerows humming with the buzzing of bees and the singing of birds. "But Amelia is not a typical lady, you understand. She rather dislikes being a Vaughn and all the restrictions that come with it."

She sounded fascinating. "And you? Do you dislike the restrictions that come with being a Vaughn?"

Nora could not help but stare as Daniel shrugged. *How did men do it?* Did they even realize how intoxicatingly distracting it was when they did that? The gentle shrug of the shoulders only drew her attention to the straining muscles threatening to burst from his shirt at any time.

The man hadn't even worn a jacket!

True, the heat was stifling, but still. A duke would never—*the earlier Duke of Thornfalcone,* Nora corrected herself, *would never have lowered himself to be dressed like a common man.*

Not like his brother.

"I am not really sure whether I know what being a Vaughn entails, now I have the burden of the title," Daniel said with his typical frankness.

He said it lightly, but Nora could read him better than that by now. "You dislike it."

"I have only been the duke for about five minutes—"

"Weeks," Nora corrected him with a snort.

"As I said, five minutes," he laughed. Her stomach lurched as their laughter mingled together. "How is a man supposed to know what he is doing in that time? How does one acclimatize? I still have two valets, for God's sake, and they are currently having to take it in turns! I can't bear to get rid of one!"

Nora rolled her eyes. "Oh, you poor thing."

"You try diverting two valets from fisticuffs over a cravat," he shot back as their steeds started to climb up the hill they had been approaching. "Then you can lecture me!"

Those words in the mouth of any other man would have simply been galling. It was perfectly clear—at least Nora thought so—that she had no servants at all to speak of and would therefore be grateful for the services of anyone who could help her.

And yet when Daniel spoke, it was not to crow about his good fortune. If anything, it was to decry it. There was something so effortlessly disarming about it all.

He was indeed a strange man.

"What about you?"

Nora blinked. Daniel had that same blazing curiosity he always affixed her with. *Really, the man could not be more obvious if he tried.*

"Oh, my valets never argue," she said carelessly, trying not to smile and failing. "No, I have them perfectly trained. If you would like, I could teach you—"

"You know what I meant," Daniel shot back with a chuckle. "Brothers, sisters. Your family. Tell me about them."

Nora's smile died on her lips.

Family.

No, that was not a good idea. In truth, she should not have brought up the topic at all. She should have known Daniel would attempt to be polite and ask her.

"No," she said softly as they reached the crest of the hill. "No, I won't tell you about my family."

"But—"

"I said that I won't," Nora said fiercely, the anger and bitterness that was always just under the surface bubbling up. "And you can't make me, Daniel!"

When she met his gaze, it was to see something most unusual.

Kindness.

"I would never make you do anything you did not wish to do," he said quietly. "Never."

Nora hesitated, her hackles raised and ready for a fight it appeared would not come.

Never? What sort of a gentleman was this, who would simply accept the word of a woman and press no further?

"You . . . you would not?"

"Confidences given freely are the only kind worth having, in my opinion," Daniel said, glancing out at the spectacular view she had promised. "Trust me. I know what it is to attempt to . . . to force a confession. It's not worth it."

Nora stared. The view she had seen before, but even if it was fresh to her, it would not have been so interesting as the man beside her who was now slipping from his horse.

Who was this man? David had mentioned a brother in passing, but she had never taken much notice. Yet here he was, entirely different from anything she could have possibly imagined.

Nora mirrored Daniel, slipping from her mare. She stepped around the beast and stood just a foot from the man who was startling her more with every conversation. She took a deep breath. *She might regret this. But he deserved it.*

"My parents died a while ago," Nora said softly, looking out at the view of Bath, sunshine glittering on the white stone. "I was . . . well, I was at finishing school then."

She felt, rather than saw, his surprise. Out of the corner of her eye she could see that Daniel had twisted to stare, mouth gaping.

"You were at finishing school?"

"Do my airs and graces not demonstrate my education?" Nora quipped, trying her best to keep the pain from her words. "You did not expect a woman living in a place like Sunview Cottage to have attended finishing school, I suppose."

She did not need to suppose. Daniel's entire body had gone rigid, and when he spoke, it was through gritted teeth.

"But—but then . . . you are a lady!"

"What of it?" Nora said, turning to him and almost laughing at the horror on his face. "Daniel, you speak as though you have gravely wounded me. You have never offended me—not really, not about anything that truly matters. You have always treated me as though—"

"But you should be in Society!" Daniel's eyebrows were so high, they were lost in his dark fringe. "Why are you not at the Assembly Rooms, why aren't you—"

"I was in Society, for a short time," Nora said, turning back to look at the town where she had experienced such scandal. Such shame. "My finishing school . . . I think they called it 'permitting me to finish early' which was a rather polite way of saying that with my parents dead and their fortune entailed, they were no longer willing to accept me without fees."

"So . . . so you entered Society? When?"

Nora tried not to notice just how transfixed the man beside her was. As though she were a most precious piece of art. As though she were important.

"For a Season," she said lightly. "I wasn't alone in being in the *ton* briefly. The Lady Genevieve Cotton-Powell—did you ever meet her? I never did, but her absence and strange disappearance was notable. And so, I like to think, was mine."

Why was she telling him this? It was madness. Nora had always known knowledge was power, always known the safest thing to do was to keep it all to herself.

So why was her past spilling from her lips? Why was she telling him—

"I don't think we ever met," Daniel said slowly. "In company, I mean."

"I would doubt it," said Nora as nonchalantly as possible, as her mind whirled back to that short time. *Was it possible?* He wouldn't have been the duke then, merely a man—

"So why aren't you—"

"Still gracing dining tables and giggling like a fool over a card table?" Nora had not intended her voice to sound so harsh.

She had also not intended to be so close to him. Had Daniel moved, or had she truly positioned herself no more than a few inches away from the man? Surely not.

"Yes, I suppose," said Daniel softly. "Why aren't you enjoying your life as you should?"

Nora swallowed. There was such heart in his words—heart she did not deserve. Certainly not heart that could be rooted in any actual knowledge of her.

"I ran out of money," she said succinctly.

She heard Daniel draw a hasty breath and knew she should not have spoken so openly about money. It was not the done thing. Her teachers at the Bath Preparatory Finishing School for Genteel Young Ladies certainly would not have approved.

But she needed to disrupt this . . . this spell that appeared to be falling over the two of them, her and Daniel. She'd played with the attentions of a duke before. She'd danced too close to the sun, and all she'd ended up with were burns. This had to end.

"But the entail—surely your uncle, or whoever inherited your parents' estate—"

"My brother," Nora said automatically.

And she froze. Her very blood became ice, and she knew—knew it was all over.

She should never have said that.

"Your brother, then," Daniel continued, stepping in front of her so he could meet her eye. "Your brother would surely have wished for you to have an agreeable Season, to—"

"The less said about my brother, the better," Nora said sharply.

She stepped away from the man who was somehow drawing all this . . . this *truth* from her. Since when did Nora Harvey admit the truth, to anyone? *This had to be the very last time,* Nora promised herself. The last conversation, the last ride, the last time she even entertained the idea of speaking with Daniel Vaughn. Because the new Duke of Thornfalcone was surely somehow like his brother. She was certain. Even if she hadn't seen the darkness emerge just yet. Even if he had given every evidence of being entirely different.

"I . . . I suppose siblings can be so different from each other," came Daniel's quiet voice.

Nora could not help but laugh. "You never said a truer word! Why, I would never have guessed that the two of you were brothers."

"Oh."

It was just one syllable. Just one.

But within it lay hurt Nora could not have expected. She turned and simply melted. There was such disappointment on Daniel's face. His shoulders had slumped, his head bowed, and he was even biting the corner of his bottom lip. A more dejected man she had never seen.

Nora acted instinctively—stupidly, in hindsight, but without any particular thought. She stepped forward and took the man's hands in her own.

She almost dropped them. The heat that seared through her was almost unbearable, as though she had grasped an iron rod which had been laying in the fire. It scalded her, burned through her fingers, up her arm, to her chest. Her very center seemed to boil with heat she did not understand, a burning she started at yet longed for.

Daniel's eyes met her own. "Nora."

"Daniel," Nora breathed. She had never felt this before, this glorious blaze. What could it be? "When I-I said you were not like your brother," Nora said quietly, looking deep into Daniel's eyes and hoping he could see the truth in her. "I meant it as a compliment."

It was still the wrong thing. Instead of perking up the gentleman, Daniel frowned. "What do you mean by that?"

"Nothing," Nora said hastily.

She dropped his hands.

The world rushed back. Birdsong returned, though where it had gone, she did not know. The brightness of the sun was now what warmed her, not the man before her. A gentle breeze caressed her arms, making the hairs stand up.

It was the breeze that did that. Nothing else.

Nora's gaze was drawn, unable to help itself, back to Daniel.

She didn't want to hurt him. The thought echoed through her so violently, so certainly, that Nora almost allowed it to slip onto her tongue and out of her lips.

Dear God. She was starting to like this man. Well, that would never do.

"Shall we return—"

"Yes," Nora said hastily, relieved it had been Daniel and not herself that had said it.

"—to our ride?" Daniel finished. "Or would you rather return straight home?"

Nora swallowed. Right now, she hardly knew what she wanted. "I . . . I don't know."

He grinned, and something of the solid determination within her melted. "Let's continue then. I want to hear all about your Season in Bath."

"There's not much to tell—"

"Make it up," Daniel declared with a laugh. "I don't care. I just . . . I want to hear you talk."

Nora almost groaned as she mounted. This was a mistake. She knew it, and Daniel knew it.

And neither of them was going to do anything about it.

Chapter Nine

23 June 1811

DANIEL HAD MANAGED to contain his excitement all the way since leaving Bath, but it was growing more and more difficult—especially as he could now see Sunview Cottage.

Just a few more minutes. Perhaps five minutes, and he would be with her again.

He saw the twitch of a curtain as the carriage pulled up, and his stomach lurched. She knew it was him. She had been waiting for him, perhaps longing to—

"Daniel Vaughn, you dolt," Nora said sharply though with a smile as she opened her door. "You know I haven't been expecting you."

It certainly looked like it. As Daniel hopped down from his carriage and, trying to comport himself in what he hoped was an elegant, refined, and altogether gentlemanly manner, he took in the pleasing sight of a Nora who had definitely not been expecting him.

The heat of the day certainly had made him leave his coat behind once again, and he was even regretting having a cravat on at all. But the thought of being without one—well, it would be scandalous.

Not half so scandalous, however, as what little Nora Harvey was wearing.

Daniel blinked, but the vision of beauty did not alter. Nora was wearing her stays, an undershift, and . . .

Daniel swallowed. *Not much else.*

"Dear God." His voice was barely more than a whisper.

Her cheeks darkened. "You stay there," she said warningly, raising a pointed finger.

The door slammed, giving Daniel the chance to do what he had been longing to do since the moment Nora had stepped out of her cottage.

He leaned against the carriage, forearm against the wood and his head leaning against his forearm. His other hand quickly rooted about his breeches and tried to make his rather stiff manhood less obvious. If he just tucked it—

"Daniel?"

Daniel whirled around, almost lost his footing, and saw with great disappointment that Nora had reappeared significantly more dressed.

"And what was wrong with the previous outfit?" he tried to quip. "I wish you had stayed—"

"If you attempt to make a jest about my stays, young man, I shall have you whipped," Nora said in a menacing tone.

It would have been far less distracting, however, if Daniel had not then been overswept by a mental image he certainly should not be permitting himself.

Nora. In her stays alone, standing over him with a whip—

"What do you want?" Nora said, leaning against her doorframe. "You'll have to come in if you wish to talk, I've almost finished kneading."

"Needing—what?" Daniel asked.

It appeared he was not to receive an answer. At least, not one with words.

Meeting his eye, Nora turned and entered her cottage.

Daniel did not even bother to consider. His feet took him forward, no thought for his driver waiting by the carriage. Nora was walking away, and he had to be close to her. She hadn't precisely invited him in, but she hadn't forbidden him, had she?

He swallowed as he entered the small kitchen. Whatever it was that Nora was doing to him, it wasn't logical. It wasn't even rational. Every part of his mind knew he had more important things to be doing that day.

For instance, he could be finally making a decision on which valet to keep.

Or he could be reading through the list of debts that had finally been sorted through on the ballroom floor. Keynes had assured him he had sent a footman to every gambling hell in Bath, and that was the lot of them. Daniel was almost ready to believe him.

He could be tidying the study, or emptying the library of the goats he had found there, or—

But no. Here he was, standing in an almost empty kitchen in a cottage which managed to smell of damp even in the height of summer, watching a woman . . . hit something squelching?

"It's called kneading," Nora explained, as though he had asked, without looking up. "K-N-E-A-D-I-N-G," she added, forestalling his question.

"Oh," said Daniel helplessly.

He stared at the thing she was hitting. It did not seem to like it, but then, it appeared to be predominately goop, so he wasn't sure it had an opinion.

"And . . . why?"

Nora looked up. "Well, how else will the bread rise?"

"Ah," said Daniel, just as helplessly. "And . . . and why will the bread . . . what on earth is that?"

She stared at his confusion, at his pointed finger at the thing she was "kneading", or whatever it was called . . . and fell about with laughter.

"Daniel Vaughn, you cannot tell me you don't know how bread is made!"

"I—I like *eating* bread," he said defensively, feeling a pang of awkwardness. "I don't have to know—"

"To think, a man who doesn't know where his bread comes from," said Nora, shaking her head with a smile and wiping her forehead. "This is dough, you idiot!"

Clearly kneading was hard work. Which might, now Daniel thought of it, explain the lack of day gown.

"I am—I have never needed to—"

"Oh, don't give me that tired old pun again," Nora said wearily.

Daniel could not help but laugh. "Accidental, this time. Look, are you going to be much longer? I have to show you something."

Nora had returned to the kneading, her knuckles forcing their way through the dough. "Do you have to show me now?"

"Yes," said Daniel, excitement returning once more. "Right now. In fact, I demand you—"

"You have never struck me as the demanding sort," said Nora, ceasing her kneading and now sort of shaping the dough. "It's one of the reasons I—well."

"Yes?" Daniel leaned forward over the table.

What had she been about to say? One of the reasons she liked him?

It was such a simple word. Liked. Daniel had never thought much of it before. There were always more important words in his day-to-day life. Like traitor. And capture. And brandy. But now there was nothing more that he wanted to hear from Nora's lips than *liked*. She liked him. Didn't she like him?

He certainly appreciated her far more than was appropriate. Daniel swallowed as his conscience rose. *She had been his brother's mistress!*

And that is why you are doing this, he tried to argue with himself. The house of Thornfalcone, as Keynes would put it, owes her something. She obviously hadn't been looked after properly by David—just look at the state of this place!

No, he was only doing what was right. This had nothing to do with desire, with the flame that had passed through them when Nora had taken his hands, with the burning need he felt when—

"You must come with me," Daniel rasped, then cleared his throat. "Now."

Nora sighed as she placed a cloth over the bread. "You Thornfalcones are all the same."

He flinched though he knew she had meant it as a tease. Well, he may not be able to match Nora when it came to sparkling good looks and witty remarks, but he could at least speak the truth.

"No, I don't think we are," Daniel said softly. "Not according to you, anyway."

He had not intended to chastise her. He hadn't, not exactly—but Nora did look up with a softened expression.

"You know, you're right. You're very different."

Their gazes met and Daniel's breath was ripped from his lungs. *How did she do that?* How did she look at him as though he were the only thing in the world? As though it was just the two of them, and if they did not hurry up and start repopulating the earth—

"Fine," Nora said briskly.

Daniel blinked. "What?"

"Fine, I'll go with you—but only because you insist," she said, brushing her hands on her gown and leaving white fingermarks all over it. "Oh, blast."

"It doesn't matter—come on," said Daniel, anticipation pouring through him.

He had not precisely thought through the logistics of this when he had left Bath. It had sounded simple when he said it to himself: take the carriage, take Nora to the house, and that would be it.

What Daniel had not accounted for was just how intoxicatingly intimate it would be, seated within the carriage during the heat of the day.

He could . . . smell her.

He had never thought of a woman's scent as a particularly arousing element. Daniel appreciated a woman's looks, the way she filled out a gown. If she slipped out of it, all the better. He liked the way they felt, the way they tasted.

The way they smelled? No, that had never featured much in his lovemaking before.

But this was different. This was Nora, and she smelled of bread and the sweetness of flour and peppermint and—

"Your brother's carriage," said Nora, then flushed as the carriage rocked forward.

Daniel tried to smile. "My carriage now, I suppose."

An awkward silence settled between them, and he was not sure how to break it. It was odd, being one's brother's heir. You never expected it to come to anything. David would marry and have heirs of his own, that's what he had always thought. But now here he was, seated with his brother's mistress, trying not to reach over and pull her into his arms.

"You were close in age, weren't you?"

Daniel swallowed. Somehow they always managed to come back to David. Was the man to haunt every interaction with this woman?

Perhaps that was only right. After all, it was not as though he could ever touch Nora, not in that way. Not after knowing she had already been given pleasure by his own brother.

"We were—are, I suppose—twins," he said shortly.

Nora's eyes widened. "What—twins? Truly?"

Daniel was rather surprised to hear her astonishment. He had always thought he and David were very much alike in appearance. When they were children, they had been able to switch at will, confusing servants and family alike.

"You do not think we look alike?"

Nora shook her head slowly. "I suppose I can see you were brothers, but . . . well, if you had not said who you were when you first came to Sunview Cottage, I would not have known."

For some reason, as the carriage rattled along, that thought gave Daniel a little comfort. He had never had to live much in David's shadow—his work for the Duke of Chantmarle, amongst others, was always enough of a distraction. And kept him out of London, away from most of his brother's friends and haunts.

But still. It was pleasant to be considered one's own person.

"So, where are we going?" said Nora brightly.

Too brightly. The knot in Daniel's stomach loosened. Clearly he was not the only one to find this discussion . . . odd.

"We are going," said Daniel grandly, "to—ah, here we are!"

He had thought the journey would not be long, and he had been right. Now he would have to hope his steward could be trusted to . . .

Daniel's shoulders relaxed the moment he glanced out of the window. *It was perfect.*

"Here," he said, opening the door before his driver could reach it. He stepped down and turned, holding out his hand. "My lady."

Nora rolled her eyes as she accepted his hand and stepped out. "You don't have to call me that, you know."

"You are a lady, even if your circumstances are a tad . . ." *Awful. Decrepit. Offensive to the name of Thornfalcone, who had taken you under his protection.* ". . . unfortunate."

Nora snorted. "Well, whoever lives here would know nothing about that. Isn't it beautiful?"

Yes, it was.

Daniel studied the rectory that was just off the main road to Bath. Impressive bay windows, a wide frontage that boasted two oriel windows above. The place had four bedchambers, his steward had told him, and a drawing room almost fit for ten guests, though he wasn't sure that would be necessary. The kitchen gardens were good and, his steward had said pointedly, there was a small stable. Just room enough for one horse, but that was all that was needed.

"You like it?"

"It's a beautiful house," said Nora, frowning. "Who are we visiting? And why on earth have you brought me to meet them?"

Then she stopped still and her gaze met his for a moment, panic in it.

"Daniel—Daniel Vaughn, you haven't—"

"Nora Harvey," Daniel said grandly, extending an arm to gesture at the place. "Welcome to your new home!"

As sunlight poured down on them, he worked hard not to speak as Nora took in his words. He would hate to interrupt her thanks, the gratitude that would surely pour from her lips. She would wish to make it clear, after all, just how relieved she was.

Her new home.

Daniel had been most definite with his steward—Nora would need somewhere she could entertain, but nothing too large. She would have an easier life: a roof that did not leak, a place for her horse to lodge. It would even have a kitchen where she could "need" all the bread she wished.

"Daniel Vaughn, you blithering idiot," came the blistering reply rather than prodigious thanks. "Are you forgetful as well as foolish?"

Daniel blinked, but the sight of Nora did not change. There was a frown across her forehead and danger in her blue eyes.

"Are you mad?"

"Mad?" Daniel repeated, taking a step backward. It was the only thing he could do to protect himself from the oncoming onslaught—one he did not understand. "Nora, you needed a home, and I—"

"Have you learned absolutely nothing from the horse?" she groaned.

Daniel opened his mouth, then closed it again as Nora strode up the path in a whirlwind of fury. "Nora!"

"Look at this—look at this hall!" Nora said, throwing open the front door and evidently despairing at the elegant proportions, the welcoming rug on the floor, the several doors leading off it. "Look at this drawing room!"

Daniel followed her, bewildered, as he walked into the spacious and well-lit room. "Yes, it's a drawing room, but—"

"Look at this—oh God, is this a dining room with a table for twelve?" Nora spluttered, as though she had been given terrible news. "Don't even tell me how many bedchambers this place has!"

"Four," said Daniel, dazed.

Nora groaned. She actually closed her eyes as she did so, as though she could no longer bear to take in the offensive sight of a drawing room where she could eat her dinner on a chair, rather than standing as Daniel presumed she did.

It made no sense.

Daniel felt self-righteous bluster rise within him as they stood in the dining room. "I don't understand—you cannot honestly think you can survive a winter in that cottage! You needed somewhere dry, somewhere safe—"

"Have you learned nothing from the horse?" Nora asked again, opening her eyes and fixing him with a glare that could have melted steel.

Daniel opened his mouth, but the memory of her words resounded in his mind.

"With what saddle? With what reins? In what riding habit, using what riding boots?"

He closed his mouth. Then he cleared his throat. "Ah."

"How am I supposed to heat a place like this?" Nora said with a sigh, shoulders slumping. "A fire in every room? That's four bedchambers, a hall, a drawing room, a dining room—"

"The kitchen and a parlor," Daniel said hoarsely. "I think there's a morning room at the back of the—"

"Daniel Vaughn!"

"I thought you would like it," he said defensively, moving toward her.

Somehow he had to make her see—and if that meant touching her, braving the scalding feeling which overtook them every time they touched, then so be it.

"Like it? How will I pay the servants required to keep a place like this clean? They won't like working for no pay!" Nora said, twisting away. "How will I furnish it?"

"You can have some leftover furnishings from my house in Bath, you've seen how much I—"

"I don't want your leftovers, Daniel!"

Nora's words rang around the dining room and Daniel staggered backward as though she had hit him. It rather felt as though she had.

Nora's cheeks were red, her eyes sparkling as though she was forcing back tears, and it had all gone wrong. All the trust, the closeness they had somehow gained over the last few days, it was all gone.

He had ruined it.

Daniel swallowed. "I . . . I am sorry, I—"

"Every time I think . . . whenever I try to give a man a chance to . . ." Nora swallowed, then stepped around him toward the door. "I need to go home—Daniel!"

What had come over him he did not know, but he had taken her by the arms, turning her to face him. All Daniel knew was that he had to make this right—and Nora could not be permitted to leave without knowing, without understanding. He may not be able to explain it with words, but she had to know.

"Nora—"

"Let go of me!" she cried, trying to tug herself free.

But Daniel would not release her, even though her close proximity was stoking a fire within him so hot he was boiling. The warmth was settling in his loins, which he had expected, but a spark had also drifted to his heart, and it was melting something in him he had not ever known was there.

"Nora, I—" Daniel swallowed. "I'm doing everything I can to show you how I feel!" The words poured from him, despite his efforts to censure himself.

Nora's eyes widened. She stopped struggling, standing mere inches away.

He could feel her heat radiating from her, her breasts heaving with the effort of attempting to escape him.

Dear God . . .

"Well," Nora murmured, her breath on his face, her chin tilted up to meet his gaze. "Why don't you just tell me, Daniel?"

They were both breathing heavily now. Daniel's breath rasped in ragged desperation, everything within him trying not to do the one thing that would show her beyond a doubt precisely what he felt for her.

A kiss.

That was all it would take. Daniel was certain, if he could just span the gap between them, he could show her. He could press it onto her lips, burn into her soul what he felt.

"D-Daniel?"

Daniel hesitated, his head leaning lower, his lips almost reaching hers. *Christ, she was so warm, so tantalizing.* He could feel her pulse throbbing under his hand which was still on her arm. A pulse that quickened every inch he grew closer.

Perhaps she wanted this. Perhaps she desired him as much as he did her. Perhaps Nora was held back only by the same inhibition that halted him. *That she had been his brother's.*

And words Daniel himself had spoken just days ago returned to halt him as he leaned in to claim Nora's lips for himself.

"I would never make you do anything you did not wish to do. Never."

Slowly, one by one, Daniel released his fingers from her arms.

"I-I want to tell you, Nora," he said, his voice rough with repressed desire and confusion. "But I can't. And I won't take—I won't force . . ." His voice trailed away. *How could he make this right?* "I am sorry."

Nora's expression softened. "You . . . you are?"

Daniel nodded. It was not manly, David had always said, to apologize, much less to a lady. But Nora deserved it. She deserved so much, even if she would not accept it from him.

"I should have thought about it. You were right, I . . . I should have learned from the horse," he said helplessly.

His head had dropped, and so he had no warning of the sudden touch.

Nora cupped his cheek, lifting his gaze to hers. "You . . . oh, Daniel. You tried. That is more than most men would ever attempt. But I think . . . I think it is time you returned me home."

Chapter Ten

26 June 1811

"Remind me," said Nora as she leaned back in the carriage. "Why am I being so foolish as to agree to this?"

It was all she could do to keep a sense of detachment in her voice. Excitement was thrumming through her so strongly, she was rather astonished she wasn't vibrating off the seat.

Perhaps Daniel did not notice because he was similarly excited. "You're not being foolish! You are accepting an invitation from a duke, something anyone with any sense would do!"

Only from the right duke, Nora could not help but think.

Thankfully, she did not say the words aloud. She had already almost been caught out a few times since he had picked her up that evening, his carriage brilliant and sparkling in the evening sun.

Why are you doing this, she had wanted to ask.

What do you want from me?

Why do you keep coming back here?

And why does my heart always awkwardly skip over a beat when I catch you smiling at me as though you are looking at the most beautiful thing?

You are not to lose your head, Nora Harvey, she told herself firmly, gripping the reticule in her hand.

The object itself brought her back to earth in a way nothing else could. "And you are absolutely sure—"

"I told you, Amelia won't even notice her favorite reticule is gone," Daniel said as he crossed his leg.

The carriage jolted against a stone. That, or Nora had left her stomach behind at the last corner.

"You did not say it was her favorite reticule!" she said accusingly.

Oh, what did it matter? The point was, the Duke of Thornfalcone had sneaked into his sister's bedchamber while she was—according to him—away in the country and grabbed a reticule from her dressing room. It was stolen. Stolen from a lady!

And now she was holding it. *Oh, goodness, this had got out of hand.*

"I could have borrowed a gown and pelisse and shoes," came Daniel's cheerful voice.

"The day I wear a stolen gown is the day you are buried in a heap of horse's—"

"The point is, no one will know," Daniel said swiftly, cutting off Nora's muttered vehemence. "And you look lovely."

Nora rolled her eyes but did not say anything.

It was difficult, after all, to argue with a duke. Any duke. And this particular duke was charm itself, more's the pity. Nora was finding it increasingly difficult to say "no" to the man about anything, which was a bad sign in itself.

Because she had to. She couldn't allow this to continue—this, this . . . whatever it was.

And the moment she returned home after the ball, Nora told herself sternly, *that would be an end to it.*

"I shouldn't be taking this risk," she said aloud.

Daniel snorted. "Why not?"

"You may not be aware of this," said Nora lightly—or as lightly as she could manage, "but my Season in Bath—"

"Your abrupt Season," said Daniel, leaning closer.

His interest was practically dripping off him, Nora could not help but think. She also couldn't help, somehow, leaning forward in turn, bringing her mouth close to his ear.

As she spoke he shivered, and a shot of power, mysterious and decadent, flashed through her.

"It was rather abrupt, yes," Nora whispered. "But the trouble is, that was because—"

The carriage came to a sudden stop. That was the only reason she flung herself forward, unable to halt her trajectory thanks to the sudden shift in the movement of the carriage.

At least, that's what Nora would have told a jury, and she would just have to hope not to then be tried for perjury. As it was, Daniel did not ask why she had suddenly landed in his lap.

The man did not look inclined to question it. "Oh. Hello."

Nora tried to smile as heat flared through her buttocks, across her thighs, and up her arms. Every part of her, in fact, that was in contact with the dazzlingly handsome man holding her in his arms.

"Hello." Her voice was quiet with a shyness she had not known for years.

The moment could have been no more than a second. Or it could have been an age.

"Ahem."

Nora sprang up so swiftly, she might have been scalded. "Ah, yes, we're here, wonderful! I had wondered how long it would be"

Her tongue ran away with her, providing her with the space to think which she so desperately craved.

Daniel's carriage driver did not quite meet her eye as he helped her down from the carriage. *Thank goodness.* Nora was unsure if she would be able to return his gaze if he had done so.

This was ridiculous. She was the guest of a duke, and that could only mean she would be welcome here at wherever . . . where were they?

Nora looked up.

Her breath caught in her throat. *Of course.* It would be totally unfair of her to hope that they could visit some nondescript place owned by a family of little importance. It had to be—

"Lady Romeril is expecting us," Daniel said brightly. "She's rather a terror I'm afraid, but I've found the trick is—"

"Lady Romeril and I are . . . acquainted," Nora murmured.

At least, she thought she did. It was hard to tell, with her head spinning and legs threatening to crumple underneath her at any moment, precisely what words had slipped through her lips.

It couldn't be. Fate would not be so cruel as to bring her here.

"Oh, you know her?" Daniel said, stepping out of the carriage and brushing his coat which had become somewhat rumpled.

Rumpled, Nora thought distractedly, *by her sudden presence in his lap.*

"Lady Romeril and I?" She had to focus on the conversation at hand—if this party was hosted by Lady Romeril, she would have to focus on *every* conversation. "She knows of me. I think that is probably sufficient—how about we get back in the carriage and—"

"Oh, we can't leave now, we've just arrived!" Daniel's disappointment was visible. "Besides, what would we do in the carriage?"

Nora bit her lip to prevent herself from laughing.

He was a man of the world, wasn't he? In their conversations, Daniel had obliquely referred to cities all over Europe, casually mentioned names of people Nora had only read about, and once tried to make a joke based on a Greek play she had never heard of.

And yet still, somehow, Daniel Vaughn, Duke of Thornfalcone, was an innocent.

What would they do in the carriage? Goodness, she could think of a great number of things. *Not things that she was going to do with him,* Nora told herself firmly. They were just—just two friends. Although, if she were being truly honest with herself, what she felt between her thighs whenever this man looked at her certainly had nothing to do with friendship.

"I thought you'd enjoy it."

Nora blinked. Daniel's face had fallen, and he had that same expression on his face as when he had tried to gift her the horse.

Oh, he meant well. He meant lots of things, most of which Nora wasn't even sure he understood. But you could mean well and still destroy your own reputation by bringing a courtesan to Lady Romeril's door.

"You . . . you do recall . . ." *Blast, it had never been this difficult.* Nora rallied. "I have been the mistress to three men in my life, Daniel. You really think Lady Romeril would appreciate me accompanying you?"

She saw the shadow of pain that swept across Daniel's face. Oh, it hurt to remind him of her past. To draw attention to her own ruined character. To point, even in passing, to what he thought she had shared with his brother. Even though she hadn't. Even though David had never touched her, except that time when he had tried to steal a kiss and Nora had managed to shove a rolling pin right where it was needed most.

"You are my guest," said Daniel quietly. "I don't think I'll be burning all my bridges with Lady Romeril by bringing you as my guest. Besides, we don't even have to speak to her."

Nora raised a sardonic eyebrow.

"We don't have to let her talk to us for too long," amended Daniel with a wide grin. "Or . . . or I can take you back. It's up to you. Your choice."

Your choice.

Nora swallowed, all the fight in her draining away as she was once again given something by Daniel that no man had ever wished her to have.

The choice.

She glanced up at the building and squared her shoulders. Perhaps it was possible, in these quiet, private parties, to return to Society. A little. The Season was essentially over anyway. Anyone of consequence, aside from Lady Romeril, would be in the country. What harm could it do?

"It's . . . it's a nice house," Nora said lamely, for want of anything better to say.

Daniel grinned. "Not as nice as the one I tried to give you, though."

She nudged him without looking around, face flushing at the memory. The things this man had tried to do for her—more than half the men in Bath had never even done them for their wives, let alone their brother's supposed mistress!

"Fine," she said briskly. "Let's get it over—I mean, let us enjoy the even—Daniel!"

His name had slipped from her lips before Nora could stop herself.

But then, what other response was possible? The man had taken her hand in his, slipping his fingers between hers, squeezed it as though it were the most natural thing in the world, then placed her hand on his arm.

"I am proud to have you by my side this evening," Daniel said softly as they walked up the steps to Lady Romeril's house. "Besides . . . this may not have been entirely altruistic."

Nora jerked her head to look up at Daniel. *Of course it wasn't.* "What do you mean?"

"This might be my first appearance as Duke of Thornfalcone," he said, wincing in clear anticipation of her ire.

She could only stare. They had stopped at the top step, the door unopened. "And . . . and you thought I would be a good distraction?"

She should have known. But she had let herself believe that he simply meant well. Why she had thought Daniel would be any different—

"I thought you would give me heart," said Daniel softly, grazing a finger down her cheek, lingering near her lips before being removed.

"You give me courage, Nora."

Nora's lips parted. Whether she was going to speak or kiss the man, she did not know.

She never found out. The door opened and light dazzled them for just a moment.

"I thought you would never get here, you naughty boy!"

Nora flinched instinctively as the roaring woman descended on them from the hall where she had clearly been welcoming her guests.

"I told them, I said the Duke of Thornfalcone knew where his duty lay, and he would most definitely be gracing my home first—but the Duchess of Chantmarle had some ridiculous idea you—"

"Lady Romeril," Daniel said weakly as Nora tried to stifle a snort. "How pleasant to see you."

Lady Romeril glared sternly, as though inspecting a horse at a show. "And you haven't bothered to visit your tailor, have you?"

Nora glanced at Daniel. It was true, the coat and breeches were perhaps worn, but as one would expect for a younger son. What was the—

Ah. Younger son.

"Really, you keep acting this way and the lower classes will begin to think they can start parading around in bonnets with feathers!" Lady Romeril sniffed.

"Well, I promise you, Lady Romeril, the moment I start to parade around in a bonnet with feathers, you shall be the first to know," said Daniel seriously.

Nora stifled a giggle.

Well. Stifled was perhaps too generous a word. She snorted, tried to transform it into a genteel clearing of the throat, and managed to choke.

"Nora?" Daniel said, immediately concerned.

Nora waved a hand as heat blossomed in her cheeks. She wished to goodness the man did not have to draw attention to the fact she was making such an exhibition of herself.

"I am quite well, I promise you—"

"Nora?" Lady Romeril appeared to swell, filling the doorway she had still not permitted them to walk through. "I do not believe we have been introduced."

And that was when Nora knew she should have said more to prepare Daniel. To give him, perhaps, a false name by which she could be introduced. After all, it had been so long ago—almost four years! What were the chances her mere appearance could remind the rest of Society of that particular scandal?

Her name, on the other hand . . .

"Ah yes," said Daniel blithely, utterly ignorant of the panic threatening to overwhelm her.

She had to warn him—had to distract him, but he was barreling forward with good intentions enough to pave hell.

"Lady Romeril, may I introduce—"

"It's awfully hot out here, isn't it?" Nora said desperately, fanning herself so violently she rather thought she might slip from the top step. "Daniel, may I speak to—"

"Miss Nora Harvey," Daniel said grandly, as though he were bringing an archduchess to Lady Romeril's door. "No, that's not right—Nora isn't your—sorry, I should have—"

"Eleanor Harvey?" intoned Lady Romeril as though uttering a curse. "No."

Nora swallowed and just about managed to keep her head lifted.

She was not going to permit her chin to drop. She would not allow this woman, this Lady Romeril who thought herself the dictator of all that was good and fashionable in Society, to make her feel small. Just because—

"Not the Eleanor Harvey who—"

"Yes, yes, I am *that* Eleanor Harvey," Nora said hastily. Less said about that, the better. "Look, I just—"

"You would bring such a scandalous woman to my door!" hissed Lady Romeril, directing her ire at Daniel with such fervor, Nora was astonished the man was still standing. "Have you no shame, sir?"

"None whatsoever," Daniel said steadily, meeting Lady Romeril's glower with such fortitude, Nora could not understand it. "You said on your invitation that Amelia and I were welcome, and as my sister was already otherwise engaged—"

"Lady Amelia is welcome, of course, any sister of the Duke of—but this is not your sister!" Lady Romeril continued to hiss in a low voice, as though terrified that those guests who had already arrived may overhear her.

Oh, this was awful. Nora had thought herself inoculated to the spiteful words of others. Had she not heard enough of them before now? But it seemed she was not. This was terrible; mortification and guilt rushed through her. She should never have permitted Daniel to bring her here.

"Nora is certainly not my sister," the Duke of Thornfalcone said, glancing sideways. "Most definitely not."

Warmth pooled again between Nora's legs as she took in the unabashed desire in Daniel's eyes. Oh, the way he looked at her: as though he wanted to slowly peel every garment from her, then kiss her all the way up from her toes to her—

"Your Grace!"

"It appears I have other plans for this evening, however," Daniel said smoothly, placing his hand on Nora's as it rested on his arm. "I do apologize, Lady Romeril, I appear to have accepted your invitation in error."

Nora glanced at the lady filling the doorway.

"B-But—but you can't—Your Grace, I—"

"Good evening, Lady Romeril," Daniel said calmly.

Nora did not have another chance to look at the woman's face as they walked away. Try as she might, she could not seem to balance sufficiently to walk without leaning heavily on Daniel's arm. The thought of tilting her head over her shoulder to see the damage he had wrought was out of the question.

It was therefore almost a full minute before Nora realized what they had done.

"We're—we're walking," she said blankly.

The street they were walking down was unfamiliar in the growing twilight.

"We are indeed."

Nora swallowed. Daniel's voice was strained. Anger had entered into his tone, an anger she had never heard before.

Daniel was never angry. On every occasion she had seen him, he had been jovial, cheerful, bright. Sometimes overly confident, always overstepping the bounds of propriety . . .

But angry?

"We're not getting back into the carriage?" Nora asked quietly.

They crossed a road, dodging a barouche of two carousing young gentlemen, and took a turning down a quieter street. Nora did not attempt to pull him in one direction or another. Daniel appeared to have a route in mind.

"I need to stomp it out."

"I beg your pardon?"

"Whenever I grow angry, I go for a walk," said Daniel shortly, still looking straight ahead. "Or a ride. Exercise of any sort. It's the only thing that helps."

Nora stared. Well, it was certainly not the most destructive method for dealing with one's temper she had ever heard of. In a way, it was almost rational. But that did not change what she knew she had to say.

"I . . . I am sorry, Daniel. I never meant to embarrass—Daniel!"

For the second time that evening, Nora gasped the man's name after he did something astonishing. This time, however, it was nowhere near as tame as just taking her hand.

Daniel had halted, twisting her around and thrusting her up against a wall. It might have hurt, if Nora could have felt anything but exhilaration and desire in her veins.

He had stepped toward her, placing his hands either side of her on the wall, pinning her in place. The street was deserted now, but that would not prevent someone from coming upon them at any moment.

"Someone will see."

"Let them see," snarled Daniel, his anger breaking through. "I want them to see—let them see me with you. Let them!"

She swallowed, half hypnotized by this passionate Daniel, this unleashed Duke of Thornfalcone who had all the same power as his elder brother but none of the malice.

Oh, he was intoxicating.

"I've been burned before," Nora breathed, wishing she had the bravery to reach out and touch him, knowing she would lose all self-control if she did. "Men who thought they knew what they wanted, thought they could accept the consequences of it."

"I will never hurt you," Daniel said firmly, leaning closer to her until he made contact.

Nora gasped, her back arching, pressing her breasts into his chest and he groaned, and oh, it was everything to hear his reaction to her.

"I will never hurt you," Daniel repeated, his fiery gaze meeting hers. "But you're hurting me, Nora. Hurting me by being apart from me every second you're not touching me."

Nora almost whimpered, but she managed to speak in a clear, quiet voice. "You're finally doing the right thing, Daniel."

His kiss was urgent, desperate, more need in it than Nora could have imagined. All breath left her, but what did she need it for anyway? She had Daniel Vaughn's lips on hers, his passion pouring onto her mouth, his tongue teasing her lips open and ravaging her own tongue for pleasure.

Nora gasped, her hands around his neck, pulling him closer. No kiss had ever been like this, no passion had ever felt like this. This aching need, this burning within her to be closer, to know him as she had never known another man before.

Eventually the kiss ended. Nora wasn't sure whether she had broken it, or he had. It did not seem to matter.

It would not be their last.

Their breathing was short as Daniel lowered his forehead against hers. "I . . . I should not have—"

"Probably not," Nora agreed, heart twisting as it had never twisted before. "I was always told . . . not to play with dukes."

Daniel's smile was lopsided. "What—play with dukes, get burned?"

"Something like that." Nora smiled as she tilted her chin and kissed him again.

CHAPTER ELEVEN

30 June 1811

DANIEL FROWNED.

Though he was not, in his own mind, a proud man, he did know what he excelled at, and he was generally able to avoid what he could not master. It was one reason he had always cared little for his lack of title. Give someone a title, and expectations of behavior, skill, and confidence are immediately placed on their shoulders.

And this was not a new propensity. When he was a boy, his mother had called it "his way". Since he had been a child, it had been his habit to only begin a thing if he knew how to complete it.

Like baking, for example.

"Not quite," said Nora cheerfully. "Come on, really put your back into it!"

Daniel stared down, utterly lost, at the dough on the kitchen table. "Put my—"

"Your back into—you know what I mean!" Nora's hair was streaked with flour again.

He tried not to examine just where one floury streak and another began. He'd already stirred up enough trouble by staring too closely at Nora. He needed to concentrate on his . . . dough.

"I will never hurt you. But you're hurting me, Nora. Hurting me by being

apart from me every second you're not touching me."

Daniel swallowed. It was hot today, was it not? Hot in the little cottage, hot in the kitchen Nora had pulled him into when he had only called to see how she was doing.

See how she was doing, sneered a voice in the back of her mind. *You know you couldn't stay away.* Try as you might, you sat in that lonely, increasingly empty home, and thought of nothing but her. Do not attempt to make this all noble. You want to—

"Look, watch my hands," said Nora, blowing away a strand of her hair that had fallen from its pins and looking confidently at the duke who had flour on his cuffs.

Daniel nodded rather than risk speaking. His gaze drifted slowly down Nora's body, lingering at some places perhaps longer than they should, but eventually reaching her hands.

They were small. Delicate. Yet the strength in those fingers was more than he had ever seen in an entire person.

"Watch," Nora murmured.

Daniel swallowed. All he could do at the moment was watch. Watch the little smile that curled Nora's rosebud mouth whenever she thought he wasn't looking. Watch the way sunlight glittered as it streamed through her hair. Watch the way Nora tied an apron, slowly and carefully behind her own back, her fingers gracing the linen as though it were silk.

And feel. Feel his stomach lurch whenever she brushed past him in the tiny kitchen. Feel the hair on the back of his neck go up whenever she smiled. Feel warmth pooling in his loins whenever he thought about—

No. He wouldn't do that again. Kissing Nora had been—God, it had been everything.

But he wasn't going to cross that line again. Brothers shared plenty of things but not that. Not women.

"See, the aim is to ensure plenty of folding, then pressure."

Daniel attempted to watch carefully, but all he could think about was how much pressure Nora had placed on his neck with those fingers, pulling him closer as—

"And then you turn it over and make sure all parts of the dough feel the same pressure. You see?"

He nodded vaguely. What he wouldn't do to feel Nora's fingers all over him, feeling the same pressure—

"You're not paying attention."

Daniel swallowed as he watched her fingers steadily move in the same pattern. How did she do it? Was it part of being a courtesan, this knowledge of precisely what she could do to overwhelm him?

"Then you eat the dough after painting it bright green."

Did all women have this skill, or was it only—

"Daniel!"

Daniel started. "Wh-What? I was listening, I—"

"Were you indeed?" Nora had raised an eyebrow, a hand on her hip. "What color paint do you need for the dough?"

He wracked his brains, carefully trying to play back the conversation he had half heard whilst staring at Nora's fingers. Red? Blue? No, surely brown if it were bread.

"Brown," he said confidently.

A puff of flour flared on his shirt.

"Nora!"

"You were not listening," she said, half laughing, half shaking her head in despair. "I said green, but—"

"Why would you paint dough anyway?" asked Daniel, bewildered. "I would have thought—"

"You are a ninny. Knead your dough."

It appeared that was all the explanation he was to be given, but Daniel could hardly complain. Not when an afternoon running over the debts his brother had accrued could have been his entertainment today.

Instead, he had managed to slip into Nora's world. *Just for an hour*, he had promised himself. Just for a bit of time with her. She needed help with the dough, after all. It would be callous of him, a gentleman, to leave a lady in distress.

Though now he came to think of it, it would be him in distress later, trying to explain all this flour to his valet.

"What on earth are you thinking about?"

Daniel started. "I'm not—"

"You're not here. Not present," Nora said lightly, though there was a steel to her voice he could not help but admire.

It was so refreshing. No one spoke to him like this anymore—it was all bowing and scraping. Only Keynes, perhaps, but even his butler was starting to do the unthinkable and be obliging. It was most alarming.

But not Nora.

Daniel sighed as he cast a look around the small kitchen. He'd tried to take her away from this, to give her somewhere better to live. Yet she refused to leave. It was galling. It was—

"Your Grace?"

Daniel stiffened. "Don't call me that."

Nora was laughing. The way her head tilted onto one side as she giggled made his stomach swoop.

"Very clever," he said with a grin, pummeling his dough as instructed. "I was thinking about . . . well, about the mess my brother has left me in, in truth."

His heart sank as he spoke. No matter how hard he tried, no matter what he did, it appeared they could not escape talking about David.

The specter of his brother hung over them, a pall over what could have been something marvelous, Daniel was sure. But David had to keep interfering. Had to keep reminding Daniel that he was not the first to find this beautiful woman, the first to want her.

"More debts?" Nora said quietly.

Daniel nodded, unable to meet her eye. "Debts of honor are now arriving, as well as requests—no, demands for money."

The debts of honor had been far more mortifying to receive than the bills. A bill could be paid, it was concrete and definite, even if it required the sale of a pianoforte. Fortunately, Daniel had a few to spare.

But debts of honor?

"What do you mean, debts of honor?" asked Nora as she lifted a sharp knife.

Daniel's eyes settled on it. *Why on earth could she want—*

She lightly scored the dough before her in a metal tray. "Daniel?"

"Debts of honor," he said hastily, trying not to watch the delicate and swift way her fingers moved. "Well, sometimes it's small things. He had three IOUs for bottles of wine at the club after losing games of billiards. His valet had an IOU for a case of cigars, which was bizarre but at least easy to resolve."

"And some of them haven't been?"

Daniel sighed. "One man was owed David's best horse. But who decides what is best? Tallest? Fastest? Most impressive to look at?"

A corner of Nora's mouth twitched. "I can see how that could be complicated."

"One woman had a promise, written by my brother, for his favorite book in his own library," said Daniel with a mirthless chuckle. "Which favorite? Which book? Damn it all, which library?"

Nora blinked. "He had more than one?"

This was not the time to discuss the magnitude of his brother's purchasing. Daniel resumed kneading the dough, finding it eased some of the tension in his shoulders.

"He was a complete reprobate," he said heavily. "I had always known David was perhaps not the man of honor I imagined him to be—"

"Certainly not," murmured Nora.

"—but I at least thought his debts of honor would make sense," continued Daniel, choosing not to investigate that comment. He had already spent far too much time thinking on something else she had said about his brother.

"When I-I said you were not like your brother, I meant it as a compliment."

"Oh, they can't be that compli—"

"One of them promised the moon to Lady Romeril," Daniel said dully. "How on earth do you think I'm going to pay that one back?"

Nora's eyes widened, her head stilling. "To—to Lady Romeril?"

He met her gaze and tried to ignore the heady rush of desire as he did so. That night . . . he should never have even contemplated taking her to Lady Romeril's. But he had. And the altercation there had led to the most incredible kiss—

"Well, I have faith in you," Nora said briskly, breaking the connection as she looked down at the dough she was now kneading. "You are the Duke of Thornfalcone. You'll find a way."

Daniel knew what he should say to such kind, placid words.

Thank you, Nora. I am sure I will.

But he couldn't. The words stuck in his throat, making it impossible to understand anything that was happening. The whole cottage was swirling, shimmering as though fading from view, leaving only Nora.

He couldn't lie to her.

He'd never been in much danger before inheriting the dukedom, not even in his work for the Crown. It was men like the Duke of Chantmarle who faced the real danger. Daniel just provided them with information, sources, solutions.

He was in very real danger now.

"I just . . ." Daniel swallowed. It felt wrong, somehow, to admit this to another soul—yet saying it to Nora also felt natural. As though he should have done so eons ago. "I just don't know how to be a duke."

She looked up. "I beg your pardon?"

"You heard me," said Daniel wretchedly, his dough forgotten. "Every other duke—they were born to it, Nora, not like me! They stand differently, sit differently. They treat people like—"

"Dirt, usually," Nora said breezily, leaning her fingers on the table and fixing him with a quiet stare. "You don't have much experience with dukes, do you?"

"I know a fair few," he said with a shrug. "It's just . . ." His voice trailed away. How could he explain it? How could he put into words the constant sensation that he was doing it wrong somehow? Every turn he made, every order obeyed by his butler or steward . . . there was always that widening of the eyes, as though they were astonished he had made that decision.

Daniel had seen it in public, too. Oh, everyone had been very polite when he had attended the Assembly Rooms yesterday. People had bowed or curtsied, a footman had brought him a drink. But no one had conversed with him. There were wide, blank smiles and genteel excuses not to remain near him too long. Whether it was the debacle at Lady Romeril's or simply that they did not view him as a proper duke, Daniel did not know. But it was disheartening in the extreme.

And how did one explain that to a woman who had, for some reason he did not know, already been turned out of Society?

"Well. Now that you're a duke, you don't have to work or do anything you don't want to do," Nora was saying. "What will you do with all that time and power?"

Daniel shrugged. "Oh, I don't know, take up hobbies. Learn to paint."

Nora snorted. "I can't imagine you with a paintbrush."

After a pause, Daniel finally spoke. "I thought it would be easy. Well maybe not easy, but easier than this." He sighed. "Lord, admitting this to you—"

"Admitting what?" Nora said. She was still leaning on the table, dough forgotten.

He took another deep breath. "My . . . my weakness."

There. It was laid out now. What woman would wish to be kissed, let alone courted by a man who was so weak?

Daniel swallowed, tasting bile and fear on his tongue. There were men out there, he was sure, who were always confident in every situation. They always knew what to do, what to say. It had never mattered that he wasn't one of those men, because he was just Mr. Daniel Vaughn. But now he was the Duke of Thornfalcone. And it mattered.

"You are not weak."

Daniel's head, which had unconsciously fallen, jerked up. "Why do you say that?"

"Because I have met weak men," Nora said decidedly. "I know them. You are not them."

"I'm just wandering about Bath hoping no one has noticed I don't know what I'm doing," Daniel admitted with a wry laugh, tension sparking across his shoulder blades. "Nora, I—"

"You don't have to be this—this perfect version of a duke that doesn't exist!" Now she was stepping around the kitchen table toward him. "You just have to be you, Daniel. You."

Daniel's breath hitched in his throat. He had not expected her to move toward him, had not considered what he would do if suddenly there were no kitchen table between them.

Like now. Nora was standing just a few feet away, leaning one hand on the table while the other hung by her side. If he just reached out—reached out and took it, felt her warmth, drew strength from—

"It's easy to feel out of our depth when we try something new," Nora said softly. "It's easy to—God, it's easy to feel alone. I know what it's like to face the world and know, deep inside you, that you're wrong. That you don't fit."

Daniel swallowed. He had never seen that look on her face before.

A strange sort of pain, a longing to be more open, yet a determination that she would only say what was necessary.

What else was Nora hiding? What else about her past did he not know?

And would she ever trust him enough to tell him everything?

"You have to keep going," said Nora softly. She stepped forward, narrowing the gap between them to only a foot. "You have to keep going, Daniel."

Daniel's lungs were tight, his whole center was burning.

He had not come here for comfort. He wasn't entirely sure why he had come here at all, except to see her, be close to her. And his bread certainly wasn't going to win any awards—in truth, he wasn't sure whether the dough would even rise, based on what Nora had said about the importance of kneading it just right.

But none of that mattered. She was so close. The temptation tingling along his fingers could no longer be denied.

Daniel reached out and took Nora's floury hand in his own.

She gasped, eyes wide, a shiver rushing over her. The obvious physical reaction to him kindled hope in him. She felt something, just as he did. That kiss—those kisses—in the streets of Bath had not been one-sided. He had not given Nora anything she had not wanted.

"It's not like I have much of a choice," Daniel said softly, lacing his fingers in hers as he spoke. "I am a duke. I am the Duke of Thornfalcone. That is not something one can step away from or give up."

"Don't give up," Nora said quietly, looking deep into his eyes.

Daniel could not help himself. She wasn't talking of his pursuit of her, surely, but he could not help but hear it that way.

He stepped forward. Now they were only inches apart. Just a gentle lean, and his chest would be brushing up against hers.

"Daniel," Nora breathed.

He leaned forward—

She leaned back, eyes downcast. "Daniel, I know all about choice. I suppose in truth, I-I know more about the lack of it, but still. You always have a choice."

Daniel leaned back, gaining his physical equilibrium as his heart shattered.

No choice.

Nora had been a courtesan. She had told him as much, had she not?

"I have been the mistress to three men in my life, Daniel."

She had been his own brother's mistress. And if Daniel was hearing her rightly, Nora had not always felt as though she could voice her own opinion, have a choice in the manner in which the affairs progressed.

And here she was, with a duke once again in her kitchen, and this time he—

Daniel hesitated. God, he wanted to kiss her again. He wanted to press his lips to hers and taste her sweetness. He wanted to push all the dough and trays and rolling pins off the kitchen table with one sweep of his hand, lift Nora up with the other, and worship her on that table.

He wanted so much. Too much.

But he couldn't cross that line again. Tempting as it was to have Nora in his arms, Daniel knew he was not that sort of man. Probably.

It was therefore with a great shuddering breath that he forced himself to release Nora's fingers and take half a step back.

Perhaps it was his imagination, but he certainly thought she almost took that step with him, before halting herself.

"I-I suppose I do have a choice," Daniel murmured, his breath ragged. "Nora, I—"

"Yes?"

He cleared his throat and thought of the numerous cold baths his two valets were going to have to prepare for him that evening. Perhaps it was a good thing he had still not found it within himself to let one go. He would need both.

"Help me choose," Daniel said in a half-strangled voice as he pointed to his abandoned dough on the kitchen table. "Buns or . . . or a loaf?"

CHAPTER TWELVE

5 July 1811

THE KNOCK AT the door was early.

"Go away!" called out Nora with a smile.

The silence on the other side of the door was palpable. Then—

"Nora?"

"I said, go away," said Nora happily, hurrying across to the other side of the kitchen and trying to pull off her apron. *How had the blasted thing managed to get so tangled?*

"But . . . but . . ."

She stifled a laugh. It really was most unfair of her to confuse Daniel like this, but really. Who turns up early for dinner? She had expected the duke to be at least half an hour late, as, indeed, any gentleman would be!

"But you invited me!" came Daniel's voice through the door, completely bemused. "I have it here—'Your Grace', it says, 'will you be so good—'"

Nora rolled her eyes. He was such a stickler for how things should be. "I said seven o'clock!"

There was a moment's silence. She managed, just, to untie her apron. Hanging it on the back of the door to the parlor, Nora paused, expecting to hear Daniel's response by now.

Then—

"It's five minutes past seven! I'm late! Are you truly to deny me entry because I am late?"

Nora rolled her eyes. "You're early!"

The stew was bubbling merrily, and there was a skip in her step as she strode around the kitchen table to lift the lid. *Oh, yes, it was perfect.* Another ten minutes perhaps, just burning off the last bit of steam, and she could add in the final ingredient.

"Early?"

Nora smiled as she heard his utter confusion.

When had she stopped being able to smile around a gentleman? She had hardly noticed, the years wearing her down so steadily and gradually. It had only been the last few days that Nora had realized she was smiling again.

Smiling. After so long. And it was Daniel who had done it.

"A gentleman knows an invitation for seven o'clock actually means half past," Nora called, carefully replacing the lid and peering once again into the parlor.

Now, had she remembered everything?

It had been a good while since she had hosted anyone in her little cottage, and even longer since she had attended a dinner in town. There were a few things missing of course, but without the funds to refurnish her little home, Daniel was just going to have to—

"Daniel!" Nora gasped.

Her head had turned at the sound of the front door opening, and there he stood.

She had known he was a handsome man. It was rather difficult to avoid: his broad shoulders, his height, the dark hair cut into sharp sideburns. But wearing that . . .

Nora swallowed. "I . . . you did not think to dress for dinner?"

In truth, she would hardly mind if the man came in almost nothing—not that she would ever let him know that. The last thing she needed was a repeat of those hedonistic kisses which were appearing all too often in her dreams. But she had presumed—incorrectly, as it turned out—that Daniel would dress for dinner. Her invitation had not specified it, naturally. Who had to?

Nora blinked at the paragon of manhood that stood before her. Riding boots. Breeches that were tight, tighter than she had ever seen over the taut thighs that led to—. *Best she not look there.* A shirt and waistcoat, and nothing more. No cravat even.

Nora swallowed, desire curling between her legs. She had never seen Daniel without a cravat. The wiry hair poking up at the top of his shirt hinted at something delectable. Something that was most certainly not on the menu for that evening.

Oh, goodness . . .

"You did not give a dress code in your invitation," Daniel said, waving her note in his hand, a teasing expression in his eye. "And so I thought, it being so warm—"

"Y-Yes," Nora managed. "Very warm."

What a shame she could not lean on the doorframe of the parlor for support. It would be too obvious, unfortunately, and make it perfectly clear that her legs were trembling, her fingers itching to touch—

"Can I help with anything?" Daniel said eagerly, stuffing her invitation in his breeches pocket. "I must say, I was delighted to receive your note."

Nora stepped toward the fire where the stew was bubbling. If she stood here, the red in her cheeks might be attributed to the heat from the flames.

"Oh?" she attempted to say airily. "Do go on into the parlor."

The words sounded stilted in her mouth, but really she was astonished she could say anything at all. There was something rather intoxicating about the way Daniel strode through her kitchen and into the parlor, as though he had been here a thousand times before.

As though he belonged here.

Nora tried to concentrate on dropping the little dough balls into the stew. *She had wanted to thank him, that was all,* she thought to herself as though mentally rehearsing what she was going to say. Daniel had—well, he had helped her.

With the dough, she reminded herself. Not with your confidence. Or your ability to smile at the world again. Or the fact that you don't approach every day with darkness.

She couldn't tell him that. *Not yet. Not ever.*

"Where's your cook?" called out Daniel's voice from the parlor.

Nora frowned. The question made no sense—she must have misheard. "There's a bottle of whiskey on the side!"

"You have whiskey?"

Her last bottle. It had been a gift, from—well, it was probably best if she did not tell Daniel precisely who had given her that bottle.

"My favorite!"

Nora winced as she set out two large bowls in which to serve the stew. *Oh, it was definitely a good idea not to tell Daniel who had given her that bottle.*

Every time she thought she had rid herself of the insidious presence of David, there was something else to remind her he had been here.

Perhaps that was why she had truly invited Daniel to dinner.

She had not known what had possessed her. Invite a duke to dinner? Here? In a cottage of four rooms, only one of which had chairs in it and was a different room to that which held a table? It was nonsense.

And yet Nora had done it. There were no more excuses she could find to go into Bath, and not seeing Daniel . . .

It was painful, somehow.

Firmly refusing to investigate that particular thought, Nora carefully lifted the stewpot onto the table, placing it upon the trivet. She lifted up the lid and breathed in happily. Oh, she had been right to add in more tarragon.

"Something smells good."

Nora's head jerked, her expression softening as she saw Daniel leaning against the doorframe, bottle of whiskey in hand.

"It does?" she said hopefully.

Nora forced herself to look away, busying herself with finding cutlery. She had promised herself the last time she had thrown David from this cottage that she was never going to permit a man's opinion of her to have greater sway than her own.

So why did her stomach flutter and her fingers long to wind themselves in Daniel's hair every time he looked at her?

"I'm afraid I couldn't find any glasses for the whiskey," Daniel said conversationally, taking a swig from the bottle. "And so I have rather helped myself."

Nora froze. *No glasses?*

Of course, she should have thought of that. Oh, it was a disaster. The last man who hadn't been served whiskey properly had—

Then her mind caught up with her.

Nora whirled around. "So . . . so you're just drinking it?"

"I hope you don't mind," Daniel said blithely with a shrug. "I did not see any point in bothering you. It's wonderful stuff, but now I'm wondering what's in that delicious-smelling pot."

Nora could not answer. *He didn't . . . care?*

Gentlemen cared about that sort of thing—doing things the right way. The *only* way.

She had lost count of the number of times a man had shouted because she hadn't had a particular fork, or she had not thought to include a cheese course. A cheese course! What did that matter?

Daniel's smile faded. "Nora? I . . . I haven't offended you, have I? With the whiskey?"

Dazed, Nora shook her head. "No, not . . . not offended."

How could she explain it? Was it even possible for him to understand what it was to be around a man who did not, even in some small way, frighten her?

"Here, let me."

Before Nora knew what was happening, Daniel placed the bottle on the kitchen table and strode over to her. He was lifting down a ladle from where it hung from the ceiling before she could speak.

He was close. So close. But not *too* close. Nora had come to the conclusion some time ago that it was impossible for Daniel to be too close to her.

The way he reached up for the ladle, his whole body leaning into hers, the smell of him, the feel of him, the sensuous way he just moved effortlessly around her kitchen . . .

Nora swallowed as he held out the ladle. "Th-Thank you."

"So, what's on the menu?" Daniel said, turning away as though there had been no moment between them. "Stew, by the looks of it!"

It was all she could do to gather herself, but Nora forced herself to do it. *She was not going to be seduced by Daniel Vaughn.* Especially when the poor man seemed to have no idea he was doing it.

"Yes, stew," she said, as firmly as she could manage.

By the time Nora had served up two generous portions of the stew, handed Daniel his choice of utensil—a spoon—and they had stepped into the parlor to settle in the two remaining armchairs she still possessed, her heart had settled.

Well. If you could call a slightly irregular rhythm every time the man caught her eye "settled."

"I asked earlier about your cook," said Daniel cheerfully as his first mouthful passed his lips. "And—oh, dear God!"

"What!" Nora looked up, fear flowing. "Too hot? Not well flavored? Too—"

"This is delicious!" Daniel's eyes were wide, his honesty tangible. "Where on earth did you get her?"

"Her?" Nora repeated. *Did the man think she had cooked up a person?* She may be on the edges of Society—well, perhaps over the edge—but that did not make her a cannibal!

"Your cook," Daniel repeated, spooning another two dough balls into his mouth in quick succession. "The person who made this. I assume she left just before I arrived."

It took a moment for Nora to understand precisely what the man was talking about. As understanding dawned she smiled, tucked her feet under herself on the armchair, and tried to keep her voice steady and free of teasing mirth. "Daniel, how do you think I could afford a cook?"

"Blowed if I know," said Daniel cheerfully. "Lord, this really is good. Do you think she'd come and work for me?"

The idea was a novel one, and for a moment, images flashed through Nora's mind. A well-stocked kitchen. With chairs. A whole staff to do her bidding. And a bedchamber under the same roof as Daniel. Dim corridors, along which anyone could creep.

"Certainly not," Nora said decidedly, cheeks pinking. "What would Society say if I came to work for you as your cook!"

Daniel stared, open mouthed. "But you don't mean to say—I meant the person who cooked this, Nora, not you!"

Was the man truly so dense? "Yes. Me. I'm the one who cooked this, Daniel."

The Duke of Thornfalcone stared. Then he flushed. "You made this?"

"What, you thought I couldn't cook?" Nora quipped, enjoying another mouthful of delicious stew. It really was one of her best. She would have to remember the mixture of herbs. "You've seen me prepare bread, Daniel. You have even—and I am using the word very loosely here, you understand—helped me on one occasion. Remember?"

"Yes, but . . ." His voice trailed away as he stared at his bowl of stew. "You made this?"

Something warm and rather disconcerting prickled inside her. For a moment she wasn't sure what it was. It did not feel particularly comfortable, but it wasn't entirely unpleasant. It stirred a vague memory of something she had felt in the past but long lived without.

Then she recalled. *Pride.*

"I made it," Nora said as lightly as possible, though a smile curled her lips.

Daniel's face split into a grin. "You should be bottling it and selling it as medicine!"

Their laughter filled the little parlor. Nora knew she was in great danger now. Until this moment, she could pretend what she had with the newest Duke of Thornfalcone was unscandalous. He was simply a man who had been attempting to repay his brother's debt of honor and, in the main, succeeded.

Paying off all her debts was wonderful. The horse had been misguided, but she had managed to sort that out with Mr. Peters, the baker who appreciated her skill with dough. The house had been a disaster. And that kiss . . .

But until this moment, Nora had been able to lie to herself. Tell herself she saw nothing in Daniel but a pleasant gentleman.

And he was a pleasant gentleman. But it was more than that for her. She found with him a heat, a need, a desire to touch and be touched. More than that, a desire to be . . . appreciated. To be seen as the woman she was—the cook, the baker, the conversationalist. Her character was opening to him, despite herself, and Daniel . . . well, he hadn't left.

Nora swallowed. She had to be careful. She had been careless before, and what had that got her?

"What I don't understand," Daniel was saying conversationally, sticking a boot onto the fender and making himself at home. "What I just do not comprehend is why you did not seek a job as a cook when you were . . . down on your luck."

That was a mild way of putting it. Nora raised an eyebrow and forced herself to speak calmly, though her stomach twisted painfully.

"You mean, instead of as a courtesan?"

Daniel's fingers slipped on the spoon. It fell into his bowl, splashing stew onto his hand.

Nora swallowed. She should not have been so bold. He would leave, unable to face the fact she—

"Yes," said Daniel softly, lifting his gaze to meet hers. "That's what I meant."

He spoke so calmly, so evenly, that Nora had to ask the question. She would go mad if she didn't, and it had been threatening to trip off her tongue the last three times she had seen him.

"Don't you care?"

Daniel's face flushed. "About you?"

"About the fact that I was a courtesan, a mistress to men who would keep me," Nora said hastily, trying not to think about his question.

"A little." Daniel placed the bowl on the floor beside his chair. Every last bit had now been scraped out. "But Nora, that was your choice. It is not my place to decide what it is you should and shouldn't do."

I want it to be, Nora could not help but think. *I yearn for you to tell me, to instruct me. To keep me safe. To tell me—*

"But do I wish you had been a cook, rather than a courtesan?" Daniel did not look away. "Yes. I think you would have been happier for it."

Nora's breath caught in her throat.

How did this man do it? How did he demonstrate his concern for her in such a selfless manner. How could he say such things and be so earnest?

What sort of a duke was he?

"You've never had to work," Nora said aloud, placing her own bowl down. Her stew was not finished, but her appetite had gone. "You don't understand."

"That's where you're wrong."

She raised an eyebrow. "The fourteenth Duke of Thornfalcone has worked?"

"Oh, not a day in his life," said Daniel with a laugh. "But Mr. Daniel Vaughn? He had no fortune, and a smallish income. He had to work. Well, in a manner of speaking."

Nora found herself leaning forward. "You did?"

The image of Daniel working did not square with the man she saw before her. But a memory of an earlier conversation rose. Had he not mentioned working with a justice?

Nora had assumed he meant in a role as a magistrate, or as the Duke of Thornfalcone he was now. But there was something else that flickered across Daniel's face. A thoughtful smile.

"I . . . let us say, I helped the Crown with a few of its inquiries, ensuring the right information was shared to the right person," Daniel said delicately with a mischievous look.

Nora's eyebrows rose. *Surely not.* "You—you worked as a spy?"

"Oh, I wouldn't call it spying," he said hastily, the uncertain charm she knew returning in an instant. "Really it was just a case of—"

"Yes, I see," Nora said, leaning back in her chair. "It's not the same."

Of course it wasn't. No man could understand, not really.

The sun had started to drift down behind the hills in the window behind him, and his expression looked serious in the dimming light. "It's not?"

"You've worked, yes. But you haven't *had* to work. You haven't needed work for your own survival." Nora did her best to keep any harshness from her voice, and he seemed to understand.

At any rate, he shrugged. "I suppose it is different."

A strange feeling was washing over Nora's whole body. She had sat here talking with him this evening about everything and nothing, matters of great import and trivialities of little consequence, and the feeling had been building the entire time. It was warm, like the desire she felt to slip onto Daniel's lap and once more accept his kisses—but it went beyond that. Really it was the warmth of . . . of companionship. Of sitting with someone into the late evening and just talking. Asking questions and wanting to hear the answers. Speaking and really being heeded.

Nora shivered. It was something new. An intimacy she had never felt, not with any of the men for whom she'd opened her legs.

"I hope you never have to fight for your survival," she said softly, taking in the handsome features, the soft, kind eyes. The way his hands twisted in his lap. *Did he want to touch her as much as she wanted to be touched?* "For better or worse, I find most people just take the route that is easiest."

Daniel looked at her, and there was no judgment there. No malice. Just . . .

Nora would not name it. She would not torture herself.

"Tell me," he said softly.

She rallied herself. "Tell you what?"

"About this cottage," Daniel said, a slow smile creeping across his face. "I would like to hear all about it."

The cottage? What did that have to do with anything?

"I want to spend the evening with you, Nora," he continued, his eyes blazing. "I . . . I never want to leave your presence."

Nora swallowed. They were dancing a fine line here. But she wasn't wise enough to send him away. She couldn't anymore.

"It was my grandmother's, a long time ago," she said with a laugh. "The story goes, when my grandfather . . ."

CHAPTER THIRTEEN

6 July 1811

"CAREFUL, MAN!"

Daniel staggered back from the malediction which rang in his ears. Most unfortunately, this meant stepping off the pavement and—

"Watch it!"

The sound of a horse neighing in distress, the awkward careering of a carriage—

Daniel blinked. The barouche he had stepped in front of had managed, just, to avoid him—but at the cost of almost running into a chaise and four coming in the other direction.

Oh dear.

"You should be more observant!" said the woman he had almost walked into, causing his rapid retreat in the first place. "Head in the clouds, sir, what do you think you're doing?"

"Your Grace," Daniel muttered instinctively.

Then his eyes widened. *Dear God, when had that become an instinct?* How long had that taken—a month? And now he was correcting people who did not address him with the right honorific?

Oh, he had always hated it when David had done that. Daniel could well remember the cringing panic he'd always felt when the idiot did it in company.

And now he was doing it?

"Your—Your Grace?" spluttered the woman, cheeks reddening.

Daniel nodded vaguely. "Yes."

That was the trouble with walking down Milsom Street in Bath without concentrating on where one was going. If he had any sense, he would stop thinking about Nora Harvey. Then perhaps he could put one foot before the other without tripping over them.

"Oh, Your Grace, I had no idea—please, do accept my apologies! If I had known . . ."

Daniel did not interrupt the woman. There did not seem to be any point—she wished to apologize, and he did not wish to offend her by seeming to refuse it.

Besides, he had plenty of other things he could think about.

Like the way Nora's cheeks had flushed when he had complimented her on her stew. On the way every mouthful had felt like a gift from her to him, something personal, something only he had shared.

Like the way they had ended up talking that evening long into the night. How the conversation had flowed without effort, their laughter mingling as they spoke over each other at times and listened quietly at others.

Like the way the sun had risen, slowly and yet suddenly, and he had still been in her parlor. And he had not touched her. Despite the temptation.

Daniel's jaw tightened.

If he were a smart man, that would be the last time he saw her. He did not need to be a wit to know it; spending the entire night with her, even if he had not touched her, was not a clever decision.

He was the Duke of Thornfalcone.

His stomach lurched. As his butler had pointed out rather obliquely that morning, he had other *obligations*, now he held the title.

"A ball?" Daniel had said blankly over breakfast. "What, here?"

Keynes had cleared his throat as he cleared the table. "It is expected, Your Grace."

"It is?" No one had mentioned anything of the sort to him. *Though that could be,* Daniel thought ruefully, *because since the Lady Romeril debacle, few people had been sending their calling cards to the Thornfalcone house.*

His butler had nodded. "You are the newly inherited Duke of Thornfalcone, Your Grace. It is customary to host a ball to welcome Society to your home as part of that inheritance."

"But . . . but no one is in town at the moment," Daniel had said, hoping to put off the damn thing until at least the autumn.

By then, perhaps he would have untangled precisely how he felt about Nora. Or at least have had a few more good dinners. That woman knew how to cook.

"Nevertheless, it is expected." His butler was sounding rather stern again. "In fact, it has been known for individuals to leave their country estates and return to Bath purposefully for such an occasion."

Daniel had tried very hard not to groan. The last thing he wanted was for half the *ton* to return to Bath just when it had got nice and quiet—and all to gawp?

No. Absolutely not.

"Not possible," he'd said aloud.

"I am afraid Mrs. Stafford and I think very similarly on this, Your Grace," Keynes had said, as though that settled the matter.

"And when you inherit a dukedom, Keynes, you may host as many balls as you please," Daniel had replied, trying not to smile. "At the moment, however, I am the duke of this particular house, and I say no. Besides, we don't even have a ballroom."

"Your Grace—"

"I mean, one not still covered in paper and parchment," he'd added hastily.

It truly was starting to become a worry. Letters were arriving from Europe now, from gentlemen on their Grand Tour who had just received the news of the old duke's death. Daniel dreaded the arrival of the post each morning. Who knew that one man could generate so many debts?

"I will host a ball when I am ready," Daniel had said firmly, seeing that unless he closed the matter, Keynes would simply go on about it. "Ask me again in September."

"But Your Grace—"

"That is an order, Keynes!"

Daniel winced even remembering it, as the woman he had almost run into continued to apologize.

"—never met a duke before, not a real one, and of course you think you'll know one when you see one but really they just look like anyone else—"

Yes, September. By then, Daniel had thought as he had left the house that morning, he would have the answers to three important questions.

First, had he finally managed to pay off all David's debts? Until that happened, the expense of a ball simply could not be countenanced. Not to mention the lack of a ballroom.

Second, had he Amelia's support? The place needed a hostess—it was impossible to have a ball without one. She'd simply have to come back to Bath if the thing was to be accomplished.

And third . . .

"—Your Grace, I suppose that is the right way to address you, I never knew—"

Third, Daniel thought as he ignored the apologizing woman, *what was he going to do about Nora?*

Because this couldn't continue. Whatever this was—this thing he had managed to get himself tangled in—it wasn't quite an affair. Though not for lack of wishing it. More like an overabundance of principles.

Daniel's hands clenched into fists, just for a moment. He wanted her. Nora. Everything she was drew him to her. Every time she spoke, he found what she said to be genuinely interesting. Every time she smiled, his stomach lurched and he promised himself he would do everything he could, for the rest of his life, to see her smile again.

He blinked. It had to be because he had been thinking of Nora. She had told Daniel several times how she loathed coming into Bath. That woman down the street, walking arm in arm with a man wearing a gaudy coat of maroon—that could not be her. It just looked like her.

Very like her.

He blinked again, but the mirage did not disappear. Her red flaming hair clashed horribly with the man's coat, but it wasn't that which ignited a fury in Daniel. No, it was the mere fact that she was with *him*, whoever he was. Arm in arm.

That was where he should be.

The thought was not rational, but it did not need to be. Daniel's feet started forward, independent of reason.

"Your Grace, I really am sorry—"

He pushed past the still apologizing woman, his eyes fixed on a completely different feminine figure. Nora and the lout she was with were not walking swiftly and it would not take long to reach her.

The jealousy pumping through him quickened Daniel's feet, giving him no time to think. Think? What was the use of thinking when he felt so wretched at the sight of Nora with another man?

Though it made no sense, though she was in no way obligated to him, though Daniel knew it was madness to display such unwarranted feelings in public, his feet drew him inexorably forward. None of that mattered.

"Nora!"

She turned, cheeks reddening the moment she saw him. "Daniel—Your Grace!"

Nora's twist had forced the man with whom she was walking to turn also. He regarded Daniel with a dark look, as though insulted that his privacy had been so grievously encroached upon.

"And you are?" he sneered.

Daniel forced back the instinct, one he had never felt before, to punch the man so hard he fell to the ground.

This wasn't about him. Not really. It was about Nora. Nora, and all the things he wanted to say to her. All the pain he'd felt in not being open with her. All the regret and anger he felt that David had found her first.

"You're being ridiculous, just let me explain—"

"Nora, come with me," Daniel said, reaching out and taking her free hand.

He wasn't sure what he had expected. Her to fly to his arms, perhaps? Demand an embrace, perhaps even scandalize the whole of Society—again—by lifting up her lips for a kiss?

These wild images rushed through Daniel's mind far too swiftly for him to fully appreciate each one, and even more regrettably, none of them occurred.

Nora's other hand was tugged from the man's arm, but she swiftly wrenched away the one Daniel held as well. "Daniel, what are you—"

"Daniel? Your Grace—ah, you're the Duke of Thornfalcone," said the man with a mocking laugh. "Yes, well. If you're anything like your brother—"

"Say a word about my brother and you'll join him," snarled Daniel.

Where this anger was coming from he did not know—and he had to stop it, had to prevent this boiling rage from spilling out.

Nora's eyes were wide. "Daniel!"

"Come with me," he repeated.

This time he folded his hand around hers and started to walk without waiting to see if she would come with him. A traitorous, masculine something roared in his chest as she came with him, leaving the other man behind.

"Miss Harvey? Miss Harvey! Where are you going?"

He had won, Daniel thought with a feeling of triumph tearing through him, head to foot. Nora could have stayed with that blackguard but she chose him. And the unexpected relief she had not refused to go with him made Daniel realize just how desperate he was.

Not just for her company. Not just her body, though that would certainly be something he would struggle to decline if it were offered. Just her. Nora. In whatever way she was willing to give of herself, he would accept it.

"You absolute fool! That was the baker I've been working with. I was trying to—"

"I don't want to hear about him," Daniel growled.

"Where on earth are you taking—"

"Here," Daniel said, cutting across Nora's astonishment.

It was not, perhaps, the most genteel of locations to have a conversation. Alleys rarely were, and this one was a little more dank than he had expected. Still, it provided some shade from the sun, and more importantly, privacy.

Daniel halted, releasing Nora's arm as he attempted to think. How could he explain how he felt about her when he was still untangling it himself? When the shadow of his brother hung over them? When she had made it perfectly clear—

"Daniel Vaughn, you are being ridiculous!" Nora said, cheeks flushed. "You have just made me look a complete fool!"

"It doesn't matter," said Daniel, excitement rushing through him. *He was with her. Alone, in an alley. Perhaps—*

"It may not matter to you, but it certainly matters to me!" she shot back. "I like you because you're *not* like those other men, those who make demands without—"

"You like me?" Daniel asked. His hackles lowered, his heartbeat slowed, and what he had just done fully dawned on him.

Oh, God. He had acted just like those idiotic gentlemen he always hated. Like David. Had he just pulled Nora from the street without giving a care to her companion, any thought to how the whole situation would look?

"You know I like you—do you think I would invite a man to my cottage if I did not? But that is beside the point!" Nora said, sparks flying from her eyes. "Why does everything have to be so difficult with you?"

"I—I don't know," Daniel said helplessly, all certainty fading.

He had been so determined not to be like his brother. To be different. Yet here he was, making his brother's mistakes with his own brother's mistress.

"You would rather see the world burn than be without whatever it is you want," said Nora with blazing eyes. "You would rather burn everything you care about, if it meant someone else couldn't have it instead!"

And perhaps it was the way she spoke, passion pouring from her, that made him do it. Perhaps Daniel could no longer hold back the desire he felt, the need for her. It was a longing he had been fighting, but he could not fight it anymore.

"I would rather see the world burn than be without you." Daniel had spoken softly, but the alley was so quiet his words might as well have been shouted.

Nora's lips parted, her tongue darting out to moisten them as her eyes widened with astonishment.

His jaw tightened. *She really shouldn't do that. It was far too distracting.*

"You . . . you would?"

Daniel hung his head for a moment, attempting to collect his thoughts. "If I—God, Nora, it's so difficult to explain!"

"Try," she said softly, taking a step closer.

He immediately took a step back, her presence itself too potent. His back hit the wall. There was nowhere else to go.

"I care about you, Nora—not just because you're beautiful, which you are—"

"You think I'm beautiful?" she whispered.

Daniel could not understand it. Was the woman without a looking glass? Had she any idea what she did to him? The way her breasts swelled and her waist curved, the intensity of the looks under those lashes, the way every part of her hummed, calling out to him—

"You are a kind, and witty, and elegant woman and you have been much wronged," Daniel managed to say. *That was it, he needed to concentrate on not being like those other rakes. That was important.* "And I care for you, Nora, more than—and I know you cannot care for me like that, not after . . . my brother, I shouldn't even . . ."

His voice trailed away.

Oh, hell. It was all going wrong. Once again David had ruined it for him—though if it hadn't been for Nora's affair with his brother, would he even have met her? What a tangled mess it all was.

A dull pain settled somewhere between his ribs. "Go on."

Nora blinked. "What?"

"Go back to your friend. I should never have—"

"I was never your brother's mistress, Daniel."

Daniel stared, shock rocketing through his body as though he had been struck by lightning.

He must have misheard.

But Nora was smiling. A sad, wistful smile, it was true, but smiling, nonetheless. She had also taken a step closer, filling Daniel's mind with thoughts of touches, caresses, kisses.

"He wanted me. Very much," she said without taking her eyes from him. "But I knew his character from the start, and he swiftly showed me he was not to be trusted."

Daniel tried to speak, found he had no voice, and cleared his throat. "Not—not to be trusted?"

Nora shook her head as she tilted it to one side. "I only took lovers

I knew could be trusted to be kind. To know when to leave. And your brother—well. There was only one occasion when he refused to leave and that was enough. I knew, then. I could never give myself to him."

History was being rewritten so rapidly in Daniel's mind that he could barely think. *Nora and David . . . they had never . . . she had never been . . .*

"You never . . ."

She shook her head. "But then I was so desperate, and I wrote him those letters, made an arrangement, though I dreaded what it would mean. And then he was gone and there you were. I . . . well, I let you believe at first that more had happened because it provided me some protection in an impossible situation and you paid my debts. You felt obligated, and I knew that if you knew the truth—"

"You were never my brother's mistress," Daniel repeated.

The world was changing, and Nora was its new center, his new axis on which his world spun. And the flames he had attempted to dampen, the burning passion Daniel had known was wrong, was suddenly right. The desire blazed through his veins, scorching every inch of him.

"Oh, Nora," Daniel murmured.

His movement was swift—that, or Nora had already been moving into his arms, he could not tell which. Their kiss was passionate, all restraint melted away by the fire of their desire. Moaning at the sensation of her breasts pushed up against his chest, Daniel's hands swiftly reached for her buttocks, cupping her closer to the aching manhood which was stiffening as he trailed fiery kisses down her neck.

"Daniel . . ." Nora breathed.

Daniel's breath hitched. God, hearing his name on her lips, hearing the longing in her breath as she whimpered, his lips nuzzling her collarbone—

Was this not everything he wanted?

Nora's passion was a surprise. Her fingers had not been idle—they had crept up to his shirt and had somehow managed to relieve his buttons of their holes. Now they were trailing down his chest, her fingertips scraping muscles as she went lower, and Daniel moaned as Nora's fingers gently stroked his manhood through his breeches.

This was a woman who knew how to make love. Who knew what it was to please and be pleasured. And—

And they were kissing in an alleyway.

Daniel broke the kiss. "Nora—"

"Don't stop now," Nora moaned, lifting up a leg against his hip and pulling back her skirts. "I want—"

"I know." *Dear God, what had he unleashed?* It was intoxicating, seeing a woman just as eager for his sensual lovemaking as he was to give it. "But not here."

Nora's eyes were brimming with lust but also something else. Something like . . . trust. "Not here?"

Daniel shook his head slowly as he swallowed. This might be a mistake, but he did not want the first time he made love to Nora to be as quietly as they could manage in an alley, while the rest of Bath walked past.

Oh no. This was going to be special.

"I want to love you," Daniel said, staring deeply into her sky-blue eyes, "love you, Nora, as you are worthy."

Nora narrowed her eyes. "And that means . . .?"

"Come back to my townhouse. Come and see what it is to be loved by the Duke of Thornfalcone as you deserve to be."

CHAPTER FOURTEEN

NORA COULD HARDLY breathe, her vision dimming at the corners as she stared up into the man's face. If it had been possible to take a step back in astonishment, Nora would have. If it were even possible to speak, to lift a hand to her mouth in shock, to do anything, Nora was certain she would have done it. But she was still. No part of her moved. Her mind was whirling, so stunned it was impossible to conceive of responding.

What could one say to such a proposal?

Nora's heart thudded painfully as tantalizing temptation coursed through her veins.

To be loved by the Duke of Thornfalcone—*this* Duke of Thornfalcone—a man who knew what it was to feel out of one's depth, who had bothered to get to know her, rather than just write her off as his brother's mistress. Erroneously, as it happened.

And now, here they were, pressed up against each other in a Bath alleyway, shadows flickering over them as people passed in their finery, never expecting that such debauchery could occur just feet away. Here, Daniel Vaughn had made her a proposition. One Nora knew she could not refuse.

It had been so long. Forever, in fact, since she had been with a man who actually cared for her. Who thought it was important she enjoyed herself in the lovemaking bed. Who knew what it was to please as well as be pleasured.

And Daniel . . . there was simply something about him. He drew her to him as no one ever had.

"I care about you, Nora—not just because you're beautiful, which you are—"

"Nora?"

Nora blinked. Daniel was looking down at her with evident concern. She had been silent too long—but then, it would have been scandalous if she had agreed too swiftly.

"I . . . are you certain you wish to . . ." Nora swallowed.

It had all been so simple in the past. She required funds, and she found gentlemen who were willing to supply them in exchange for . . . company.

She hated calling it that, but she could hardly call it love. It wasn't like this . . .

Nora splayed a hand gently, seductively on Daniel's chest. This man, this darling, ridiculous man. A man who had been handed a title and riches beyond compare. Most men would have discovered an arrogance within them second to none, but Daniel?

Daniel *worried*.

There was something about a man who cared that much, Nora thought wildly. *A man like that was worthy of love.*

If only this had all happened differently. If only they had met without his brother's memory haunting their steps. If only her reputation had not been ruined and they had met at a ball, perhaps, or bumped into each other on Milsom Street. If only their story could be like the hundreds of others around them.

But it wasn't. And somehow, Nora knew it never would be.

"Certain? Wish to? Dear God, woman, can I not be clearer?" Daniel lowered his lips to hers once again.

Nora surrendered to the connection, marveling in the way he could so easily create such warmth between her legs with just a single kiss. No other man had ever managed it. In truth, no other man had—

"Oh, Nora, please give me an answer," Daniel groaned, releasing her lips and dipping his head to her shoulder. "I'll respect whatever you decide but I can't—I need—no, I want—"

"Yes."

It was just a breath. At first, Nora was unsure whether or not she had actually spoken it.

Yes. Yes to lovemaking. Yes to love. Yes to Daniel and to throwing caution to the wind and risking everything. Not her reputation, Nora was well aware that was long gone. But risking her heart. Risking her head. Risking being burned by a man who could cast her aside at any moment.

What was it he said—or she had said? She could not recall . . .

Play with dukes, get burned.

"Yes?" Daniel blinked, lifting his head. "Did you say—"

Nora could not help it. Her need for him, her desire propelled her forward, capturing his mouth and sliding her tongue between his unprotesting lips. He shuddered, clutching her tightly as Nora tried to pour into the kiss all her excitement, fear, and desperation for more.

When the kiss ended, they both stood there for a moment in silence.

"Right," said Daniel with a dazed expression. "My townhouse. At once."

Nora nodded and silently lowered her leg back to the ground. Surprisingly, it did not give her any greater sense of balance. The world was lopsided. She was going to make love to Daniel Vaughn, Duke of Thornfalcone—and without the promise of money. She loved him. She—

She loved him?

Nora swallowed. *She loved him.* It wasn't something she could have predicted—but the kind, thoughtless man had somehow slipped into her heart and now she had no idea how to remove him. Or, indeed, if she even wanted to.

His gaze had dropped to his shirt, waistcoat, and jacket, buttoning them up hastily with shaking fingers. Only when he was moderately more presentable did he look up and reach for her.

Daniel squeezed her hand. "Ready?"

Nora chuckled dryly as she squeezed back. "Born ready."

He rolled his eyes before they started back toward the alley mouth. They almost reached it, too, before Nora gave into the temptation and pushed Daniel against the wall again.

"Nora!"

"I can't wait." Her eager lips found his equally hungry mouth.

Their passionate kisses threatened to remove every last thought of decorum from Nora's mind, but she didn't care. Every moment not spent kissing Daniel Vaughn was a moment wasted.

His eyes were dark with longing as he finally pulled away. "We need to—"

"I want—"

"Nora, my townhouse is but three streets away. Do you think you can keep your hands off me until then?"

Nora whimpered, leaning her forehead against his broad chest.

With any other man, it would have been a simple question. With any other man, it would not have truly been a question at all. Of course she could. But no one had ever tempted her like this, enticed her like this, made her want—

But if she couldn't control herself at least a little, they'd never reach his house.

"I can manage it," Nora said brightly, straightening and placing her hand on the duke's arm. "Just—just don't make me wait, Daniel."

It was his turn to groan as they stepped out of the alley and back onto the street, into Society, into respectability. "You're killing me, Nora . . ."

She was killing him? Nora had never known such intensity. As they walked arm in arm down the street, their pace swift, she could not bring herself to meet the casual glances of anyone they passed.

Did they know? Could they tell? Was it obvious, simply radiating from their bodies, what she and Daniel planned to be doing in just a few minutes?

"Here we are," gasped Daniel, as though he had been holding his breath.

Nora raced up the steps in an attempt to keep pace with him. The man's steps were rapid, and the slam of the front door behind them was satisfyingly echoey in the large hall.

Well, they were here. In his townhouse. They were alone, they could do anything they—

"Your Grace," said a tall, severe-looking man—the unwelcoming butler she had encountered on her first visit here. "We were not expecting you for another hour, but your arrival is fortuitous as we have discovered another pile of letters which—"

"Everyone out," Daniel commanded in a ringing voice.

Nora clutched his hand tightly, conscious that the butler was looking disdainfully at her but thankful he did not consider her worthy of his official notice.

As she looked properly, it was not only the butler there with them in the hall. Two footmen, a maid, and what appeared to be a housekeeper had all been busy in the large open space.

Now they were staring.

What on earth was Daniel thinking?

"Out, Your Grace?" repeated the servant. "I do not think you understand. It is Saturday, that is carpet beating day, and—"

"Every single servant in this house needs to leave," said Daniel in a firm yet kind tone. "Go to my townhouse, take the day off. That's an order."

The servants leaving? But that would leave them . . . completely alone.

The butler seemed just as astonished as she was. "Your Grace!"

"And an additional week's pay for everyone," said Daniel, striding toward the stairs as though it did not matter if the entirety of the Duke of Thornfalcone's staff knew precisely what he planned. "Off you go,

Keynes! All of you!"

"But—but—"

"Thank you, Keynes!" called Daniel cheerfully over his shoulder.

It was all Nora could do to keep her countenance as Daniel pulled her down a richly decorated corridor, their footsteps dulled by the luscious carpet. How could Daniel so blithely do something so scandalous? There would be talk—heaps of it—and—

And . . . what did that matter? What did it matter if the world gossiped? The duke had taken a mistress—well, wasn't that expected? Did not great men do that all the time?

"Nora," Daniel said suddenly, halting dead in his tracks.

Nora moved closer to him, hearing some sort of desperation in his voice. "What is it, Daniel?"

His growl was short lived. Nora gasped with delight as Daniel turned, thrust her against the wall, and began kissing her once again.

Oh, even his need for her was exciting. Nora had never known anything like it. This wasn't a craving for release, it was desire for her: Nora Harvey. His kisses lit flames wherever his lips touched her skin, and the warmth between her legs was growing—growing to such a pitch that in a way, she hardly knew what to do.

Well, that wasn't entirely true.

When alone, she had supplied herself the deficiencies of the men who believed they had satisfied her. Though Nora would never have dared to suggest anything so wild with any other man, why could Daniel not do so now?

Trembling slightly at her own boldness, Nora returned Daniel's passionate kisses while also reaching for his right hand. He accepted her touch eagerly, evidently wanting every possible connection—but his eyes were wide in shock as he pulled away when Nora brought his hand to—

"Nora! I—God, are you sure?"

Nora arched her back against the wall as she guided his hand under her gown and toward her secret place. *So sure.* "You . . . you know how to please a woman, Daniel, don't you?"

She knew the truth in his eyes before he could speak. *Of course he did.*

"Yes, but—"

"But what?" Nora held his splayed fingers against her inner thigh as she waited for him to speak. She watched Daniel swallow, watched him fight the temptation to move his fingers.

"I've never stroked a woman against a wall before," he admitted with a roguish grin. "I—oh, Nora, you're so ready for me."

His last words were groaned, not spoken. Nora had brought his fingers up to her secret place, pressing his fingers gently against her.

Oh, she wanted this. She wanted him. She wanted to feel her pleasure build, feel it cascade through her.

"Nora," Daniel murmured, lowering his lips to her.

She willingly accepted his kiss, allowing her moans to rise in her throat as his fingers slowly started to stroke her. Oh, it felt wonderful, delicious tingles flickering through her, growing in size and intensity as Daniel's stroking fingers started to build a rhythm, and—

And then she gasped in his mouth. Daniel had slipped a finger into her, gently grazing her nub.

Nora whimpered, clutching his lapels. "Daniel . . ."

Somehow the audible sound of her enjoyment spurred him on. As she tilted her head back, unable to do anything but accept the worship of his fingers, Daniel lowered his lips to her décolletage.

It was fortunate indeed she could lean against the wall, for as the sensation built, Nora was uncertain whether she would have been able to stand on her own. Oh, it was building, the pleasure, the scalding heat in her. As Daniel started to gently circle his thumb around her nub as his finger slipped deeper inside her, Nora could not help but breathe her joy.

"Oh, like that . . . yes, Daniel, yes, faster—oh God, faster—Daniel!"

The climax came from nowhere. Nora's body buckled under the

ecstasy which flowed through her, burning every inch of her, shaking her body as it had never shaken with a man before. It dimmed her eyes and drowned out all sound, and all she could do was feel. Feel Daniel's fingers inside her, feel his breath on her neck, feel his strength as he held her up with his free hand, feel his very presence burn within her.

As it subsided, Nora blinked. Light returned and the sight of Daniel Vaughn, Duke of Thornfalcone appeared before her, a look of great satisfaction on his face.

"I have never brought a woman to pleasure like that before," he murmured, eyes flashing with delight. "I think I rather like it."

Nora could not stop the words slipping from her mouth. "I have never been brought to pleasure by a man before," she admitted. "I think I rather like it, too."

Daniel's face dropped. "You—you have never—no one has ever—"

"No man has ever cared about my pleasure," Nora confessed, feeling shamed by the admission. She had never spoken so openly about it before. "Nor knew what they were doing like . . . like you."

He cupped her cheeks and kissed her deeply. Nora clung to him, knowing he was the only man she would ever love. When they finally parted, both their breathing was ragged and Nora could feel warmth between her thighs again.

"Well I care a great deal about your pleasure," Daniel said gruffly, grabbing her hand and pulling her forward. "Let's make you cry out my name again."

"Daniel!"

Nora flushed as he opened a door and pulled her inside. *The very idea of saying such things! She had thought herself unable to be embarrassed, but he . . .*

He had pulled her into the most splendid bedchamber she had ever seen. A high ceiling covered in gold leaf. A bay window with resplendent velvet curtains. Marble statues of various nudes, all kissing their partners, and paintings—

Nora's eyes widened. "I have never seen such—"

"I had them all put here, in the state bedchamber, because I thought they may offend future guests," Daniel said with a grin, not releasing her hand. "But I thought they might be suitable for us."

She nodded, trying not to peer too closely at a painting that appeared to be of a woman being gratified by a man's tongue.

Did men really do that? No man she had ever taken to her bed had wished to even consider such a thing, even on the two instances when she had hinted at it.

"Nora . . ."

Nora turned and saw the desire burning in Daniel's eyes.

"You wished for something, Your Grace?" she teased, stepping into his arms only to lean back and start to unbutton his jacket.

Daniel groaned. "I wish for a great number of things, all with you."

Nora smiled. "Well, in that case we had better get started. You've got a long afternoon ahead of yourself, Your Grace."

"I wish you wouldn't call me that."

His voice was low, eager, earnest. Nora looked up as she finished unbuttoning his waistcoat and saw the truth in his eyes. Daniel could have the world bowing and curtsying, scraping and obeying, and he didn't want that. He only wanted her. He only wanted to be treated as a man.

Well, that she could do.

"In that case, Daniel," Nora said, mischief in every syllable, "we have a problem."

His face immediately fell. "We do?"

"We do." She kept her voice low and suggestive, slipping his jacket off his shoulders and allowing it to drop to the floor. His waistcoat soon followed. "You are severely overdressed."

Understanding dawned as merriment rose in his voice. "Oh, well, we can't have that."

"A true scandal," Nora whispered, pulling apart his cravat and dropping it onto his waistcoat as Daniel's fingers scrabbled at his shirt buttons. "What can we do to rectify it?"

"I think if we just strip me as swiftly as possible," Daniel said, his voice quavering. "Then we'll have to address the second scandal in this room."

Nora shivered with anticipation as the white shirt dropped to the floor, revealing a broad muscular chest with hair trailing down to his breeches. "And—and that is?"

Daniel's grin became wicked. "You have not cried out in ecstasy in at least five minutes."

"Daniel!"

But he did not reply—not, at least, in words. Pulling off his boots and swiftly unbuttoning his breeches, Nora gasped as Daniel became completely naked.

And what a sight he was. His manhood stood erect, plainly aching for her. It twitched slightly as she beheld it, as though conscious of her gaze.

Nora reached out a hand. She wanted to know what it felt like—

"Daniel!" she cried in shock.

Once again he had moved so quickly, she had been unable to prevent it. Not that she wanted to—it was rather delicious to be swept up in his arms, carried over to the bed, and—

His eagerness could not be contained. Nora saw desire flash across Daniel's face as he pushed up her skirts, not patient enough to undress her, and he was in her!

Nora arched her back, welcoming the delightful sensation of his manhood pressing into her, filling her, brushing past those sensitive spots that throbbed to feel his rub again.

"Nora?"

She hadn't even noticed she'd closed her eyes, but that didn't matter. As she opened them, she saw nothing but affection, care, desire—and a need to ensure she was as comfortable with what was happening as he was.

Love blossomed in her heart. No man had ever—none of the men she had been with had ever cared whether she herself enjoyed it at all.

Until now.

"Love me," Nora gasped, clutching Daniel's bare shoulders and reveling in the sensation of a naked man around her, above her, within her. "Love me."

And he did. With subtle movements, teasingly near to her desire but not quite bringing her to climax, Daniel started to build a rhythm.

Nora's fingers dug into Daniel's shoulder blades. "Daniel, please—harder—"

"You'll come." His voice was uneven and his eyes dark. "When I say you can, you'll come."

The soft, low vibrations of his words were almost enough to push her over the edge. So commanding, yet such reverence! Such softness, yet such grit! Nora moaned as Daniel dipped his head to press a scalding kiss on her lips, increasing his thrusting pace as his manhood jerked within her.

And then she fell apart. Pleasure as she had never known, ripples of sensation spreading to every part of her body, Nora's climax shook her body. It forced away all control as she lost herself in the heady decadence of being worshipped for who she was, not what she could provide.

It was not long, or perhaps it was an age, Nora could not tell.

Daniel grunted. "God, Nora, Nora!"

He spilled into her, warmth rushing inside Nora as she welcomed the man she loved into her waiting arms, Daniel's breathing rough and his control finally—completely—lost.

They lay there, in silence, in privacy, and in joy, for some time.

Then Daniel lifted his head, and Nora looked up and saw the man she knew she could love until the end of her days.

And he grinned. "Again?"

Chapter Fifteen

7 July 1811

Daniel was not completely sure on this—after all, he had not been a duke long. But wasn't a man supposed to wake up well rested, not more tired than he was when he went to bed?

He groaned, the noise echoing around the cavernous bedchamber.

Cavernous bedchamber?

Now, that didn't make sense. The only truly massive one in this huge townhouse was the large state bedchamber, which Daniel had viewed as something of a joke. Surely no one would actually consider sleeping in such a monstrosity of a bed?

Apparently, it had been designed for royalty, though no royalty had ever come. Why would they? The dukedom of Thornfalcone was a small, unimpressive, and—most importantly—dull dukedom. Daniel could almost hear his father's words ringing in his ears. And according to Keynes, no one had actually slept in it.

Until now.

Daniel blinked. The distant walls of the state bedchamber appeared, hazy in his vision.

Now this wasn't right at all. Why on earth would he have slept here? It didn't make sense—the bedchamber he had chosen for himself was perfectly—

Something moved in the bed beside him.

Daniel swallowed. Then he blinked again as he took in the slumbering and delightfully naked form of the woman beside him.

And all of a sudden, the memories of the previous afternoon and evening rushed back.

Nora. Nora in an alley, kissing him, her hip straining against his own. Their haste to go back to his townhouse, his ordering of all servants to leave. Their lovemaking. Their raid on the kitchen, bringing nibbles upstairs, eating and talking until they could no longer refuse themselves, and they took their pleasures yet again.

"Daniel, please—harder—"

"You'll come. When I say you can, you'll come."

Daniel's lips pulled into a smile. He may have woken up groggily, exhausted, but it was well worth it. He had bedded Nora Harvey—no, that was not quite right.

He had made love to her.

Sinking back into his pillow and grinning happily, he watched the slow and gentle breathing of the woman beside him. She had fallen asleep nude, refusing all offers to hunt down a nightgown.

"I prefer to be naked in bed," Nora had said at some unlawfully early time that morning. "All the better to wake you in the morning."

Daniel's jaw clenched as he attempted to prevent his manhood from standing to attention at the mere thought.

How had he ever managed to deserve this? How had he managed to convince her, to show Nora just how much he cared about her? How had he managed to entrance a woman so witty, so beautiful, so dazzlingly decisive, so stringently independent?

"I was never your brother's mistress, Daniel."

Daniel sighed, happiness radiating from every pore. After all his frustration, his certainty he'd never cross the line with Nora, to discover that she had never—she and his brother had not—

"You look rather pleased with yourself," said an amused voice.

Daniel glanced down, smile broadening as he took in the fine blue eyes, the laughing expression.

Nora grinned. "Good morning, Your Grace."

He groaned. "Don't call me—"

"You know, I think we're going to have to create a new nickname for you," Nora said, lying on her front and looking up at him. "I'm not sure I can call you Thornfalcone."

A discomforting feeling settled in Daniel's stomach. "No, definitely not."

There was something rather depressing about outliving one's father and brother. The last thing he wanted was to be given their name.

"Vaughn is a little too formal, and Daniel . . . well, I can't keep calling you that, not after that mouth has been where it's been," Nora said in a low, teasing voice.

Daniel swallowed. He was not about to permit his desire to run away with him. He was not going to—

"Perhaps I should call you 'lover'." Nora reached out for him.

Her hand on his bare chest was more than Daniel could resist. In a swift movement, he'd pulled Nora into his embrace, groaning at the sensation of her soft skin against his, and captured her lips with his own.

"Lover," Nora's voice was low and sultry.

Daniel growled. "You say that one more time, and I won't be held responsible for—"

"Lover—"

An hour later, both Daniel and Nora lay back against the pillows, breathing hard.

"Now that," Nora murmured, "I did not expect."

Daniel was rather surprised he had it in him after yesterday's exploits, but he wasn't about to admit that.

"That's the trouble with waking up in a bed with a naked woman who is the most beautiful thing you have ever seen," he said quietly.

He glanced at Nora and caught a look of genuine embarrassment.

There was something about her he just did not understand. How could a woman go about the world looking—*well, looking like that*—and not realize she was so startlingly beautiful?

"Well, I accept the compliment. Both of them," said Nora. "I suppose you have had your fill for today."

Daniel permitted himself a quick dart of his gaze down Nora's neck to her—

"I wouldn't be so sure of that," he said ruefully. "Though I suppose the servants are back. We'll have to be more discreet."

She raised an eyebrow. "More discreet than you arriving at your townhouse, hand in hand with a known fallen woman, and ordering all your servants to leave the entire house until the next day?"

Daniel opened his mouth, thought about it, then closed it again. He sighed.

Nora giggled. "That's what I like about you, lover."

A strange sort of possessive shiver went up his spine at the sound of the word. On the lips of anyone else, it would have been a cliché. Tired. Dull. Awkward.

Slipping through Nora's lips, however, it was a badge of honor. Something he had earned, something powerful. Something tantalizing, promising something more in the future.

Dear God, something more? He could barely recover from what Nora did to him now.

"What you like about me?" Daniel repeated.

She nodded, fire red curls tumbling down her shoulders. "You don't think beyond the moment."

It was difficult not to feel crestfallen. It was not, perhaps, the compliment she thought it was. "Oh."

Perhaps that was the best he could hope for. He was the younger brother, after all, albeit by a few minutes. Less loved, less educated, less expected of him. Perhaps a lack of thought was attractive in the eyes of some.

"I mean, you're not calculating," Nora said softly. She caught Daniel's eye and smiled, all her mischief gone. "You don't do things, say things because you wish to gain something. You're not in the habit of manipulating others for your own benefit."

Daniel frowned. "Who would do such a thing?"

All too late, he recalled precisely who might do such a thing. His own brother, for a start. He had attempted to manipulate Nora, though she had resisted him.

And perhaps even Nora. Out of necessity. Out of hunger.

There were fine pink dots in Nora's cheeks as she said, "There's no shame in it. But I will admit, I like its absence in you."

Something strange was happening in Daniel's chest. Where it had been puffed up with pride, it was now . . . well, unseasonably warm. Even for July. A delicious, covetous warmth was taking root within it, growing every time he glanced at Nora or heard her voice.

"I suppose things will be different now," Nora said lightly.

Daniel turned on his side and leaned on his elbow to better look at the woman who was fast stealing his heart. Those words had been spoken far too lightly to mean nothing.

His instinct was true. There was a strange sort of shyness on Nora's face he had never seen before. It made her look . . . not younger. Perhaps more inexperienced.

"Different?" Daniel repeated. "Why would anything be different?"

The very thought sent panic coursing through him. *Different?* He had only just managed to get things how he wanted them—or at least, get Nora where he wanted her. Naked and gasping for pleasure in his arms. That was hardly an easy feat.

And now she wanted something different?

"I mean, now we've—now that . . . after bedding me—" Nora said, uncharacteristically shy.

Daniel blanched. "I made love to you."

"You did?"

It was astounding. The woman was the most spectacular he had ever met, and she appeared to have no concept of how deeply he cared. Which was probably his fault. It was so obvious to him, it had to be his error that made it difficult for her to believe.

It had to be.

"Nora, I made love to you," Daniel said slowly, picking the words prickling carefully as he said them. He had never said them to another. "Dear God, was my devotion not obvious?"

Her cheeks flamed. "It's just—"

"You think I would bring any other woman here?" he continued, fixing his eyes on hers even as they dropped, unable to meet the intensity of his gaze. "You think I could feel anything like what I feel for—you think I would just . . ."

Daniel swore under his breath as words failed him. *This was the trouble with falling in love.* One minute you were totally coherent—fine, not coherent, but far more coherent than this—and the next minute—

Wait. Falling in love?

Daniel's stomach swooped as he took in the delicate curve of Nora's neck, the swell of her breast, the hint of delights at the arch of her hips.

But it was more than that, this feeling inside him. This need to be with her, to just be in her presence. This joy that blossomed whenever she smiled, the fierce knowledge that nothing could ever happen to her.

Dear God.

"I am in love with you," Daniel all but whispered.

Nora's eyes widened as they snapped to meet his. "I-I beg your pardon?"

There was nothing for it now. "I am in love with you," he repeated, certainty filling him as he said the words once again. "Nora, I am in love with—"

"You can't mean that," Nora said breathlessly, pushing away. "You—"

"I can mean it, and I do mean it," said Daniel, reaching out swiftly and preventing the woman he loved—*he loved her!*—from retreating. "Nora, listen—"

"No, you cannot say such things," she said, twisting in his grasp and almost escaping, the bedclothes tangled around them. "I don't want to hear it—you can't say such things then disappear—"

"I am not going to disappear," Daniel said firmly, bewildered at her sudden change.

Just moments ago they had been lying in bed enjoying the sweet thrill of having made love again. And now? Nora was acting as though he had promised her the world, only to take it from her.

Her lip quivered. "I-I was—when I first came out into Society, I met—he said . . ."

Nora's voice trailed away. Daniel's jaw set.

Blast it all to hell. She had hinted at some sort of great scandal, something which had precipitated her fall from grace, but he had assumed she was being frivolous. Surely nothing could have actually happened—there would have been someone to protect her! Had she not mentioned a brother?

"He said he would marry me if I . . . and we did. And he left, and I never . . ." Nora swallowed. "My brother refused to fight on my behalf, but even if he had, the blackguard had already left Bath and the name he had given was false, and no one knew . . . No man has ever said he loved me. Not said it and meant it."

And Daniel's heart broke.

How could it not? It was clear as day what had happened. Seduced on the promise of matrimony, Nora had been abandoned by a rake and her own brother had not thought her important enough to defend.

It was all he could do not to roar out of the house, find the reprobates, and have them both flogged. The thought of harming any woman like that was abominable. To do such a thing to Nora?

Reprehensible!

Daniel realized his hands had clenched into fists. It took a great deal of mental effort to uncurl them. That was not what Nora needed in this moment. She needed comfort and reassurance. She needed to know she was worth fighting for.

Daniel took a deep breath. An easy task, then. "Nora, I—"

"And here I am, in bed with a duke," Nora said, breathing a laugh. "Play with dukes, get burned, isn't that what they say?"

"It's what we said," Daniel pointed out, bewildered.

Where on earth was this conversation going? Why was it so difficult to keep track—

"And I will completely understand, now you have bedded me—"

"Made love to you," Daniel interjected. "Really, Nora, you must believe me."

"You can return me now to my cottage, and I will—"

And that was the last straw. The thought of Nora going back to that place—barely mended, and with its debts only just paid—to live alone, unprotected, without his affection?

No. It could not be borne.

Clearly Nora had been let down in her life, and Daniel could see why she would believe she could expect nothing better from any man. But he wasn't just any man. He was the man in love with her, and though saying it seemed to have little impact, that only meant he had to show it.

And he could begin now.

"You will not be returning to your cottage!" Daniel said grandly. "If you don't want to," he added swiftly, seeing a flash in Nora's eyes.

She frowned. "I won't be?"

"I want you here."

"Here?" Nora repeated. "In this state bedchamber? Am I a prisoner?"

Daniel took a long, deep breath. *This was because she had been be-*

trayed by a gentleman before, he told himself. *This was her defense, to be wry and dark and assume the worst.*

Soon she would see him and assume the best.

"You are not a prisoner, you are my guest," he said softly. He brushed his fingers against Nora's cheek and was pained when she leaned back. "Nora, I . . . damn it, I love you. I want you to stay."

"You can't love me," Nora said blankly, sitting up abruptly and leaning against the headboard. "No one loves me."

And his heart broke again. She should never have been allowed to believe that, and he would spend the rest of his life helping her to understand how wrong she was—if she would let him.

"I love you." Daniel raised himself and shifted in the bed so he was looking directly into Nora's eyes. "Nora, I love you. The joy you bring me, the way you challenge me, how every encounter teaches me something about you or myself—"

"You can't mean that," she said in a small voice, eyes brimming with tears.

Only when one fell, slowly trickling down a delicate cheek, did Daniel reach out. To his great relief, this time she did not lean back.

It pained him to his very core to see her so upset, but he had to keep going. It was vital she understood.

"I love you. You, as you are, with all your history and your nonsense and your baking. Nora, I've had my fingers burned with you—"

That made her laugh. "The feeling is entirely mutual."

"And I want to keep burning, burning away all the dead growth of my life before you, and revel in the blaze of passion we share," Daniel said, hardly sure where the words were coming from, desperately hoping she accepted them the way they were intended. "Nora, I—"

"You love me," she said softly, blue eyes brilliant.

Daniel's manhood lurched, but so did his stomach, and so did his very soul. All of him wanted her, yes, but he needed her. It was a new sensation. One he rather liked.

"My life is so much more full than I could have dreamed," he said softly, "when you are in it."

Nora's slow smile warmed him. "You know, if I were feeling in a sentimental mood, I might just say I was in love with you."

"Well, don't let that stop you," Daniel quipped, his heart skipping a beat. *Did she? Did she love him?*

She pushed back a curl behind her ear, and he resisted the urge to pull her back down into the bed and make love to her again. Perhaps that would show her—

"But what I would really love right now," Nora said, her voice low, teasing, tantalizing, "is to get wet. Very wet."

Daniel leaned closer. "Yes?"

He could barely stand it. How was he supposed to get anything done with Nora—

"In fact, I want to get so wet . . ." breathed Nora.

Daniel's whole body was taut, stiff with the anticipation of kissing her, tasting her, loving her once again. *Oh, this woman—*

". . . so would you pour me a bath?"

Daniel's head hung as he chuckled in dry frustration. "I thought for a moment—"

"I do not know what else you could possibly think I would be referring to," Nora said blithely, stepping out of the bed and making Daniel groan again at the sight of her naked body. "It was quite evident I was asking for a bath."

He could do nothing but shake his head ruefully. This woman was going to be the death of him—and oh, what a sweet death it would be!

"You can get the horses ready."

Daniel blinked. "The—the horses?"

Nora smiled blithely as she pulled his shirt around her, leaving a teasing view of her buttocks just beneath the hem. "Yes, I rather fancy . . . a ride this morning."

Unable to bear it any longer, Daniel lowered his head onto the bedclothes and groaned. "Nora Harvey!"

"Yes, a ride would do me very well," continued Nora. "Perhaps, if you are very good, I'll ride you after my horse."

Now that got his attention.

"A ride," said Daniel, staggering out of bed and hoping to goodness she could not see the very obvious physical evidence of his—

"I can see you are quite interested in a ride, too," said Nora with a faint flush. "Your bathing chamber, is it—"

"That door," groaned Daniel, pushing down his disobedient manhood and planning all the ways he was going to make Nora pay for this later. "I'll go down and order a bath and get the horses ready."

Nora stepped over to him swiftly, before he could prepare himself for her heady scent, and moaned as she pressed her lips to his.

"Thank you." She pressed her forehead against his for just a moment. "I . . . I care about you, Daniel."

"Nora—"

And she was gone, disappearing into the connecting bathing chamber, leaving Daniel naked and alone in the empty room.

After a long, deep breath, he managed to put one foot in front of the other. Getting dressed was a mite difficult with such a stiff member for the woman in the other room, but Daniel managed it. He also managed to slip out of the bedchamber, walk down the stairs, and have an almost reasonable conversation with his butler.

"A bath, Your Grace?" said Keynes with raised eyebrows.

Daniel knew precisely what the man was asking and was not going to give him the satisfaction of revealing who it was for. "In the state bedchamber, yes. Send Mrs. Stafford. I am just going to—"

"And will your guest be staying with us long?" asked the servant, his eyebrows disappearing upward.

Forever, Daniel wanted to say. *She'll be here forever.*

"For a time," he permitted himself. "Now, I need to see to the horses."

"The—but you have two grooms for that!"

But Nora's instructions were ringing in Daniel's ears, and he was not about to disobey them. If one ride was not to her liking, perhaps the other would be cancelled. *Heaven forbid.*

"I'll do it," Daniel said cheerfully. "I've not been a duke so long that I can't remember how to tack a horse!"

The stables were quiet. He took a deep breath and tried not to think of the very wet and very soapy Nora just a few yards upward from where he stood.

No, all he had to do was—

A noise.

Daniel looked around. There did not seem to be anything there. How odd.

He turned back to the riding tack hung up by his horse and—

Chapter Sixteen

Nora could not recall luxuriating in a bath quite like this, and she relished the opportunity to do so now. Especially as it would drive Daniel absolutely wild.

"In fact, I want to get so wet . . . so would you pour me a bath?"

She smiled as she picked up the soap and lathered it in her hands. The place was filled with the sound of water dripping back into the bathwater, echoing around the bath chamber.

Bath chamber, indeed. This room was probably as large as her cottage, with palatial pipes leading into a bathtub the like of which she had never seen before. Nora had groaned as she had stepped into the scalding water.

Oh, the last time she'd had a bath . . .

Well, it had been nothing like this. Her tin bathtub, which hung on a nail on the back of her bedchamber door in the cottage, took far too long to fill with the small kettle she had. One of hot, and the rest cold from the pump in the garden, that was all she ever permitted herself. It was rather pleasant in the summer, but in the winter it was a misery keeping clean.

But this? This was heaven!

Nora marveled at the pile of fresh towels waiting for her, the three different kinds of bar soaps all smelling divine, the way the water was scattered with rose petals. Though she tried not to think too much about why there were such provisions set out—*undoubtedly David's doing*—it was impossible not to enjoy such luxury.

Anything like this was in rather short supply in her world. But now she was in Daniel's world.

"I love you. You, as you are, with all your history and your nonsense and your baking. Nora, I've had my fingers burned with you—"

"The feeling is entirely mutual."

Nora swallowed as she rose from the bath, water cascading, and wrapped herself in a towel.

Never before had a man spoken to her like that. Never before had she wanted a man to speak to her like that.

It was bizarre. Since she had endured such absolute betrayal, she had learned swiftly to guard her heart. And she'd learned that her physicality could be used to get, mostly, what she wanted. The idea of truly opening up to another man again had been ludicrous.

But Daniel had somehow managed to creep under all the protections she had built around herself, slowly taking them down brick by brick. This was no explosive, demanding love, but a gentle, caring love. An affection that surprised her, burning away all protestations and making it impossible not to care for him that deeply.

Because she did, didn't she? She may not have said it properly, but Nora knew how she felt.

As she slowly dressed, other words they had shared echoed in her mind.

"I've never stroked a woman against a wall before. I—oh, Nora, you're so ready for me."

Words of desire, passion, yes, but also affection. Was that not love?

As Nora buttoned the last part of her gown and gave up on sorting her hair without pins, a loud shout somewhere in the townhouse echoed up the corridor. It was impossible to tell precisely what the man—for it had been a man—was saying, but it sounded hurried.

Perhaps it was a servant preparing a picnic, Nora thought with growing delight as she sat on the end of the bed to wait for Daniel to return.

Oh, how lovely it would be to ride out with Daniel for a picnic. Perhaps, if they could find a secluded grove for their luncheon, she could ride her second beast of the day . . .

More shouts grew about the house as Nora waited. She was not completely sure how busy a house this size should be. It certainly sounded like busyness. But as the minutes ticked by on the longcase clock opposite her and the shouts grew and Daniel did not return, something akin to fear curled inside her.

Those shouts. They sounded like panic now, not preparation. Uproar, not unconcern.

Nora swallowed and rose from the bed. It had been nearly half an hour since she had stepped out of the bath, and she must have been in there for almost an hour. Why would Daniel not have returned?

He was the Duke of Thornfalcone, the master of this place. Anything could be put off by such a man, could it not?

Steeling herself, Nora stepped forward and clasped the door handle. Though it would be mortifying to go out and meet Daniel's servants, there was nothing for it. She needed to know whether or not they were going on a ride—whether or not she was still welcome here.

She felt a flutter of panic but pushed it aside. She was not going to disbelieve Daniel so swiftly after his declaration. That was what Nora of yesterday would have done. She was a new woman now. His name was branded on her soul. She had been scalded by his passion, yes, and changed by it.

And she needed to be brave.

The corridor was deserted. Now Nora had stepped through the door, the shouts from downstairs were louder and definitely more panicked. She could not help herself. She strode toward the noise, and when she reached the bottom of the staircase and stepped into the entrance hall, it was to see absolute bedlam.

An older woman, perhaps the housekeeper, was sobbing. Two maids were trying to console her, but one also had tears in her eyes.

There was a footman pacing anxiously to and fro, turning on his heels whenever he reached a wall, his eyes narrowed. Three other footmen were talking to an elderly man wearing a wig, and the butler Daniel had so imperiously ordered about only yesterday was sitting, head downcast, on a chair.

Nora stared. *What on earth had—*

"That's her," said the butler suddenly, lifting his head and pointing a finger. "That's the woman the duke returned with yesterday afternoon!"

Every eye turned to Nora.

She swallowed, hating the heat creeping into her cheeks at the intensity of their stares. She had known this was a mistake. Not coming downstairs—being here at all. She should have taken Daniel back to her cottage when their ardor threatened to overwhelm them. True, it would not have been so luxurious, but at least they could have enjoyed true privacy.

Instead—

"Is it, indeed?" said the man wearing the wig seriously, approaching her.

The sniffles in the room increased in volume. Nora stepped back as the man drew near. This was a mistake. She should leave, now. Whatever had happened?

Nora's gaze darted about for Daniel. He would protect her—he would explain her presence away with an excuse that would save his reputation. After all, plenty of gentlemen had mistresses. And she should know.

But he wasn't there. Despite all the noise which had surely drawn every person in the place, Daniel was not there.

Something ice cold slipped into Nora's lungs, making her gasp.

"Where's Daniel?" she gulped.

The man narrowed his eyes. "That is precisely what I was going to ask you."

"Who are *you*?" Nora shot back, trying to pull herself up.

It was rather difficult to do for three reasons. Firstly, because her hair was undone in a most scandalous manner, something she was highly aware of as curls fell past her shoulders. Secondly, she was not supposed to be there. When dukes took mistresses, it was supposed to be discreet. And thirdly, because the man was significantly taller than her.

Nora swallowed. "I asked—"

"My name is Judge Snee, and I have . . . worked with Mr. Vaughn before," the man said coldly. "Before he was His Grace."

Her eyes widened. Daniel had mentioned this before, hadn't he? The "help" he had given the Crown when the occasion called for it. He had been rather circumspect about it all, and despite her great interest, Nora had not pried. If a man wished to tell her something, he would. There was no point in attempting to force it.

And now Daniel was not here and a justice had arrived?

"What has happened to Daniel?" Nora breathed.

Her worst fears were realized as she saw the magistrate exchange a glance with the butler.

"You don't know he was abducted by a ruffian not an hour ago?" Judge Snee asked.

Nora did not know what happened first: the panicked gasp from her throat, the painful agony twisting her up inside, the giddiness, the falling—

"Careful there!"

"Dear Lord, she's a fainter!"

"Get a smelling bottle, Mrs. Stafford!"

Nora blinked. The ceiling swam in and out of view, as did the numerous faces. It was impossible to tell just how long she had been unconscious for. Her back was cold. She was lying on the marble floor of the hall.

She blinked again. "D-Daniel?"

"He's gone missing," sobbed the voice of what could be the housekeeper, just to Nora's left. "Snatched from his own stable!"

"I saw the blackguard, thought he was helping His Grace to a carriage," came a male voice from the other side of the room. "I thought he had an appointment, if I'd known—"

"No one is blaming you, Keynes," came the calm, soothing voice of the magistrate.

Nora pushed herself upright and the two maids leaning over her pulled back hastily. "Daniel—Daniel has been taken?"

"Abducted," said Mr. Snee, shaking his head as he stood by the front door. "Terrible business."

Terrible business? Was that all the man could say?

Nora forced herself back onto her feet though her legs felt like jelly and her head was still swimming.

Daniel, abducted. Taken by a man. Forced into a carriage. An hour ago—an hour ago?

"Daniel." Nora seemed unable to say anything else.

Panic was washing over her, but it was accompanied by an even more painful emotion: guilt. This was her fault, wasn't it? Her fault. She knew precisely what had happened, who had taken him, and why—and it was because of her. She should never have allowed this, this whatever-it-was with Daniel Vaughn, Duke of Thornfalcone, to get this far. She should have known his proximity to her would put him in danger.

". . . check the stables for any clues as to the duke's whereabouts," someone was muttering. Nora could not tell who, her mind was whirling. "And question the woman, whoever she is . . ."

Nora almost laughed, it was so ridiculous.

She had been so desperate, so eager to be cared for that when her brother had returned to her cottage a few months ago, apologizing for not protecting her, she did what anyone would. At least, she thought so.

She had trusted him.

"—could be anywhere by now," the butler was saying in a low, panicked voice. "An hour? We don't even know what direction they went in. His Grace could be—"

"If it was a ransom job, we will hear very soon," Mr. Snee was saying. At his words, a maid broke into loud sobs. "I would ask you, Keynes, whether you have a store of money easily accessible—"

"You wish to pay before we have attempted a rescue?"

"I think we should consider all possibilities to ensure His Grace's safe return . . ."

Nora leaned against the banister of the stairs, unable to take any more in. *His Grace's safe return. Daniel's safe return.*

But this had all happened because he was not the first Duke of Thornfalcone to come to her cottage, was he? It was because of his brother, David, that this was happening. If only she had never revealed to her own brother just how frustrated she had been with David's unwanted affections. If only she had censured herself, not been so open with her irritation at the man's persistence. If only she had told her brother the man's full name, and not spent an entire evening complaining only about the Duke of Thornfalcone.

And the thought that something terrible could happen to Daniel—and if it was truly her brother who had taken him, something terrible already had happened—rushed through Nora's mind.

She fell, heavily, onto the bottom step of the staircase. "Daniel."

The men halted their conversation. Nora's cheeks burned at their attention, but she could not take back the word, nor alter the way she had spoken it. Devotedly. With reverence.

With love.

Oh, he had been bold enough to reveal his true affections for her—and she had not. Why had she missed that opportunity? Why, when Daniel had poured out his heart to her, had she refused it?

"I love you. You, as you are, with all your history and your nonsense and your baking. Nora, I've had my fingers burned with you—"

"The feeling is entirely mutual."

"You know something about this, don't you?"

Nora looked up.

The butler, Keynes, had raised a finger again and was pointing malevolently. "She probably let them in, this kidnapper," continued the butler bitterly, glaring. "You snuck your way in here with charm and your feminine wiles—"

"Mr. Keynes!" said the woman Nora presumed was the housekeeper, placing a hand over her heart. "The maids!"

"I'll call it how I see it, Mrs. Stafford," the butler spat. "This woman came here yesterday and ordered all the servants to leave, rendering the master helpless—"

Nora went cold. "It wasn't like that—"

"—presuming upon my master's better nature, purposefully separating him from those who would have defended him—"

It was all going so horribly wrong. "It was Daniel's idea to—"

"Once you put it into his head," snarled the butler, taking a step closer.

Nora rose from the step but could not think what to do or where to go. Had it been her idea? She could barely remember—that afternoon and evening had been spent on nothing but joy and pleasure.

But the memories were bitter now. Why had she not told Daniel how she felt about him?

"But you didn't escape with your accomplice! Now you've been left to take the fall—"

"I have to go after him."

Nora looked around for a moment to see who had spoken those determined, quiet words. Only when she saw that every eye in the hall was once again on her did she realize the only person who could have spoken was . . . herself.

"She's mad," whispered one of the maids.

"Of course she'll go after him," muttered a footman. "She knows where he is."

Nora swallowed her retort that she did know where Daniel was—or at least, she only suspected. But not for the reasons they thought. Quite the opposite.

"You cannot go after such a ruffian!" Mrs. Stafford, the housekeeper said in a breathless voice. "You'll be killed!"

"You'll be abducted too!" cried one of the maids.

"It would certainly not be advisable," added Mr. Snee with a frown. "You are a mere woman, Miss . . .?"

Nora glared. "Miss Harvey."

She should have given a false name. She realized that the moment the magistrate's eyes widened. *So, even amongst the law, I am notorious*, Nora thought bleakly.

"You are? Any relation to—"

"I have to go after him and bring Daniel back safely," Nora said, cutting across him. *The less said about her brother, the better.*

"You can't," blustered the butler. "You are—"

"I am not about to wait around here for some magical information to fall into our laps and tell us where Daniel—where His Grace is," said Nora forcefully, allowing her temper to rise just enough to give her the boldness she required. "I—we all care about Daniel, His Grace I mean, and we all want him to be safe. I need him to be safe, because I—I didn't tell him—he said that he, and I didn't . . ."

Her voice trailed away as heat seared her cheeks.

He had said he loved her, and she had not told him she loved him in return. Perhaps that chance was gone forever, but Nora was not going to let it be so without a fight.

She swallowed. "What would you do, Mr. Keynes?"

All eyes, thankfully, turned to the butler, who flushed. "Wh-What would I—"

"You seem to think I should not go after him," Nora said, her lungs constricting as she thought of what Hamish could be doing to Daniel right now. "Do you have a better idea? A more immediate solution? Any thoughts on the matter whatsoever?"

She was being too harsh, she knew, but she could not help it. She had to put this fiery frustration somewhere, and the butler had hardly been kind to her.

Keynes swallowed. "I—I would suggest that Mr. Snee—"

"Oh, I haven't the faintest idea what to do," the magistrate interrupted with a helpless shrug. "I am the person people bring ruffians to in court—I don't go chasing after them! Besides, I'm from London. I don't know the streets of Bath at all. I only arrived yesterday to speak to the damn man about his brother, and I got lost twice today coming here from—"

"Get me a fast horse," said Nora as sternly as possible to the nearest footman.

The man immediately looked at the butler.

Keynes glared at Nora. "What do you need a—"

"Damn it man, a fast horse, two strong men with their own steeds, and . . . and a pistol!" Nora said with far more confidence than she felt.

She had always hoped it would never come to this. That Hamish would be smart enough to leave Bath, leave her alone, stop attempting to gain coin through nefarious deeds and actually find himself a profession.

But that hadn't come to pass, and now she and Daniel were paying for it. Paying for her indiscretion in complaining to her brother about the Duke of Thornfalcone.

The butler was still blustering. "—cannot see what good that would do! A pistol is not the sort of thing for a lady, and—"

"I ceased being a lady when I was caught in a scandal," Nora said harshly. "I'm just a woman. A woman determined to go and save the man she loves, so unless you can help me, Mr. Keynes, I suggest you get out of my way."

For a moment, just a moment, the older man met her glare with one of his own. Nora stared him down, seeing the rage and the panic she felt mirrored in the butler's eyes.

Then he looked to the footman. "You heard, man. Two pistols for the lady."

Nora released her breath in a rush, hardly aware she had been holding it. "And a fast—"

"The horses will be brought around in but a moment. Johns and Simkin will accompany you," said Mr. Keynes stiffly, as though he had been previously prepared for this unlikely eventuality, like any good butler. "And the three of you will bring His Grace home safely."

Nora nodded curtly. "Time to bring the fire."

Chapter Seventeen

8 July 1811

"Chrissake, whaat the . . ."

Pain as Daniel had never felt before was drilling through a part of his skull just behind his left ear. Ripples of agony shot through his head as he tried to move. As he tried to speak. As he tried to open his eyes.

Shapes, blurry and swimming, appeared before him. His mouth was dry. Daniel tried to swallow, but his jaw appeared to have been glued shut.

Ye gods, his head hurt. It felt as though he had been hit severely with . . . with something. Something hard.

Daniel blinked, but his vision was still blurred. *Christ, his head hurt.*

He lifted a hand to the pain.

Rather, he *tried* to lift a hand to the pain. It was only when he tried to move his hand that he realized he couldn't.

Not because Daniel was too groggy, although that was a tempting conclusion. No, far more worryingly, it was because his hand seemed to be bound. Tied to his other hand. Both were behind his back, but more than that, they were behind . . .

Behind a chair.

Daniel blinked again. This time his vision started to sharpen. He was no longer in the stables.

Which made no sense. He had been in the stables—he had been about to tack up a horse. Two horses. One for himself, and one for—

Nora.

Daniel stiffened then looked down at himself in panic.

He appeared to be tied, quite securely, to a chair. It was not a chair he recognized. It was a wooden chair, one that had seen better days. It was resting on a flagstone floor he did not know. Could it be part of the servants' quarters, a kitchen or scullery he had not been in before?

But no, that did not make sense. Daniel's thoughts started to rush through his mind, increasing in speed as he shifted from unconsciousness to agonizing wakefulness.

Why would any of his servants have tied him to a chair?

He shifted as best he could, and another stabbing pain split his head. Now he thought about it, Daniel was almost sure he could feel dried blood behind that same ear.

So, he had been hit over the head.

The thought unlocked something in him. He had been attacked—kidnapped, perhaps. Where was he?

Daniel looked up and saw to his despair that there was nothing here he recognized. The room he was apparently bound in was small. Soft daylight drifted through the small, cracked windowpanes. It was either evening and he had been here for a few hours . . . or, more troublingly, it was morning and he had been here all night.

The soreness in his muscles told him it was likely morning. So did the sodden rag he now realized was in his mouth, gagging him.

As Daniel looked around, he took in more details. The room was poorly furnished, but it was set up as a sort of parlor. A sofa was just to his left, a fire to his right. Two small tables, one with a stained teacup, the other bare.

There was a strange chill in the room, though perhaps that was in his bones. Perhaps being bound and gagged here on a chair, the rope used to tie him up eating into his wrists, had chilled him.

Daniel tried to swallow as he took in the most important thing not in the room.

Nora.

The thought of her stirred him, forcing him to sit upright again. Where was she? Where was Nora—had she been attacked too? Was it possible, though the thought brought him nothing but pain, that she was somewhere else in this ramshackle house?

A terrible idea struck him, a knife of ice slicing into his gut.

What was the blackguard who had tied him up doing to Nora?

"Nora," Daniel muttered.

He was unsure if the word would have been comprehensible to anyone, even if he were not alone. The gag made it almost impossible to speak.

But he had to. He had to do something, try to escape—make sure Nora was safe. The idea she could be somewhere, in pain, unable to reach him—

It was enough. Daniel started to struggle against his bonds. Perhaps the rope would snap, though it did not feel as though it would. Perhaps someone would hear him, though he could not tell whether he was still in Bath. Perhaps—

"I wouldn't struggle," said a calm, quiet voice. "You might hurt yourself."

Daniel froze.

It was a man's voice. Of that, he was certain, though he was not certain of much else. The voice had come from behind him, though his head ached so much he could not bring himself to turn.

A man's voice, then. A young man, from the sound of it—at least, probably not much older than himself. Not a voice he recognized.

Or did he? Daniel tried to wrack his brain to think whether he recognized any syllable of the voice, but his head throbbed and it was impossible to tie it down to a particular person.

There was something about it, though. A lilt he recognized,

though Daniel could not place it. As though it was the voice of someone he had met once under an unusual circumstance and then forgotten.

"Where's Nora?"

At least, that was what Daniel attempted to say. The gag made it almost impossible to form any coherent words. He coughed into the horrible material.

The man behind him chuckled. "I wouldn't speak, either. I don't fancy your chances escaping from that gag or the ropes."

Daniel tried to stay calm, tried to push back the panic threatening to overwhelm him.

He had to stay calm if he was going to escape—and he was determined that he would. What possible reason could this man, whoever he was, have done such a thing as this? Attacked him from behind, dragged him off somewhere, and trussed him up like a chicken?

Daniel attempted to scour his mind for all those who may wish him ill. The trouble was, whenever he was helping some agent of the Crown—usually the Duke of Chantmarle—he, Daniel, only got involved in a very small way. Finding informants, passing on messages, that sort of thing. He had never got involved in the important bits.

For just this reason, he could not help but think darkly. It was his brother, David, who liked the idea of adventure. Who gambled. Who had to be rescued from brothels, who bought copious amounts of art without any idea of where he would put it, who promised Lady Romeril the moon.

That wasn't him.

"But I suppose it would be terribly dull not having anyone to speak to," came the man's voice dryly. "Perhaps I will give you this small gesture."

Daniel could not think what the man meant, but he did not have to wonder for long. Rough fingers scraped against his cheek and he cried out, or tried to, but the gag prevented—

Then it was gone.

Daniel gasped, fresh air passing into his mouth, and his head sagged with relief. It was gone, the gag was gone. He could finally speak.

It took almost a full minute by his reckoning, however, for him to swallow enough times for his voice to have any power.

"Where is she?" he gasped.

The man was still behind him, but Daniel could feel how close he was. The skin on the back of his neck prickled uncomfortably.

He was proven right when the man spoke softly into his ear. "She?"

"Nora," said Daniel, hating that he had to speak her precious name to this ruffian. "What have you done with her?"

The man hissed, a sharp intake of breath that grated on Daniel's nerves. "You dare speak her name?"

This made no sense. Daniel's head was still swimming, he was parched, his neck was stiff, his wrists were sore, and he would stay in bed for a week if this ordeal ever ended.

When it had ended. Yes, that's what he had to keep thinking about—when it was over. This wasn't going to be how this Duke of Thornfalcone died.

Daniel twisted his head and caught sight of—

A man. Just a man. If he had walked past him on the streets of Bath, he wouldn't have given him a second glance. He was tall with reddish brown hair and a crooked smile. *He looked altogether too pleased with himself,* thought Daniel grimly, *and there was strength in those shoulders.* Even if he hadn't been bound to a chair, he wasn't sure whether he could match him.

It was an unpleasant thought.

"Good morning, Your Grace," snarled the man, stepping around to finally face Daniel.

It was odd. After all this time, after asking people time and time again not to call him "Your Grace", it was only now he realized that the title had offered him some sort of protection.

Protection he would very much appreciate just now.

"Untie me," Daniel said, in as reasonable a voice as he could manage. "We can forget this—I don't know you, or where I am, and—"

"I am not going to let you go," snapped the man, dropping onto the sofa and eyeing Daniel malevolently. "You think I would do such a thing, after what you've done?"

Daniel blinked. *What he'd—*

Dear God, the man must be mad. *There could not be a more tame duke in the whole land*, he thought ruefully. There was no rhyme or reason for him being kept here like an animal.

And he still hadn't answered Daniel's question.

"Where is Nora?" Daniel said, his heart skipping a beat at the very thought. "You haven't—you haven't done anything to her, have you?"

The man glared, thunder on his brow. "Me? Oh, it's you that's done the terrible things to her, Your Grace. You bastard. You accuse me, when it's your own filthy behavior that so distresses her?"

Daniel stared.

Perhaps it was the blow to the head or perhaps he was just very dim—but Daniel could not fathom what on earth the man was talking about.

His filthy behavior? Nora, distressed but what he had done?

Guilt crept in at the edges. Fine, perhaps he had not been quite so considerate in his early encounters. Perhaps he had not understood her then as he did now. Perhaps he had been a little thoughtless.

The memory of the horse flashed in Daniel's mind, and he closed his eyes for a brief moment.

All right, he had not been perfect. Far from it. But surely nothing he had done deserved this?

And besides, Daniel thought, starting to consider more clearly. *That was weeks ago.* He and Nora had shared so much since then. She had been open with him, vulnerable, and he had been the same in return.

God in his Heaven, they had shared a bed just four and twenty hours ago. He loved her, he had told her he loved her!

So why did this lout believe him to be so terrible?

"You deny it?" spat the man. "You deny that you have treated Nora ill?"

"I-I do deny it," Daniel said, his voice hoarse. He swallowed and said more strongly, "I have never wished for anything but Nora's good! I have only ever loved—"

"You call your pathetic attentions to her *love*!" cried the man, glowering at Daniel. "You disgust me!"

And I am beginning to understand, thought Daniel.

Well, Nora had never told him much about the gentlemen she had . . . befriended in the past. He had not wanted to know, and she had not wished to volunteer the information. The last thing he had wanted, after all, was to be reminded of the ways she had been forced to survive. He did not blame her. Now he knew she had been tricked into giving up her virtue, Daniel did not blame Nora at all.

He had wanted to think about her future. Their future. A future together.

So, was this man a jilted lover of Nora's, Daniel wondered, trying to take in every detail of the man. It made sense, but it did not quite explain precisely why he was so determined to protect what he thought was Nora's honor.

"What's your name?"

The man frowned. "You think I would be stupid enough to tell you my name?"

Daniel sighed. Not really, but it had been worth a try. "I love Nora."

"You dare sully her name in your stinking—"

"And I think you know she cannot love you," Daniel continued, trying to twist his wrists again. If he could only find a weak spot in the rope—

It was then he noticed the man's frown had transformed into one of confusion.

"You're disgusting. You think I'd want to love my sister as you love her?"

Daniel's mouth fell open. "Sister?"

Nora's brother nodded. "You've disgraced my sister, you blackguard! The Duke of Thornfalcone, she told me. Continuously coming round to her house, begging her to lift her skirts for him! Refusing to take no for an answer!"

Daniel stared.

Oh, dear God, it was worse than he could ever have imagined. Nora's brother. She had mentioned the brother, spoken of their estrangement, but she had revealed few details about him. Only yesterday had Nora felt safe enough to explain that her brother had not protected her when she had lost her virtue—that he had not called out the blackguard, forced him to marry her. And now . . .

Daniel groaned. Now Mr. Harvey was attempting to do just that. Put right the past. Protect Nora as he had not done before.

"You're Nora's brother," he repeated, as the truth sank in.

And then Daniel's stomach lurched.

"The Duke of Thornfalcone, she told me. Continuously coming round to her house, begging her to lift her skirts for him! Refusing to take no for an answer!"

Dear God, had Nora truly been that repulsed by him? Had she found his gestures of devotion so lacking, been so nauseated by his presence?

Everything Daniel thought they had shared, every moment of heat, every glance of desire, every touch—had it been wonderful for him and awful for Nora? So awful she had actually complained to her estranged brother about him?

Doubt and guilt swirled within him as he tried to take in this new information. Had she only gone to his townhouse yesterday because she felt obliged? Worn down, perhaps, by his constant attentions? Daniel had been certain she wished for his touch, craved his lovemaking. But then, he had been open about his affections, hadn't he? And what had she said?

"I love you. You, as you are, with all your history and your nonsense and your baking. Nora, I've had my fingers burned with you—"

"The feeling is entirely mutual."

Dear God, he was the worst sort of dunderhead. Even worse than that—he had been so blinded by his own desires, his own needs, he had not even realized that Nora—

Then something shifted in his mind.

Daniel looked up sharply. "The Duke of Thornfalcone?"

"That's what I said," Nora's brother spat. "And that's what you are, aren't you?"

Daniel's mind was whirling. He was not the only Duke of Thornfalcone who had desired Nora Harvey, but he was certain his attentions could not be described as "begging her to lift up her skirts for him". Even if he had wished it, he would never have been so coarse.

His brother, on the other hand . . .

"Ah," said Daniel weakly. "Oh dear. I think there's been some terrible mistake—"

"No mistake! You are the Duke of Thornfalcone, are you not?" said Mr. Harvey fiercely.

Try as he might, Daniel could not think of a way to easily explain the confusion. For it had to be David that Nora's brother had mistaken him for.

"I had a brother. A twin brother, actually," Daniel said wretchedly. *Oh, it all sounded so fanciful! The man would think he was spinning him a yarn.* "And the funny thing is, although I suppose it's not that funny now I think about it, but my brother—"

"Shut it," snapped Mr. Harvey. "I'm tired of your blathering! You were the one who pestered my sister, a helpless, defenseless woman!"

Daniel bristled. It was most unpleasant to have such unfounded accusations thrust at him. And it was particularly awkward to know they were probably true of his own brother.

His irritation, therefore, was probably what made him say what he did without a thought. "She was only defenseless because you had abandoned her! Your own sister! You—"

Daniel was unable to continue. It was so much more difficult to speak after a man had punched you solidly on the jaw.

Chin aching and stars dancing in his eyes, Daniel fell against the chair as his gaze drifted across the room to the window.

To the window where he could see Nora's face.

Daniel blinked. The face was gone.

He had been dreaming. Well, not quite dreaming, but the blow to his jaw from Mr. Harvey's fist must have made him think he saw . . .

There she was again. Nora, two footmen whose names he could not remember, and—

No, he must be dreaming. There was no possibility that Keynes was at the window.

"Consider that a taste of what's to come," snapped Nora's brother, wringing his hand after the hefty punch. "Nothing is too good for my sister, and I'll never allow her to defend herself alone again!"

Daniel nodded, hardly aware what he was doing. "Yes, yes, good . . ."

Nora was here to rescue him—that, or he was hallucinating. But no, there were footsteps outside—he could hear them.

Blast it all. He was supposed to be the one rescuing her!

The footsteps were getting louder. His kidnapper looked around at a particularly loud tread, and Daniel knew he had to do all he could to distract the man.

Even if it meant another blow to the jaw.

"You mistreated your sister far worse than I ever did," Daniel said, abandoning all attempts to explain that it was a completely different

Duke of Thornfalcone who had so pestered Nora Harvey. "You were the one who should have protected her when she was ruined, but all you did was abandon—"

The second blow was harsher than the first. Daniel moaned, blood dripping from a split lip, head lolling on his shoulder.

Christ, he would have to hope Nora wasn't merely a dream and that she had brought a few men with her. He wasn't sure how much longer he could put up with this.

"But I love her," Daniel said thickly, his voice a mumble under all the pain. "I love Nora Harvey, and I would marry her if she would have me. She's the most beautiful, most modest, kindest, gentlest—"

The door before him banged open and Nora appeared, a pistol in each hand, a fiery rage in her eyes.

"Move," she said in a ringing voice, "and I will shoot you."

Chapter Eighteen

NORA COULD HARDLY breathe as she led Daniel's servants closer, step by step, toward her brother's old cottage—the last and most remote of his haunts they had to check. She had begun to despair last night, as darkness had fallen and they still hadn't found where Hamish had gone to ground. But the carriage he'd used to kidnap Dnaiel was still sitting in front of the cottage, and she could see the horses in the small pasture. Her brother was here. She trembled just a little.

Surely he could hear her heartbeat. Surely Hamish would notice her, spot her in the courtyard. The windows may be small, but any moment now he would look out and spot—

"There he is!" hissed Keynes.

Nora immediately pulled the well-meaning servant into the shadows. "Hush!"

"But I saw—"

"Good, then we are in the right place," murmured Nora, trying her best to calm the exuberant butler. Against her protestations, he had insisted on coming with them this morning. In the end, she'd given in just to save time.

"His Grace was there, bound to a chair—"

No. Nora could not permit herself to think too much about that. *Daniel would be fine.* He would be safe—as long as he was still alive, there was every chance she could have him back in her arms within a moment.

As long as the servants she had brought with her did not spoil everything.

"Take a look in the window, Miss . . . miss," whispered the older man. "I . . . well, my eyes aren't what they used to . . . I would hate for us to be in the wrong place . . ."

Nora caught the butler's gaze and saw real shame in his eyes. "You didn't actually see?"

The guilt was palpable on the man's face. He'd been looking straight in the window. If he really didn't know if he'd seen Daniel, it was because he couldn't know.

It seemed clear to her that the butler hadn't mentioned his poor vision to anyone, and she could understand why he wouldn't wish to. If his eyesight truly was going, he would have been terrified about losing his place, and that meant—that meant the person he had seen in her brother's cottage, bound and likely gagged, could have been another.

Trust Hamish to have an entirely different man kidnapped in his home.

"Stay here," Nora said in a low, warning voice.

Mr. Keynes nodded, and she crept away from him toward the small window. The echo of every footstep echoed louder than an elephant's in her ears, and she was certain her breathing must be audible even through the glass. Surely any moment she would be discovered.

It was certainly her brother in there. There was no mistaking that red gold hair.

And there, tied most uncomfortably to a chair, blood tangled in his hair, was—

"Daniel," Nora whispered, forgetting herself.

For a split second, Daniel's gaze flickered. Their eyes met, and her heart constricted with agony. He was in pain, he was injured, he—

She ducked down.

"Was it him?" blustered the butler quietly, coming close to the window. "Can you see—"

"Mr. Keynes, I need you to do a great service for me—for His Grace," amended Nora hastily, pulling the man away from the window and toward the front door.

God help her for this, but if the man insisted on coming inside with them, their chances would be ruined.

"Oh, I will do anything for His Grace! Whatever you need from me, I will do!"

"Stand here," said Nora firmly, placing him just to the left of the door.

Mr. Keynes blinked as the two footmen followed. "Here?"

Nora nodded firmly. It would be good to have a lookout, after all, and she did not like the older man's chances inside her brother's cottage. No, far safer to have him out here.

And, she could not help but think bitterly, *if something happened to her and the two footmen but they were able to free Daniel . . .*

Well, the Duke of Thornfalcone would run into the waiting arms of his butler. Hopefully the two of them could get to the horses and be away, back to Bath, back to civilization. Back to safety.

"Right," said the butler, catching her eye. "Right. Here."

Did he understand why she had done this?

But there was no time to wonder about such things. Every moment that passed was another chance for Hamish to severely injure—perhaps kill!—Daniel.

She would not permit herself to even think about it. She was going to save him—a rescue was the only way this day could end.

She swallowed, tasting her own fear in her throat. *Play with dukes, get burned.*

But it was Daniel, wasn't it, facing the consequences of their liaison? Daniel who had somehow managed to get caught up in her brother's foolish nonsense.

"Follow me, and be ready for anything," Nora whispered, reaching under the doormat where she knew her brother kept a spare key. "And give me two pistols."

The weapons were heavy in her palms, but Nora did her best to show the men she was more than capable of managing them.

The fact that she had never fired a gun before needed to be of little consequence today. Probably.

Raising one pistol to her lips in a hushing motion, Nora received the nervous nods of the two footmen. What were their names, Johns and Simkin? Did they have families waiting for them—wives, children? Families who did not even realize their loved ones were in danger?

Nora forced herself to concentrate on creeping along the corridor which she knew led to the little parlor where Daniel was being held captive. She winced as she heard one of the footmen stumble slightly and take a heavy step, hoping the sound hadn't given them away.

How had it come to this—creeping down corridors with pistols in her hands? Well, if she were honest, she might not know why, but *how* she knew full well. Her brother's approach to problem solving had always been far more violent and aggressive than she had thought wise.

And now she might lose the man she loved, to the man who had never cared for her as he should.

The three of them halted just by the door to the parlor. The two footmen took deep breaths, readying themselves. How did one prepare for such a moment? Nora's mind was whirling so rapidly, it was almost impossible to think. All she could do was hear, and all she could hear was—

"You mistreated your sister far worse than I ever did." Daniel's voice was low, pained, and clearly directed at her brother. "You were the one who should have protected her when she was ruined, but all you did was abandon—"

Nora gasped—the noise of a blow had been unmistakable. Daniel was tied up, bound. That meant it had been Hamish who had struck, and therefore Daniel who had received the pain.

There was a moan.

Tears prickled in the corners of Nora's eyes. He was hurting Daniel and she could not help him, not yet. She had to make absolutely sure she was ready.

And hearing such words of affection and love from Daniel was heady. He cared for her in a way that her older brother never had. Hamish should have protected her. When he had not, he had abandoned her to the caprice of the men she could entertain for a while. And Daniel—Daniel—

"But I love her. I love Nora Harvey, and I would marry her if she would have me."

Nora's breath caught. She had to slow it down, she had to stay calm and ensure she was in full possession of her faculties before she entered the parlor and attempted to save Daniel's life.

But how could she stay calm when he was saying such wonderful things? As his love poured out, despite the circumstances, despite the danger.

She should have told him, when she'd had the chance, just how deeply she cared.

"She's the most beautiful, most modest, kindest, gentlest—"

Nora couldn't stand it any longer. If Daniel did not quiet, then Hamish was liable to do something reckless—and that could mean the loss of the one man in the world she truly loved.

She looked back at Johns—or was it Simkin?—and gestured at the door. It was now or never. He nodded his understanding and, as Nora tightened her grip on the pistols, he threw the door open wide with no consideration for the wall. Nora took a deep breath as she stepped forward, attempting to plaster a look of supreme confidence across her face.

"Move," she said clearly, "and I will shoot you."

It took just an instant to look around the room and get a clear idea of what had happened.

There was Daniel, wrists bound together behind the back of the chair, ankles tied to the legs. There was blood in his hair, across his face, dripping from a split lip.

There was Hamish. He was wringing his hand after so recently punching the Duke of Thornfalcone. There was such a look of malevolence in his eyes that if the circumstances had been different, she would have stepped back.

But she couldn't. And not just because directly behind Nora were the two footmen.

No, she'd had enough of stepping back. Stepping away from Society, away from those who may have helped her. Stepping out of Bath itself, into the cottage left to her by her grandmother. Stepping away from any hope of true connection, away from the feelings Daniel stirred, away from the devotion she was terrified to slip into.

Today, Nora had to step forward. Even if she was burned in the encounter.

Rushing toward her brother, she was astonished to see Hamish take a hasty step back.

"Nora! Nora, I—I only did it to help you—"

She did not actually intend to do it. The pistols Mr. Keynes had procured were far heavier than she had supposed, and Nora stumbled on the long hem of her gown as she hastened across the parlor.

Unfortunately, this meant her right hand flew up, catching the side of her brother's head with the heavy pistol.

Hamish went down like a sack of bricks.

Nora halted, breathing heavily, looking at the prone form of her brother.

Help her, indeed! What sort of help was attacking the man she loved, taking him prisoner?

"N-Nora?"

"You—You killed him!" spluttered one of the footmen.

Nora was hardly listening. Not as a man's shaking voice said her name. "He's only knocked out cold, he'll be fine. Daniel—"

"Nora?" croaked the Duke of Thornfalcone.

Nora dropped the two pistols instantly as she stepped toward the man she loved, caring little that the two heavy weapons hit the ground right beside her brother. She thought she saw a footman hastily scoop them up, but she had lost all care or interest in the matter.

Nora dropped to her knees by the chair Daniel was tied to as tears prickled the corners of her eyes. "You are hurt! Oh, Daniel—"

"It doesn't matter—you are uninjured?" asked Daniel swiftly, his gaze raking over her as though desperately worried that she too had been attacked.

Nora swallowed her tears as best she could as her fingers scrabbled to the rope binding him. "I am fine, no one has hurt me—though I admit, Mr. Keynes has said some cutting—"

"You know, I thought I saw him outside," Daniel said, his head lolling on his shoulder. "I must be going mad! It must be the blow to the head, there is no possibility—"

"He's outside, standing guard. I thought it best to keep him there, out of harm's way," said Nora in a rush, wishing to goodness she could free him from this bondage. "Daniel—"

"Here, miss," muttered a voice near her.

Nora blinked. She was so focused on Daniel she had almost forgotten that there was anyone else in the cottage, but of course there was. The two footmen.

They had lifted up her brother and placed him on the sofa, and one had thankfully retrieved her two pistols. The other had stepped forward and was now offering her something.

Nora blinked. His hands came into focus. He was holding a small knife.

"For the ropes," the footman said, as though she had forgotten why they were there in the first place.

Grasping the knife hastily, Nora nodded and turned back to her beloved without another word. Her fingers started to work on the ropes. Anything to keep her hands busy. Anything to keep from thinking about what could have been.

She needed to be close to Daniel, helping him, loving him.

Except, of course, that they were not alone.

"You, both of you," Nora said swiftly, looking up. It was rather odd to see the two men stand to attention, as though she were some great lady accustomed to giving orders. "Take my—take that man outside and place him in Mr. Keynes's keeping. Then check the rest of the house for other miscreants and then . . . then wait for us. By the horses."

If the two footmen thought anything was strange in her instructions, they did not say. Nora was almost sure they exchanged a look, but the moment was so brief it was over before it had begun.

"Yes, miss," they muttered together.

Taking her brother's arms over their shoulders, the two footmen half-dragged, half-carried "the miscreant" out of the room. The door closed behind them.

Nora's shoulders sagged. *They were alone.*

"Now let's take another look at those ropes," she said, as bracingly as she could.

When she turned back to Daniel, however, it was to see a fiery glint in his eye. "How dare you come here!"

It was so unexpected, Nora almost tilted back on her ankles as she knelt on the rug. "I beg your pardon!"

"You should have stayed as far away from danger as possible," Daniel said fiercely. "Yet here you are, barreling into a dangerous situation—"

"All to save you," Nora pointed out.

Her heart was singing, despite the gruffness of Daniel's voice. *He cared about her.* He wanted her to be safe. Though she knew those emotions should not be rare, they were. And she deserved to be with someone who wanted those things for her.

"I mean it, Nora, I'm cross with you!" Daniel was saying as Nora cut his wrists free. He groaned as he stretched out, bringing his hands back into his lap. "I consoled myself with the thought that you were far away from that madman!"

"How terrible of me," said Nora wryly as she cut both his ankles from the ropes tying them to the chair. "I really must—Daniel!"

It had been impossible not to gasp. Daniel had suddenly moved, far swifter than she could have predicted after being tied to a chair for so long. His hands grabbed at her arms, pulling her onto his lap.

Nora looked into Daniel's eyes and saw—

Pain. Panic. Fear. Terror.

All the terrible emotions one felt when they thought someone they loved was harmed.

Nora knew them well. They had settled into her chest the moment she had heard Daniel had gone missing. It was only now, as she felt his strong fingers encircle her arms, that she could finally start to let those bitter, piercing emotions go.

He was safe. They were together.

"Nora," said Daniel seriously, looking deep into her eyes. "I . . . I could have lost you."

There was utter silence in the parlor save for their words. Nora wanted nothing more than to sink into his embrace and receive his affection.

Even if the whole idea of being so vulnerable terrified her.

"And I could have lost you," Nora said simply, reveling in the love she could see in Daniel's eyes. "I should never have played with your affections—"

"You never did, you were always direct and honest with me," Daniel said, cutting across her. His brow crinkled as he grinned.

"Though I have to say, I am relieved you came to rescue me, even if it has bruised my pride somewhat. I don't think your brother was going to believe that I wasn't the man he was looking for."

It took a moment for the duke's words to sink in. "So he did think you were—"

"The Duke of Thornfalcone, yes," quipped Daniel, though how he was managing to be so blithe about the whole thing, Nora did not know. "He was utterly convinced you had complained about *me*. Was tired of my *pestering*, I think was the word—"

Nora groaned again, closing her eyes for a brief moment.

She should never have been so foolish as to open up to her brother. Where had that ever got her in the past? Nowhere—and this time, it could have meant the accidental murder of the man she truly loved!

"He thought you were David," she said softly, opening her eyes.

Daniel shrugged, then winced. "I suppose he did. I think he believed he was doing right by you, though of course I have rather a different idea."

Nora shook her head with a dry laugh. "Hamish has never had a good idea in all his days, though I suppose I should be grateful he didn't do anything worse."

"You're right there. I suppose he could have just turned up at the stables, shot me—"

"Daniel!" Nora said, horrified. The very idea—the very mention of such an idea was enough to turn her blood cold.

His strong arms encircled her and Nora's eyelashes fluttered shut as she welcomed his embrace, his strong arms around her, the way his hands tightened as though they would never let go.

Yesterday this would have awakened desire in her, desire to kiss and be kissed—and though she would certainly not say no to that, this embrace was different. It could last the rest of time, if possible, and Nora knew she would never tire of it. Never tire of him.

Daniel's best efforts, his foolish ideas, his adorable enthusiasm: all had led to this. To a man tied to a chair and her desperately trying to rescue him.

"It could have been so different," Nora said in a muffled cry into his shoulder.

Daniel pushed her back to look in her face, and she swallowed another whimper.

"We have each other now," he said firmly. "And I hope you are going to make an honest man of me. Marry me?"

Nora breathed out a shaky laugh. "What, you think you could put up with me forever? My temper, my baking, my insistence of getting myself into trouble?"

Daniel's eyes sparked. "That sounds perfect."

Their kiss was warm, reverent, an aching desperation to be close. Nora gently cupped his head, pulling him closer but painfully aware of the dried blood in his hair.

He was hers, and she was his.

"Now," said Daniel with a roguish grin, pushing her up off his lap and then slowly standing, wincing as his legs straightened. "Don't I have a butler around here to solve all my problems?"

Nora smiled as she rose. "Just outside."

"In that case," said the man she loved, "he can wait a few more minutes while I kiss you again . . ."

Chapter Nineteen

22 July 1811

"Just—just stay there. No, like you were before—Nora, you're doing it on purpose!"

Daniel's voice rang out across the garden, and though he attempted to sound severe, it was impossible to do so when looking at Nora Harvey.

She was resplendent.

No, that wasn't quite the right word. No woman had ever looked like her, Daniel was sure. No one had ever been adorned with such a garland, or had hair that glittered so in the sunlight, or—

"This is ridiculous," said Nora firmly, lowering the elegant vase from her shoulder.

Daniel shook his head. "You're ruining it!"

"You should have more imagination," she shot back, sunlight glittering in her eyes. "You've had me here for over an hour! You don't think you have committed my person to memory yet?"

Something low in Daniel's stomach—or perhaps even lower—stirred at her words. *Well, yes, she had a point.* Whenever he closed his eyes, he could easily see the outline and form of Nora Harvey. All of it. Sometimes, she didn't even have any clothes on . . .

"You looked wonderful," he said, trying to focus on the real Nora before him, rather than the splendid form of Nora he was half certain he would delight that evening. "I was doing so well!"

"You try holding a vase over your head for an hour!" said Nora, eyes flashing with mischief. "See how you like it!"

It had been his idea, Daniel freely admitted. A chance to learn a new hobby—something that as a duke, he would apparently have to take up. There could be no more danger for this duke, no more secrets, information passed, or missions undertaken.

At least, not until he and Nora had been firmly able to put the escapade with Hamish Harvey from their minds.

That meant he needed something else to fill his time. Painting, Mrs. Stafford had suggested.

"Very good for the soul," she had said firmly. "Moral scenes, you know? Stories from the Bible. Exhortations—"

"I think I have just the idea," Daniel had said, cutting across her yesterday afternoon as his gaze alighted on Nora. "The perfect idea."

He had expected it to be far more difficult to persuade Nora than it had turned out to be. Daniel wasn't sure if every woman enjoyed being looked at, or if Nora had a particular penchant for being adored.

At least, adored by him.

And Daniel had quickly encouraged Nora to wear something that approximated a Greek toga as she stood in his garden by the pond holding a vase above her head.

But apparently she had not expected his painting attempt to take more than about ten minutes.

"It isn't that heavy," he shot back now.

"Then you try it," Nora said, thrusting out the vase. "Go on—give me your pocket watch, and we'll see how long you can manage it."

Daniel grinned as he placed his paintbrush back into the jug Mrs. Stafford had reluctantly lent him. "Give it here."

He was half tempted to allow the vase to fall to the lawn and smash instead of taking it from her, just so he could pull the sensuous

Nora into his arms. Really, it was too difficult, given how wonderful she was looking.

The bold pink toga had perhaps not been one that anyone would have predicted would suit a woman with fiery red hair, but Daniel was transfixed by the clash of the two shades.

His fingers slipped.

"Careful!" teased Nora, plucking his pocket watch from his waistcoat and grinning.

Daniel groaned. Just for a moment, her fingers had been flush against this chest. Just for a moment, he could have grabbed her and directed their afternoon away from painting a beautiful scene—and toward making one.

As it was, the terracotta vase was safe in his fingers and Nora was examining him with a raised eyebrow. "Come on, above your head."

Daniel grinned. There was no one like Nora for teasing him, but this particular jest would be in vain. Why, the vase was not heavy in the slightest! Why was she complaining so?

"And what will you give me?" he asked with a smile as he lifted the vase above his head. "When I stand here for more than an hour?"

Now that was the strangest thing. Somehow the vase seemed to have doubled its weight. What had happened?

His eye caught Nora's. She was grinning. "Heavy, isn't it?"

"No," lied Daniel swiftly. "Perhaps a little."

This was ridiculous. Nora had already held the blasted thing over her head for a good thirty minutes. He had not yet held it a tenth of that time and he could already feel his forehead perspiring.

It was the heat, Daniel told himself. It had not been so hot when Nora had been holding it. Why, when they had first come out into the garden there had even been a few clouds over the sun and—

"Feeling the burn yet?" teased Nora pleasantly.

Daniel had opened his mouth to say he had no idea what she was talking about, but the moment she said it, he could feel it. A strange sort of burn in his shoulders and wrists. Why, the vase was now at least three times as heavy as it had been when Nora had first thrust it into his grip.

How had this happened? And how on earth was he going to keep it aloft for even twenty minutes?

"How long?" he said gruffly.

Nora grinned. "Two and a half—"

"It has to have been at least four times that!" Daniel blustered.

Dear God, he was going to die here, holding a vase over his head, merely because he had told a woman that she should be able to manage it!

"Give up?"

Daniel threw all caution—and pride—to the wind. "Yes!"

He groaned as he allowed the vase to fall, catching hold of it just as it passed his knees. Oh, his back! His shoulders were burning as though a torch had been placed behind him. How on earth—

Nora was laughing. "Did I, or did I not, say—"

"Yes, yes," said Daniel with a smile. "I can admit when I am wrong. Most of the time. It's because I was tied to that chair, you see, my strength—"

"Don't give me that," said Nora, placing his pocket watch on the easel and approaching to take the vase back. "That was weeks ago. You just underestimated me, that's all."

He had to give her that. "Not for the first time."

They shared a heady moment when Nora reached for the vase. Daniel pulled it into his chest, denying her until she came close and he breathed in her scent. His manhood lurched and his stomach swooped as Nora placed a delicate kiss on his neck as she took the vase from him.

"Not for the first time," she agreed in a breathy voice. "And undoubtedly not the last, if I know you."

Daniel was dazed in the brilliant summer sunshine as Nora returned to her place where he had been painting her.

Not the last? Oh, no. If he were to have the rest of his life with this woman, there would almost without doubt be plenty of occasions when he would underestimate Nora Harvey—Eleanor Vaughn, as she soon would be. That was the trouble with a wife who continued to dazzle him. When he was with her, he couldn't see straight.

"I think I'll stick to painting," Daniel said ruefully, stepping back to the easel. "You know, I think I've almost captured you."

"Oh, you captured me a long time ago," teased Nora with a shake of her head. "I just didn't know it."

Joy swelled in Daniel. *She hadn't, and neither had he.* The two of them had barreled forward in a rush of emotions and desires, hardly realizing what they would mean to each other. Hardly aware what depths of devotion they would find.

Now here they were, in his garden—soon to be *their* garden—and nothing could touch them. Nothing at all.

"I heard you have a new gardener."

Daniel looked up from his pathetic attempt at painting Nora and saw her wry smile. "You did?"

Nora nodded. "I hear Mr. Keynes makes an excellent Head Gardener."

Try as he might, Daniel could not help but roll his eyes.

It had been Nora who had noticed, of course. No one else in the Thornfalcone household had, and for that he'd felt rather foolish, but there it was. Keynes had simply grown accustomed to hiding his failing eyesight and few would ever argue with the man.

And so it had been up to Daniel to have the rather awkward conversation. After all, the man couldn't continue as butler. It would be ridiculous. On the other hand . . .

"It was your idea," said Daniel, mixing some blue paint on his palette. "I never would have thought of it."

"You are not the sort of man to throw a servant out onto the street," said Nora, the vase delicately balanced on her shoulder. "Even a butler."

"Still. I would never have considered offering him such a position," Daniel admitted.

It had been rather clever. The gardens at the Thornfalcone Bath townhouse were impressive but not large. They had a gardener who could quite sufficiently care for them—but Keynes as Head Gardener could potter about, pick roses, order people around, and snooze in his potting shed every afternoon.

A match made in heaven.

"You're going to make a wonderful duchess," Daniel said, dabbing the blue paint onto the canvas. Yes, that was a perfect color for the sky. Almost. "I will never have to worry about household management again."

There was a snort on the other side of the easel. He stifled a laugh of his own.

"If you think I am going to spend all my time worrying about—"

"Well, what are you going to do, then?" Daniel asked cheerfully.

There was silence from the other side of his painting. A rather astonished silence, from what he could tell.

"Do?" Nora repeated. "I'll bake, of course. Scandalize Society, naturally. And when I have any spare time . . . I'll love you."

Daniel peered around his easel. Nora was smiling a little more shyly than he had expected, her cheeks pink, but her eyes shone brilliantly.

"Good," he said softly. "That's all I want."

She was all he wanted, though he did not need to say that. They both knew. His adoration for her was matched only by her devotion to him, something Daniel had never thought he could experience.

How had he managed it? The bold, brash, and completely brilliant—and independent—Miss Eleanor Harvey had been a mystery to him from the moment Daniel had met her. The instant he had seen her he had wanted her, though that wanting evolved and grew to something more akin to affection.

And now he had her. Sometimes Daniel could hardly believe it.

"What foolish thing am I dressed up as, again?"

Daniel chuckled. *And sometimes, he could believe it.* "A fire nymph."

There was a snort from his elegant model. "Of course I am."

"They are supposed to be sisters of the water nymphs," said Daniel, frowning in concentration as he attempted to get the blue paint to spread evenly across the canvas. "Though I am not sure who their brothers are."

He wasn't able to catch himself in time rethink the wisdom of the comment, but when he glanced up, Nora's smile only slightly faded.

"That is the problem, I suppose," she said. "Too many brothers."

Daniel attempted to return her nonchalance with a smile, though it was a struggle.

Yes, too many brothers. His brother had been a reprobate of the most elevated kind: the rich, titled kind. He had overspent and overbought, bedded women and called out men in duels, and caused such a ruckus that he had begun to hear whispers in the *ton* that it was a blessing David died when he did.

And then there was another brother, Hamish. Nora's brother. He had made bad choice after bad choice, and then had done something Daniel would never forgive: he refused to help his sister. And for that, the two of them had fallen into disrepute, their lives irrevocably changed. The sister had been forced into a life of courtesanship, and the brother it appeared, kidnapped and held to ransom. Just because of one mistake.

In a way, it wasn't fair.

But then he hadn't been the one, Daniel reminded himself, *who had kidnapped an unarmed man, tied him to a chair, gagged him, accused him of the most terrible things, then punched him.*

"Daniel?"

Daniel forced another smile. He had permitted himself to become morose, and that simply wouldn't do. Not on a day like this. Not with a woman like this.

Evidently Nora could still see the pain in his eyes. Her look was affectionate as she stepped forward.

"Stop!" Daniel commanded.

Nora froze. "Why?"

"My art!" he said dramatically.

She giggled, rolling her eyes. "Your art is terrible."

"How dare—"

"And I want to kiss you," Nora added with a wicked glint in her eye as she placed the vase on the lawn. "Are you really willing to deny me?"

Daniel swallowed. "No."

Deny her—deny Nora? Never in his life would he do such a thing. Tell the woman he loved she could not have what she wanted, do what she wanted, go where she pleased?

As though it were even possible to say no. As though she would pay him any mind if he did.

Daniel's fingers itched to take her as Nora stepped forward. His paintbrush fell to the lawn, unheeded, as Nora stepped into his arms.

Their kiss started calm and quiet but did not long remain so. Daniel was unsure how he would ever stop kissing Nora once they began, tendrils of delight curling around his heart, her fingers curling around his neck. The world stilled, all sound ceased, as Nora's lips pressed against his.

Daniel's tongue darted past her lips, causing ripples of pleasure to move through his body as Nora whimpered and clutched him tighter.

Oh, God, she was everything. Burning with unresolved passion, Daniel's hands moved to her buttocks and—

"We probably shouldn't," Nora said as she broke the kiss.

She did not, however, step out of his embrace.

Daniel grinned. "We probably should."

"Anyone could see!"

"Let them watch," growled Daniel, pulling her closer.

But to his great regret, Nora slipped from his embrace with a flushed smile. "Walk with me."

He groaned. "You think I can walk with all this stiffness—"

"Walk it off," said Nora, entwining her fingers in his and squeezing his hand. "Come on. Show me this garden of yours."

It was on the tip of Daniel's tongue to beg for more—to tell her just how desperately he wanted her, how waiting until they were married was tearing him apart from the inside out, and if she did not succumb to him then he would—

Well. He wasn't entirely sure what he would do. But it would probably be something drastic, and that never ended well.

Nora's eyes danced. "You make me so happy, you know."

And just like that, all Daniel's ability to think faded. "A walk, you said?"

"In your garden," Nora said with a nod. "I . . . I don't want to be overheard."

Curiosity piqued and fingers burning from the contact with hers, Daniel nodded.

The gardens were not overly large, but they were sufficient to provide a number of places where two people could meander and have a private conversation. What she wished to speak of, he did not know—but he could guess.

And he was correct.

"I-I wanted to apologize," said Nora awkwardly, as they stopped under the large oak. "Again. For my brother."

Daniel braced himself. This was not going to be an easy conversation. "No. Not unless you want to be subjected to all the apologies for mine."

He had still not forgiven David, not completely. The lengths to which he had gone to pester Nora were still unclear to Daniel, but if she had been so affronted as to complain to her own estranged brother . . .

Well. It did not bear thinking about.

Nora nodded ruefully. "Brothers."

"Who would have them?" agreed Daniel. "Oh, my sister Amelia is all right. You'll be meeting her soon, you know."

Was that a flicker of fear across Nora's face?

"And you don't . . . you don't think she will be mortified? Having to meet me, I mean. A *fallen* woman."

"She'll be meeting my future bride and future matriarch of this family," said Daniel fiercely. "Besides, if I know Amelia, she'll be absolutely delighted and will ask you a great many impertinent questions."

Which reminded him, he would have to have a talk with Amelia about that ahead of time. He really couldn't allow—

"What kind of questions?"

Daniel sighed, shaking his head under the broad, shadowy canopy of the oak leaves. "Questions about . . . gods above, about . . ."

He couldn't bring himself to say it. *What brother could?*

It appeared, however, that Nora did not need him to speak the precise words to understand what he meant.

A giggle escaped her lips. "You think your sister will want me to tell her—"

"Please, don't tell her," Daniel begged. *The thought of his sister knowing about that*! "The longer she's kept in ignorance—"

"If you think any woman is that ignorant, you are lying to yourself," Nora said. "But I suppose if that is the greatest challenge we have now to face, we're doing quite well."

Daniel's chest swelled as he took in her beauty, her brilliance, the way she so effortlessly adapted to any situation.

Yes, she was right. They were doing quite well.

"In fact, I don't think we have anything to worry about now," said Nora lightly. "Well, except . . ."

Despite the heat of the day, Daniel went cold. Surely, after all the misunderstandings they had shared, the mistakes he had made, the danger they had both been in—surely there could not be something else!

"What?" he asked urgently.

Nora's smile should have told him instantly there was nothing to fear. "Why, how many diamonds I want, of course."

Daniel's laugh was half merriment, half relief. Was it himself, or Nora who had first said that those who played with dukes got burned? Well they both had certainly been through the fire. But they had both also come through that fire, scorched but not burned. And now all they had to worry about were diamonds.

"You are already the perfect duchess," he said softly, kissing her forehead and wishing to goodness their wedding day would hurry up.

Nora's eyes sparkled. "I know. But I want the diamonds to prove it."

EPILOGUE

15 August 1811

"YOU HAVE ABSOLUTELY no need to be nervous," came the stern voice of Lady Romeril, giving quite the opposite impression. "You're about to become a duchess! You're covered in diamonds!"

Nora smiled weakly. Everything that the impressive woman said was true.

Well, most of it. She was about to become a duchess. In just under an hour, she would be walking up the aisle in St Michael's Church and marrying the man she adored more than she thought possible.

And marrying Daniel Vaughn, Duke of Thornfalcone, had some rather obvious consequences. Because Lady Romeril was right—she was covered in diamonds. She had not expected Daniel to take her jest quite so literally, but it was rather hard to argue with a man showering you with glittering jewels.

Even if it was quite ridiculous. *Her, Nora Harvey . . . diamonds?*

But on one matter, Lady Romeril was wrong. She had absolutely every need to be nervous.

"Come now, chin up," ordered Lady Romeril brusquely. "I have never seen such a dour bride in all my life!"

And that was what finally got to her.

Nora turned from the looking glass in the bedchamber Daniel had insisted she take over the night before the wedding and glowered at the interfering, irritating, unwelcome busybody—

"That's better," said Lady Romeril approvingly. "We've got to see that spark, Miss Harvey. A bride needs a little fire in her on her big day."

Nora opened her mouth, thought better of arguing with one of the most esteemed women in all Society, and turned back to the looking glass.

It was all very odd. A few months ago, she could not have conceived of such boldness within her—at least, boldness that was expressed. She had never been short of brash thoughts, nor a temper that was difficult to quell. Of course, most of her ire at the beginning of summer was against fate, Society at large, and a few gentlemen in particular.

And now . . . now . . .

"Here, let me help you with your veil," said Lady Romeril in a tone that brooked no opposition.

Nora sighed. She was still not sure what the woman was doing here in the first place. No one had told her Lady Romeril was going to be assisting her before her wedding.

In truth, she was not sure whether anyone else in the Thornfalcone household knew. She had been helped into her dress by a maid, then left alone to choose her jewels, and then Lady Romeril had barged in.

"I really don't need any help with—"

"Nonsense," Lady Romeril said firmly, picking up the elegant veil and wafting it through the air. "I am always so helpful at weddings. Everyone says so."

Nora bit down the response that no one would dare say anything else and permitted the doyenne to carefully place her veil upon her head. And she had to admit, from what she could see in the looking glass, Lady Romeril did a superb job.

"There," said Lady Romeril dramatically. "A woman fit for a duke!"

Nora's smile faded somewhat.

Fit for a duke? Perhaps. But fit for Daniel?

No woman was. She certainly could not live up to his kindness, his ineffable joy in life, his ability to try his best at everything though he so often fell just a little short.

She loved him all the more for it, of course.

Nora's stomach squirmed. And she was not alone in thinking herself not quite sufficient for a man like Daniel. Oh, Society thought it was because he was a duke and she had lost her reputation entirely. But she knew it was more than that, deeper than that.

Was she truly worthy of a man who was so . . . good?

"You'd better get to that church, you know."

Nora blinked. Lady Romeril was examining her closely in the looking glass's reflection. There was a knowing look on her face Nora was not sure she liked.

"The church?" Nora repeated blankly. *Oh goodness, was she late?* "I did not think the time was so—"

"Oh, I think you'll be early, if you leave now," said Lady Romeril airily, lounging on the chaise longue at the end of the bed.

Nora frowned. *Early. A bride, early?*

She may have broken most of Society's rules, but she wasn't about to break that one. The bride was always late! It was one of the few times, in truth, that a woman could be late and not be considered rude.

Lady Romeril's smile was far too significant. "You know, I believe the quality of a lady is revealed in how desperately a man wants her."

Nora's cheeks burned. *How could Lady Romeril be saying such things to her?*

"And that man," continued the older woman, waving a hand in the vague direction of the church, through the wall, "that man, if you ask me, will not complain if you arrive early. He's burning up for you, that man. All of a dither."

Though the flush in her cheeks deepened in color, she was sure, Nora could not help but allow herself a grin.

Lady Romeril was right. Daniel could barely keep his hands off her, but it was more than that. He wanted to spend every minute of the day with her. He truly listened to her. He had even mediated an agreement between her and Cook so she could spend time in the kitchens baking. If arguing with your own Cook wasn't a sign of love from a gentleman, she didn't know what was.

"He loves me," Nora said softly.

"Hmmm," said Lady Romeril. "I suppose he does. I look forward to making your better acquaintance, Your Grace."

Nora had not thought she could blush any deeper, but apparently she could.

In a flurry of skirts, Lady Romeril had left the room, leaving Nora to her own thoughts. But not for long.

"Come on, then," said Amelia briskly as she stormed into the room. "I would say my damned brother won't wait forever, but then you know perfectly well that he will. The ruddy man's besotted with you!"

Spoken by anyone else, it could come across like a snipe, but Nora had already got to know Daniel's sister well enough to know she spoke from the heart. A sarcastic heart, sometimes, and one that was absolutely determined to have its own way, certainly. This was a woman who would be a most interesting sister indeed.

"Well, then," Nora said as she rose to her feet. "I suppose it's time."

Amelia grinned. "You look like you're burning up, Eleanor. Are you quite well?"

It was all Nora could do not to grin. *Burning up?* Oh, she was, but not in a way she could explain to Amelia, sister of Daniel or not.

They had been . . . good. That was what Daniel had called it. Nora had called it unreasonably restrained.

The point was, as he had reminded her often, they were increasing their anticipation for the wedding night. And abstinence, he had said, made the heart grow fonder.

Nora had threatened to make it absence and return to her cottage. Daniel had obliged with a compromise that was most pleasing to her—very pleasuring, in fact. She had never known a man with such clever fingers.

But being in his arms was not the same as feeling Daniel move inside her. Nora tried not to think about it too much as she followed Amelia down the stairs and out into the fresh summer air.

Soon.

The church was packed. Nora was under no illusion; she knew St Michael's was mainly full of those curious about the woman who had captured the attention and the devotion of the new Duke of Thornfalcone.

But she did not care. How could she, when Daniel turned and gave her that gentle smile that belied so much passion?

Nora could barely concentrate through the wedding service. Oh, certain parts stood out. Her fear when the vicar asked whether anyone objected, half expecting to hear Hamish's voice. Her excitement as she and Daniel exchanged vows—such words of devotion, words she had never expected to hear, let alone hear before an audience. Her surprise at the rather stunning gold ring that Daniel gently slipped onto her finger.

"Oh my, it's—"

"Burnished gold," Daniel said under his breath, merriment in every syllable. "I thought it rather fitting."

And fit, it did. Nora could not stop looking at it as they left the church to the cheers and well-wishers of those she had never met—and those who had once looked down on her. She could not drag her eyes from the ring as they walked back to Daniel's townhouse. *Their townhouse.*

And it proved quite a distraction on the receiving line, when Nora was supposed to be welcoming guests into her new home, and instead kept marveling at the way the sunlight caught the burnished gold.

"Nora," coughed Daniel, his hand squeezed hers.

Nora looked up guiltily. "I beg your pardon?"

There appeared to be only one person left to welcome. A tall man, with dark hair and a foreboding look. There were silver hairs tinging his temples, but there was strength and power in his expression. Despite his good looks, however, Nora had never seen a man looking more morose.

"Ashcott," said Daniel in an awed voice. "I did not expect the honor . . ."

Nora tried to hide her smile. That was one of the things she adored about Daniel—her new husband. Despite being born the second son of a duke, despite being brother to one, he had never expected to rise to such a title.

And even though he now had, Daniel presumed the world was uninterested in him. He was still easily awed—and that, Nora was certain, was a very good sign indeed.

The man her husband had called Ashcott shrugged lazily. "I was in the area, and thought I might see—but then, you do not know her. If you had known her, you would have invited her."

Nora stared blankly up at the man, then glanced at Daniel, whose face was red.

"I am afraid—well, in truth, Your Grace, I did invite her."

Your Grace? Surely this could not be another duke?

But as Nora examined the man's attire, his nonchalant arrogance, the way every eye in the hall was being dragged to him . . .

Yes, he was most certainly a duke.

"You invited her?" Ashcott's interest was piqued. "And she did not come?"

"Her . . . ah, her brother came," said Daniel, the tension in his voice rising. "Erm . . ."

Nora looked between the two men in absolute confusion. What on earth were they talking about? Who was this mystery woman that they were talking about? And why was Ashcott—the Duke of Ashcott, that was—acting so strangely?

"Ashcott," said a cold voice.

Nora turned as one with Daniel, and they both stared at another gentleman who had approached them. He was just as tall, just as handsome, just as commanding. He was also glaring most furiously at Ashcott.

"I did not think you would be bold enough to come here," said the new gentleman in clipped tones.

Nora watched, amazed, as Ashcott bowed low—far lower than would have been warranted for a duke.

"Dulverton," he said quietly.

"And you'll notice that my sister is not here," said Dulverton curtly. "I am keeping her far away from you. You've done enough damage."

Nora saw Ashcott's face darken. "I promised her—"

"Your promises are worth nothing, and I do not want to hear them," Dulverton said sharply.

Someone who could only be his wife approached and placed a hand on his arm. "Henry, I think—"

"I think I should be going," said Ashcott stiffly. "Good day, Your Graces."

And with a stiff bow, he was gone.

Nora turned, open-mouthed, to the Dulvertons—but they had already stepped away. She looked instead at her husband. "Now what was all that about?"

Daniel looked rather discomforted. "I forgot."

"Forgot what?"

"All that had happened between those two families," he said in a low voice. "Between Ashcott and Dulverton's sister, Lady Margaret."

Understanding very swiftly dawned. "Ah, I see . . ."

"The engagement was not official," Daniel said wretchedly. "It was very brief. At least, that's what I heard. A verbal agreement only."

Nora raised an eyebrow. "And is there any other kind?"

Her husband sighed. "I should have thought about it—should have told them to wrangle the guest list somehow."

A cancelled engagement! Nora could not help but wish for further details, but this was not a day to be prying into the affairs of others. Not when her own affairs were so fascinating.

"Well, it's not my problem," she said, squeezing Daniel's arm as the last few of their guests wandered into the ballroom where Mrs. Stafford had laid out a resplendent luncheon, leaving them alone in the hall. "And it's not yours either, Daniel, so don't you get all worried about it. I know you."

Daniel's worried expression melted into a grin. "That you do."

"After all," teased Nora, warmth spreading through all the way to her fingertips. "You have much bigger problems."

Her husband raised a quizzical brow. "Goodness—a bigger problem than you have been?"

Their laughter mingled in the echoing hall and Nora could not believe she could be so happy. How was it possible that a woman like her who had lost everything, even her own self-respect, could be so fulfilled?

"I am afraid so," she said, excitement leaping. "I am only one person to manage, and soon you will have two."

Daniel groaned and Nora's joy died. *Was it possible—could she have been so wrong as to misunderstand him?* They had talked about it, naturally, as something that would happen in the future. But was it truly so bad that it had happened now?

"No, please, I beg you," Daniel said with a sigh. "I am not sure if I could survive having Amelia move back into this house!"

Nora's shoulders sagged with relief. "I meant I'm going to have a baby, you dolt!"

Daniel stared, mouth open, eyes transfixed, still as a statue.

She waited for what felt like an entire minute. Then she gently poked her husband in the stomach. "Daniel?"

"A . . . a baby?" the man said faintly.

"It is a rather common side effect of what we've shared, yes," Nora said ruefully. "You . . . you aren't upset, are you?"

The words slipped from her mouth. The instant they did, she saw her fears were baseless.

Daniel pulled her into a tight embrace, kissing her cheek, her forehead, her lips, anything he could reach as his breath shuddered. "A baby! One of ours!"

"I'm almost certain you're the father, yes," Nora teased, joy rushing back to replace the momentary fear.

Oh, was there any happiness greater than this? Was it possible that the rest of her life could be like this? Full of embraces, and kisses, and joy? Relying on a person she completely trusted, knowing that he would always be by her side? Being content, knowing that the man who loved her was a good man?

Daniel's eyes were shining. "Nora, we're going to have to build a nursery!"

"We are indeed!"

"And we're going to have a baby!"

Nora nodded, eyes swimming with tears. "We are."

"And you never know," said Daniel with a mischievous grin. "I was a twin. There could be two in there!"

Nora's face fell. "You . . . you think?"

It was a rather startling thought. One baby was going to be more than enough of an adventure—but two?

"Whatever happens, we'll be together," said Daniel, allowing his hands to drift to her buttocks. "And speaking of together, something we have not truly been—not in the way I have wished—for several weeks . . ."

He could not be serious. Their wedding guests were just in the ballroom to their left!

"Daniel Vaughn," Nora quietly scolded, not pulling away. Why would she? Every place his fingers touched her tingled with anticipation.

"Nora Vaughn," Daniel quipped in a ragged voice. "Just a few minutes in the drawing room? It's got a lock—"

"Daniel!"

"I can't stay away from you any longer," he moaned, causing flickers of longing to cascade through Nora.

She could hardly breathe. "Play with dukes, get burned?"

"Play with duchess, get burned, is more like it. You can't lose your reputation now," her husband pointed out, one hand meandering up past her waist to brush against her breast.

Nora closed her eyes, just for a moment, in exhilarating expectation of the pleasure they were about to share.

Then she opened her eyes. "Can't lose my reputation? Not if we don't try hard enough . . ."

About Emily E K Murdoch

If you love falling in love, then you've come to the right place.

I am a historian and writer and have a varied career to date: from examining medieval manuscripts to designing museum exhibitions, to working as a researcher for the BBC to working for the National Trust.

My books range from England 1050 to Texas 1848, and I can't wait for you to fall in love with my heroes and heroines!

Follow me on twitter and instagram @emilyekmurdoch, find me on facebook at facebook.com/theemilyekmurdoch, and read my blog at www.emilyekmurdoch.com.

Made in the USA
Middletown, DE
04 February 2024

48510783R00136